Mafia Billionaire Daddy Series

CROSS TO BEAR

(Book 1)

S.E. Riley

The Redherring Publishing House

CROSS TO BEAR

*A duty-bound seduction, unplanned secrets, an arranged marriage...
and yet, a real love against the backdrop of the mean streets of Chicago.*

AUTHOR'S NOTE: This book contains cussing, gun violence, murder, and mild physical violence, as well as conversations on drugs, prostitution, theft, bribery and assault.

Table of Contents

Prologue

Mira

I found it uncanny that Saint Riccini possessed the same cutthroat danger in the blueprint of his eyes, just like my father.

A kaleidoscope of flashbacks filtered through my mind as I thought of Simon, my first boyfriend at sixteen. He'd made the mistake of talking back to my father, Frankie Saliano.

"What did you say, you little bitch? Don't you ever question the motherfucking Don of Chicago! You're not fucking good enough to date my daughter."

Simon's face had transformed from All-American handsome to a pummeled mess, courtesy of my father's closed fist. Shaking off the nasty memory, I sipped my champagne, leaving the imprint of my fuchsia-stained lips on the Cristal glass. I lowered it carefully as the Parisian server left our table. We sat in the middle of Guy Savoy in Paris, oblivious to those around us. We were in a bubble of love, and only we were inside it.

The glaring difference was that Saint's blue irises were like cool, icy pools, unlike my father's dark obsidian pupils. I rubbed my stomach discreetly, not understanding why a pile of knots had taken up residence and were destroying my stomach lining.

Saint interrupted my concerns, reaching across the table, the warmth of his ruthless fingers wrapping around mine. A destroyer to many but tender-hearted to me. The man had no idea of my real identity. To him, I was Claudia, a university student from Brussels enjoying my time in Paris. How wrong he was.

"I wish things were different, Claudia. We come from completely opposite worlds, and you're too pure. Too goddamn sweet for the brutality of a man like me. It's not right for me to corrupt you."

Tingles flushed through my pussy. I'd gotten so used to Saint's deep husky voice over the weeks of knowing him that I could hear it reverberating in my head every minute of the day when we weren't together. His muscular arm draped casually over the back of my chair as he whispered as gently as a summer breeze into my ear.

A pang of guilt knifed through my stomach as I sheltered my eyes from Saint, toying with my food.

"Maybe. Or maybe I'm not so sweet," I pouted.

If he knew who I was, he would have killed me. My father had managed to keep me hidden in my younger years. Only a few high ranking mobsters could put my face to a name.

"You're going to boarding school, Mira. I don't want you around the house right now. There's too much going on."

I hated the creaky wood floors and the catty, bitchy girls, but I'd gone—though not without protest.

"Why can't I stay and go to public school?" I had whined.

My father had scowled, putting me in my place. *"You have no idea what I do, and I never intend for you to find out. Know your place, Mira. Babies, school, looking pretty—those are the things you're destined for.*"

I'd resented every notion of this. I wasn't stupid. I saw the men coming in secretly every weekend, dressed in all black. I'd known all along my father was a mobster.

Saint scoffed in disbelief, unfurling his fingers from mine and skimming a hand through his close-cropped jet-black hair. He cut an imposing yet sinful figure, his white linen shirt open at the top, the outline of his chest muscles visible, with a black blazer and black tailored pants finishing the outfit.

"Sweetie pie, you couldn't be fuller of honey if you tried."

If only you knew, Saint...you would point the barrel of a gun in my face.

"I've loved our time together. I don't want to go. You're wrong about things, Saint." I hinted, but my subtle warnings held no weight with him.

I had to dip into my acting skills to appear older than my twenty-three years of age. With an extra coating of foundation, lips the color of bloodshed, and my sleek champagne chignon, it worked a treat on Saint.

Even though my virginity was intact—other than a few sprinkled moments of masturbation—my pussy ached for the man to touch it. For weeks, I'd gotten to know him, weakening his defenses for the final blow, but the joke was on me because I was the one falling...

I licked my lips unconsciously as Saint groaned in appreciation, smiling at my slightly parted mouth. He rearranged the watch on his arm, sneaking glances at the other patrons.

My heart hammered hard in my chest as he stroked a finger down the back of my hand, his hot breath blowing on the tip of my eardrum.

"If you knew the dirty thoughts running through my mind right now, especially when you lick your lips like that..." He chuckled, his sandalwood and cashmere scent almost making me drool. I clenched my thighs together, and Saint kept his eyes forward while I admired his tight jawline and two-day stubble. His hand slid into the groove between my legs under the long tablecloth.

Gasping in shock and a flood of fervent desire, my eyes flew around the packed restaurant. Patrons could have cared less about us, but the server was fast approaching with our bill. I was wearing a tight dress, and a wet patch had pooled thick and fast between my legs. Saint had barely grazed my pussy with his open palm. Reluctantly, I wriggled slightly to the left with a giggle.

"Saint, come on, we're in the restaurant." Although I clamped my legs shut, trapping Saint's hands between the apex of my shaky thighs, one of his fingers tickled over the top of my lace panties. I controlled myself by biting down on my bottom lip.

"Damn, you're fucking wet there. Let's get out of here. I can't let you leave Paris without a send-off." His brusque tone dropped an octave lower, and all I wanted him to do was keep his hand in position and get me off.

I smirked, smoothing down the side of my hair, trying to keep control of my tumultuous emotions. I fingered the silver cross around my neck, knowing the sacrilege of offering my body. I was going to sleep with a man nearly ten years older than me and lose my virginity to a family enemy.

Gulping down my secret guilt, I watched as Saint slipped his black card into the leather pouch, eyeing me for dessert.

"Are we going to end the night at yours, Saint?" I breathed seductively.

"Do you want to? I don't want to pressure you, but I can't lie and say I don't want you in my bed tonight. I want you badly. It's more than sex—it's us. But you're too good for me."

Saint cupped my chin, teasing my lips lightly with his Scotch-tainted lips. Shuddering, I pulled back, covering my shoulders with my shawl.

"Yes," was my only answer.

You can do this, Mira. Do it for the Saliano bloodline.

Saint escorted me out of the restaurant, eyes on us as we left, my pussy throbbing for Saint's body.

As he beeped open the door of his cherry-red Maserati, I knew this decision would forever change the course of my and my family's life.

By the time we arrived at Saint's lush apartment, my hands were trembling—not only from desire but from what was about to go down.

"Here, let me take your shawl." Saint eased my perfumed shawl off my slender frame, revealing my bare shoulders. I sucked in a hard breath. Saint's lips touched the heated skin. My lips parted as Saint unpinned my hair, its mid-back length cascading down my spine.

His hands massaged my skull, back and forth, a pleasurable groan escaping my lips. Saint pressed an insistent hand over my flat stomach, pressing me into him. His hard-on dug into the small of my back, causing me to feel both alarmed and excited.

"You are the most incredible woman I've ever met, Mira. So elegant and innocent. So willing...and you're interested in a brute like me. I don't understand what I've done to deserve these last few weeks with you, but I'm sure as hell going to leave my mark so you never forget me."

My knees buckled slightly as I turned to face Saint. His lean, solid, 6'2" frame held mine close as my arms involuntarily linked around his neck. We were so wrapped up in one another that Saint forgot to turn on the lights of his apartment, but I could make out his imposing shadow.

"You're a beautiful brute, and I want you as much as you want me."

On the tip of my tongue was the fact I was a virgin, but I found myself too insecure to give that truth away. I wanted Saint to think I was experienced and in control, even though deep inside, I was a murky mess, unsure if I was doing the right thing.

Saint led the way to his bedroom—a decadent ensuite layout, but all my focus was on him. He clicked on the lamp beside his bed, shedding dim light into the room that reeked of his masculinity.

Everything in the room oozed of rich, dirty class, something I'd grown up with. He unbuttoned his shirt, and I watched. I drifted towards him, letting my fingers do the work to reveal his sculpted chest. I ran a finger over a raised circular scar resembling a bullet hole near his nipple.

"Wow."

"See why you don't want to be involved with me?" A deep-coated thickness spilled from his thick lips. He thought I was a university student on holiday, but nothing could have been further from the truth.

I placed a hand on the side of his face. "No, I don't see why." Saint silenced me, crushing his silky, fleshy lips over mine, and our bodies magnetized together. His hands cupped my ass, his erect cock digging into my thigh. I let him take over me, knowing what I was about to do. I let him strip me bare as I stood before him, offering myself on a platter while he did the same.

"My God, you are fucking beautiful, Claudia...you're all a man could ever want or need." I reveled in the rawness of Saint, his palpable, violent power. I expected rough handling and aggression, but Saint's gentle caresses reminded me of floating atop ocean water.

I fell back onto his bed, my hair spreading around me. He bent his head, his mouth flicking over my erect nipples, drawing them out even more. I could barely breathe with all the sensations running through me. When he finished, his generous mouth planted firelight kisses down my hip bone, his tongue grazing my skin ever so often. Closing my eyes, I allowed myself to let go. As his lips got closer to my pussy, he kissed and licked at my inner thighs, bringing a shudder to my sensitized body each time. I'd never been touched like this before, and the experience blew my mind. His lips led a salacious trail down to my throbbing pussy

I opened my legs, wanting his whole face between them. The tickle of his bristles between my thighs only added to the moment as his tongue snaked into my wet folds. Pressure began to build in waves as he lapped a flat tongue against my clit.

Yes. Yes. Yes. I can't go back now. I can't. I want this. Saint Riccini. You're not the enemy tonight. Tonight, I'm your lover, and I'm giving everything to you. Please forgive me for what I'm doing. I have to do it for my famiglia.

My pussy was burning up like a furnace, and I could no longer fight all these feelings for this man. At first, he was gentle, but the more my hips writhed, wanting him to dig his tongue deeper, his pace increased until my body morphed into overload, all my clit nerve endings zinging into orgasm. I cried out, with Saint panting and coming up for air.

"Wow." My eyes flew open, shocked at my body's reactions, and it was still pulsing with pleasure. My first lover was a sworn family enemy, but I did not want it to be so.

How could we be anything more?

He grinned. "I'm only getting started, Claudia. We've got all night, baby."

His touch lit my body on fire, and for a moment, I tightened before he entered me, swallowing the sharp pain as he stretched me. My hymen broke, and I watched his pupils dilate in surprise, but Saint didn't skip a beat.

Please don't say anything. Please don't say anything.

He didn't speak any word of breaking me in. He gently pulled back then placed the tip of his thick cock into my dripping folds. I winced in temporary discomfort, but still, my pussy throbbed.

It's for the family. It's for them. You have to do it, Mira.

I was so wet that it only hurt for a few seconds. The more he buried himself inside me, the deeper I fell in love with him. I wanted to cry because this was our last hurrah together. I'd fallen into a dark abyss and couldn't drag myself back out.

Saint's fingers interlocked with mine as the bed rocked with his thrusting rhythm. I pinned my legs around his back as he groaned, breathing heavily in time with me. The more he penetrated, the more I opened like a flower for him.

Sweat intermingled as sweet tenderness soaked us both. A ball of anguish tightened in my throat as my suppressed feelings climbed to the surface.

I wish it were different, too, Saint. I do, but we have this moment.

I dug my fingernails into Saint's back, remorse forcing me into a weeping mess. Both of us were climbing to euphoria. Saint's expression contorted as he panted heavily, lost in our fake world, a volcano about to erupt.

A drop of Saint's sweat slid between the crevice of my breasts as he swelled inside me, the friction unbearable on my clit. I sang out in ecstasy and sorrow as my body shook in a simultaneous orgasm with Saint.

He broke me in, taking me over the cliff face to the edge of an orgasm I'd never had with a man. Simon and I had never gotten past my father's fists, and I doubt he could have made my body sing the way Saint had.

We exhausted one another in the best possible way with a second round after that.

Less than two hours later, I listened to the soft snore purring from Saint's lips before I made a move. Carefully, my heart beating in my throat, I donned my clothes, grabbed my purse, and left the room, glancing behind me only once. One more look and I wouldn't be able to go. With a sob in my throat, I padded lightly through the house to the kitchen.

Top drawer. That's where he keeps it.

The stutter in my chest almost undid me as I pulled my phone from my purse. My iPhone slipped devastatingly close to the floor. Watching the hallway, I half-expected Saint to be standing in the doorway, catching me in the act. But my fears remained unrealized. Gripping my phone tightly, I eased open the top drawer to the holy grail of trade secrets.

I blew a shaky breath, thankful I didn't need to search for it. I'd only been to Saint's apartment a handful of times. He'd had the notebook in hand two of those times while making dinner and slipped it into this drawer without thinking twice.

Without ever suspecting my motive. Without ever seeing me as a threat.

He had trusted I didn't know what the notebook contained.

He had trusted me.

I swallowed, not wanting the guilt of betraying him to manifest.

Page by page, I snapped photos of the sepia-colored pages, risking my life for my famiglia.

Snap. Snap. Snap. By the time I was done, beads of sweat were dripping down my spine from fear.

After reaching the last page, I placed the notebook back where I found it, held my breath, and ran out of the door, grabbing my discarded heels on the way out.

Outside, several blocks down the road, I hugged my arms around myself, standing in the cold as I waited for my Uber to my hotel. I had to give my body away...didn't I? Shivering, I agonized over my decision. It was the only way Saint would let his guard down even more.

Five hours later, with the imprint of Saint firmly between my legs and a wide-open crack in my heart, I boarded the plane to Barcelona. Only then did I text my brother Marco.

It's done. I got the information. Check your messages.

Chapter 1

Saint

Five years later

Pigeons flapped through the open cracks of the dilapidated warehouse roof. My fingers dropped to my Glock—force of habit. Gravel crunched underfoot as I walked into open slants of light shining onto the hard cement floor. I eyeballed the tattered blankets in the corners of the warehouse. Only the homeless and crack addicts feeding their demons were its occupants.

"Saint." The thick Russian accent of my main Fentanyl and coke supplier echoed through the empty vandalized hangar as I stepped toward the center.

"Boris." A skint head, 6'5" bruiser emerged from the shadows. Boris was both a hitter and a supplier. My father had broken him in young, and he'd been duly rewarded. Loyalty was everything to the Riccinis, and Boris had upheld his end of the bargain so far.

I eased my hand off my Glock, checking the perimeters, but kept my hands out of my pockets. I never missed a step. Friends turned into enemies and enemies turned into friends in the thick of the drug trafficking business. The pressure had been compounding on my shoulders since my father's death three years ago, but such was mob life. "Do we have a problem?"

Boris skimmed his hand over the back of his head as I stared at the black spider tattooed on the back of his left hand. I was never one for tattoos; I preferred my body clean. I waited a beat for his answer. "Yeah, Englewood. Donato's sniffing around, but I've got you covered."

My jaw clenched as I closed my eyes briefly. I knew why. Five years ago, I'd made the best and worst decision of my fucking life. *Mira Saliano, or should I say Claudia Enmore.* I didn't find out who the devil incarnate was until I showed my capo a photo of her the day after she left my bed ice-cold.

"You don't know who the fuck that is? It's Frankie Saliano's daughter! You got caught with your dick in your hand."

I let the conversation with Falcone rest, focusing on the new one instead.

"What now?" I spat out. Our drug warehouses had been hit too many times for me to count, and we were losing drug mules faster than I could replace. "I just switched up our warehouses last week."

Boris nodded, dipping his head to the ground. "Yeah, yeah, I know. The Salianos offered me a route in Boston. They're expanding. Marco, that little ratfink bitch is tracking me. Popping up everywhere. It's risky meeting, but I had to tell you face to face. Watch your crew, run it through your capo because Salianos are whispering sweet-ass nothings to dealers. Alright?"

"I got it." I gulped down the bitter pill that was triggered by the slip of my dick. Shaking my head, I continued, "You got movement on their locations? I gotta move stock every few days, and time is fucking money. It's screwing up the schedule."

"Right. Donato trusts me for some reason. He outright offered me my region. Gotta tell you, his deal was real nice. We're in talks, but I followed one of his street crew, and the sucker led me right to their stash house. I watched them stack the bricks myself, right behind the Family Dollarmite store in Englewood. You know the one?"

"Yeah, I know the one," I answered quietly as Mira's pretty face materialized to haunt me. She'd been doing that ever since that fateful day she'd left me in Paris. "When do they ship out? Got times, dates?"

"Tuesday nights, like clockwork, right after twelve. Two schleps. Sloppy, too. Been watching them for weeks. Careful when you send capo in—it could be an ambush."

Frowning, a surge of anger filled my veins. "Why the fuck are they talking to you? Don't they know I'm going to talk to you? These are my fucking streets, Boris. You hear me!" My blood pressure was rising because Mira Saliano had tunneled her way under my flesh, and I couldn't erase the traitorous minx from my memory banks.

"No doubt, and you're doing a hell of a job. They're stupid is the best bet. You hitting the warehouse?"

"You better believe it. I've been waiting for a breakthrough, and you've come through. Check your bank account tomorrow. There's a bonus in there." I reached up, clutching the back of Boris's neck with a wry smile—both a warning and a gesture of street endearment. If Boris fucked me over, I would shoot him and his whole family dead without blinking.

"Thanks," he replied gruffly.

"Keep your phone on. I'll let you know when it's done." I walked off, the pigeons circling at my departure and Mira taking up residence in my brain.

I recalled her evocative, sensual scent of Chanel No. 5 invading my nostrils as my lips glided down her swan-like neck. I'd wanted to ravage her, to fuck her brains out, but something stopped me. Instead, I had made love to her, my heart wrenching as I had popped her cherry. I hadn't ever made love to any woman. I called them, dicked them down, and got back to mob business.

Not with Mira. Her demure naïveté had captivated me. I loved how her champagne locks had spread out on my bed as her back arched in orgasm, her tits on display.

Fuck, I wanted her back. What I wouldn't do to touch her ivory skin...and to wring her neck, all at once.

"I wish I could stay here forever with you." Her velvety lies had broken me. She'd been so fucking convincing. Big innocent caramel eyes, just like a deer. Her effervescent laughter, her pearly straight teeth, her hot lithe body against mine.

I'd listened to the plans she'd had for the future. She'd been like a bright light, a respite from the unwelcoming world I cradled myself in, but it turned out she was even more cold-blooded than me.

I'd known the next morning. The kitchen drawer where I kept my address book was open. I'd closed it, not wanting to believe the dupe, but deep down, I'd known she'd seen it.

No responses to my text and missed calls had left my heart stone-cold.

I spat onto the curb as I emerged outside, texting Falcone, our capo, for the pickup. He rounded the corner seconds later as I slid into the passenger seat, fuming, my slain father's words stinging like venom in my ears.

"I told you pussy is the downfall of a man. You took your eye off the ball to a slippery Saliano snake. Fix it, Saint."

A sharp stab pierced my heart as the sedan pulled off the curb. My father had never got to see me fix it, and ever since Mira, blood had spilled from both sides every other week.

Falcone's beady eyes drank in the street as he turned the radio down. He had a gun sheltered in his lap. That's how hot the streets of Chicago were. "Verdict?"

"Double cross. Salianos are after Boris. They're moving into Boston, just like we wanted to. I need you to torch the warehouse behind Family Dollarmite. They're running product out of the warehouse in Englewood. Torch it to the motherfucking ground and shoot if you need to. I want to send an obvious message to the Salianos. I want to personally handle a couple of things there, so I will come through."

I grit my teeth, tapping on the middle console, rage and sorrow simmering in my soul for Mira Saliano. If I ever had the opportunity to see her again...

"Wait...you wanna torch it, boss? No product? You know you ain't gotta be there. We got it."

My eyes glazed over as I rubbed the pounding out of my temple. "No. Don't worry about the product. This is personal." Chicago traffic was crawling, doing nothing for my terrorized nerves. "I need a fucking Scotch."

Falcone chuckled, turning the corner to the gated community of North Central Chicago where I tormented myself every day about Mira and how she'd crept into my heart.

"They might have Boston, but so do we. You believe Boris. Is he solid?"

Now it was my turn to chuckle. "There's one thing I know, Falcone, and that's never to trust. We just have to adjust. Heard from Jimmy?"

"Okey dokey. Just say the word. He's alright. Doc stitched him up and he's back home. I got a few new recruits I'm breaking in, but it's gonna take time to get 'em up to speed. We're losing men, Saint."

I never heard Falcone complain. He dealt in street war, but even his resolve was waning. We were being hit from every angle possible, but somehow still pulling in revenue from various sources.

"Good to hear. Hold tight. It's gonna take time to break the Salianos, but we will, little by little." I didn't even know if I believed my lie, but it was my job as Don to prove it.

"Yeah, alright, boss. Tuesday."

I sat back, eyes glazing over.

Mira fucking Saliano.

If I wasn't so pissed off, I would have been awestruck by her. She had used one of the oldest tricks in the playbook.

My phone beeped. A message from my twin sister Riza.

Where you at, Saint? I'm feeling like a pizza and some blackjack with my twin. Need a pick me up?

I smiled as I sent a quick reply. She could always sense when I needed to forget the whirlwind of shit I was in the middle of.

Like you wouldn't believe. Two minutes out from mine. Come through. Bring your checkbook. It's gonna be a long night for you!

***

Tuesday night came around quicker than I wanted it to, with

another two of my soldiers underground. I sat tight, my leather gloves shielding my hands, waiting for the green light from Falcone. "Alright. We caught one. Saliano's man, guy's already shitting himself. You wanna do the honors?"

"Sure do. When it's done, I want you to send a present to Frankie. Make sure it gets to him. Understood?"

"Understood, boss." I dropped the black balaclava over my face so only my eyes were visible. Exiting the car, the bright city lights of Chicago skyscrapers illuminated the navy-blue skyline.

The back street I'd parked on led straight to the back side of the warehouse, where dumpsters and the loading dock were situated. My heart thumped for a minute, my blood running cold when I thought of my deceased father. Nick Riccini.

A sterling night for a killing, especially a Saliano killing. I pulled my gun, my finger firmly locked on the trigger, jogging across the street to the back of the warehouse.

Two of my men were standing, gesturing at a small opening to a side door. I could barely make them out in the shadows, but I knew Falcone's cut anywhere. "Come on. Roscoe's on the pickup."

"Good." I charged forward, a dark-haired man's head reeling in a chair as my target. I raised my hand, fire raging through my veins. "This one's for my father."

A horrified scream rang out—the type I heard every man make before I shot them between the eyes. I squeezed the trigger, the Parabellum bullet flying straight to his temple, piercing a hole through his skull. Target practice.

My team ran in and I pivoted calmly, my gun back in its holster. Job done. Sure, the sirens of Chicago P.D. screamed, but half the cowardly bitches were on the Riccini payroll, so it didn't matter, anyway.

"Now you're a real Riccini." My father's words punched through my skull. I saw my father's proud, craggy face upon my first street kill. It was a guy who'd tried to take my cousin Rico's marijuana stash at sixteen. I'd accidentally shot him with my father's gun, my unchecked temper flaring.

The first kill was the hardest to overcome. I'd broken out in hives for weeks after waking up in cold, drunken sweats, but it got easier as time moved forward. Now, I could shoot a man down like a ten-pin bowling ball and keep walking.

Chapter 2

Mira

"Enjoying your salad? Your mother used fresh herbs from the garden she's got going."

I stabbed at my cherry tomatoes, letting the balsamic vinegar hit the back of my tastebuds. I had trouble looking into my father's eyes these days, but still, I had to face the tornado's worth of damage I'd caused. I coughed, shifting uncomfortably in my seat, clanging my fork to the side of the plate.

Bravely, I stared over the family dinner table at my father who'd finished eating, his eyeballs boring into mine with silent contempt. His fat fingers picked up a toothpick and he dug it between his teeth.

"It's good. She's done a great job," I mumbled. Five years of distance wedged between us due to one man, but I couldn't turn back the hands of time. He locked his fingers in a steeple, assessing me as he bobbed his head, now full of salt and pepper strands.

"Good. Let's talk. So, I've tried to keep you out of harm's way for so long, Mira. It's not what I wanted for you. All you had to do was look pretty like your mother, pop out babies, and mind your place."

The chauvinistic tirade flying off my father's tongue made my cheeks bloom crimson. Forcing my face upward, my eyes glowered with anger.

"I did what I was told to do to help you. I got what you wanted, and now you've brought in more than a million dollars to the famiglia."

I held my chin high, smoothing my golden strands behind my ear.

My father belched, rubbing his belly as I observed the angry battle scar over his bushy left eyebrow.

Frankie Saliano was a 5'9" savage and cunning adversary for any mob family to come up against. I expected nothing less of him. It's all I'd ever seen him be. He sat upright, throwing his napkin on top of his food.

"You know nothing, and this is precisely why a woman has no business in men's business." My pulse quickened as I fixed my mouth to protest.

Even at twenty-eight years old, I was still a girl in my father's eyes—a girl who knew nothing of the world.

My father immediately placed a hand up. "Let me finish. That fucking million you earned us has gone down the drain. I've had to replace foot soldiers because of you. Our Englewood warehouse that raked in over two hundred thousand for one region got hit by your little boyfriend, Saint, and his cronies. Not so saintly now, is he? You've brought darkness to the heart of Chicago streets, Mira."

He paused, letting the bricks of guilt stack up in my stomach.

"You've fucked up in ways you can't comprehend. So tell me about the half a million I've had to recoup because I'm listening."

He gestured with a dismissive hand and an ugly snarl.

"It's not my fault. I wanted to help. Why can't you understand that? Marco told me it would be the right thing to do! He said if I got the information from Saint, you would be happy about it." I strained my voice, trying my best to get my father to understand for the one-hundredth time.

But letting Saint Riccini take my essence had made lasting repercussions.

He shook his head, sipping a small nip of port. "You're fucking stupid to think that," my father snarled, shocking me.

I'd seen and heard him be scathing towards others, but for him to give me a dose of that medicine hit me in the stomach—the same way I'd felt when leaving Saint in Paris.

"We have now lost more drugs and have to set up a new operation. I've had to pull out all the stops and hire a whole new security team before I start moving into Boston. What part of this don't you understand? You're making us look reckless out here."

Flummoxed by his answers, I tried again. But tears were welling in my eyes, and it wouldn't be long before they dropped—not from sadness, but from sheer frustration.

"You told me to do this!" I yelled back. If he was going to launch an attack, I wasn't going to just sit there.

"How do you think I told you to do this? How, huh?" My father leaned forward over the table.

"Marco..."

My father's chair screeched as he pushed himself up, disgust etched on his face. We'd had this conversation many times, and each time, my father never believed me.

"Marco this, Marco that. You can't be serious, Mira. Take some responsibility for what you've done! You've cost the family, but I'm dealing with it, and I'm gonna make it work for us. Fucking a Riccini?"

He pushed his chubby index finger into the expensive oak wood table.

"No, no, you couldn't have thought I would want my daughter to do that. That's not our way, but you've made your bed. Now you gotta lie in it. Saint's got a sister, and since he wants to take what's mine, I'll take what's his."

Crushed by the salt my father was grinding into my wounds, I wiped the flowing tears away angrily and kept trying to eat. "Torn" wasn't strong enough of a word.

What will you do? What will you take?

I asked these questions in silence because the truth was, I didn't want to know. All I knew was what I had with Saint was real.

His rugged face still kept me up at night, and he'd embedded himself into every molecule of my being.

Light footsteps entered the room as I heard liquid pouring. My father was getting himself another drink, and the shaming rant would continue if I stayed too long.

My trembling fingers tried to lift one more cherry tomato to my mouth, but my appetite was lost.

"What's all the yelling in here? I can hear you both from the living room," my mother complained, worry lines carved on her strong yet feminine features. I modeled after her, often wearing sleek monochromatic colors.

She folded one arm over the other. Her long, bone-straight blond hair hung in perfection, her pink cheeks were rouged up, and her French-tipped nails were immaculately done.

"Mira and I were having a conversation about the business since she wants to be so involved."

I stared at my father's back as he lifted his glass, before turning to our sprawling yard. We lived in an upper-crust gated community just outside of Chicago and wanted for nothing, naturally. The tears dried up soon enough because not even one of them cared that I'd put my body on the line to advance the famiglia.

My mother stood behind me, taking strands of my hair in her hands and stroking it.

"Ah, Mira, Mira, Mira. It's not what we wanted for you. This is why I sent you to boarding school and houses abroad. You were never supposed to be involved this way. There are so many other things we had planned for you," she coaxed softly.

I jolted my head sideways, so my hair slipped out of my mother's fingers. "I told you—Marco told me to do it! Why won't you listen to me?" I protested, standing up from the table.

My father half-turned to look at my mother. "See, this is why I didn't want you to spoil her."

"Don't talk to your daughter that way. She made a mistake, and you're the last person on earth to talk about mistakes being made," my mother lashed out.

The Salianos were not without their own family skeletons. My father had a pussy problem, and although he tried to hide it, I'd heard my mother weeping in the bedroom corner more times than I could count.

The room fell silent as a 6'o" frame took up the majority of the doorway. My blood boiled as Marco, the younger doppelgänger to my father, strolled in, light as a feather.

"What's to eat?" he asked casually, raising his eyebrows and his dark eyes, ignoring the pain in mine.

My father adjusted his body, facing Marco as he sat back at the table.

"We've gone over this enough times. Marco didn't force you to do anything, Mira. You have to look in the mirror and see this is what you've done. Nobody else, and your actions have cost the famiglia dearly. *Wake up!*" my father yelled, his face red as I jolted in my seat. I forced myself to go numb. I didn't want to fight anymore. I knew what I'd done had cost me in more ways than one.

"This again, Mira." Marco rolled his bloodshot eyes. "You're lying. You can't keep pointing the finger. Your nose is getting longer, like Pinocchio's." I wanted to erase Marco's smug face, but I fought back instead.

My throat clogged with emotion as I banged my hand down on the table.

"You're the only liar, Marco. You told me it would help. I got you the book with all the fucking dealers across Chicago that the Riccinis use. You can't put a price on that. You might not be making money now from them, but you will."

My father's eyes stayed trained on Marco, who simply shrugged his shoulders, but a heinous smirk curled on his thin lips. An image of me banging his head on the table filtered through my brain as I blinked rapidly.

"All you gotta do is seduce him, Mira. Saint's a ladies' man. Pop will be so proud of you. I know you wanna sit in on all the meetings. I can feel it. I know you want to. Why not? You've got nothing to lose." He'd winked at me that day as we sat downtown, watching the Chicago lights. *"Sleep with him, and get that black book. You'll know it when you see it. He keeps it close. He carries it everywhere. That's the word on the street. Take pictures of it and I'll get the info to Pop. That's all*

you have to do. Easy. I guarantee he's going to be so happy with you. It will make his day."

I dragged myself back to the present, a burst of fire lighting me from the inside out. I flexed my fingers and got up from the table. I heard the beeps from the outside and knew a meeting was going on.

"Like Pop said, we've been over it. Drop it. You have to accept the shit you've dropped us into. That's not something I would tell you to do. Give your body to a Riccini—no way." Marco scoffed.

I turned on my heel, walked out of the room, and headed for the safety of my bedroom, where I could mentally torture myself about Saint's role in my life.

"Mira, I can't get enough of you. You're the type of woman I could spend forever with."

Tingles dotted down my spine as I drudged up the loving sentiments from Saint—the only man I'd let enter my body and burden my soul. I threw myself onto my bed, covering my head with my pillow. It was bad enough that my father knew I'd slept with a man, let alone my brother talking about it as if he didn't manipulate me into the situation.

Minutes later, I let the anguish dissolve, staring at the woman I'd become in my nightstand mirror. Hollow cheekbones, a shattered heart, longer hair, and another day more hardened to the life of being a Chicago kingpin's daughter.

I picked up my charging phone and called Ella Jones. She was the key to keeping me sane amid all the mess I'd created for myself.

Chapter 3

Saint

Two weeks later

A sea of black. Muffled tears. A dark day that ripped my heart in two. My twin sister Riza was about to be buried six feet under. Street religion was my only code, but I made the cross symbol over my chest, watching them lower her wooden casket into the dirt.

I covered a hand over my heart, grimacing from the heartbreak. I could feel my sister. When Riza was sad and in trouble, I knew it. That's the life of a twin. She had the same feelings about me. She knew when Mira had left Paris because I'd moped around for months.

"My brother is in love. Never thought I'd see that in my lifetime. I knew somebody changed you."

Tears trickled down my face as the priest spoke, and the sun beat down on the back of my neck. I hid my pain behind my sunglasses as my mother held onto my arm, weeping. I was the anchor, soothing and vowing to protect her and the rest of my family. Too much. It was too much now. We'd played the game long enough, and the knife had cut to the bone.

I tightened my grip on her shoulder, a grim line forming on my lips. "It's gonna be okay. I won't let it go any further. RIP Riza," I said hoarsely, clutching onto the last fibers of my strength.

I had to be strong for the Riccinis.

My mother's heart-wrenching wails and her near-collapse fucked me up.

As soon as I heard about Riza's murder, my instincts told me it was a direct hit from the Salianos. Payback for the Family Dollarmite raid I'd orchestrated. I cast my eyes to the heavens, watching my stoic family members look on as the priest tipped holy water over the casket.

I flashed back to last week, the same week that changed my life.

"Riza's been hit. Saliano crew. Cops found a cross symbol marked on her lower back. It was them. Has to be." When I received the fateful call, I'd been on my way back from negotiations for a commercial property acquisition on the Southside of Chicago.

"What?" I'd barked as Falcone delivered the news.

"Sorry, Saint. Riza's dead. One shot to the back of the head. Straight through. She's gone."

My head had spun, and the room blurred as I steadied myself. Riza. Gone. Is that what he said? The fuck she was. My twin.

No. No. No.

"You're fucking lying to me. Get off my phone." Delusional, Falcone thought that shit was a joke, but I rang Riza's phone only to receive an empty dial tone. I must have rung it ten times before I let the reality of Falcone's call sink in.

Anger flourished inside me, setting the wheels in motion for revenge, swiping papers off my desk in rage. I've lost friends and family in this street game, but in all my 39 years, I'd never felt such pain. A part of my soul was gone in the ether.

I rang Falcone an hour later, tipsy from nursing a bottle of premium Scotch.

"I want you to find that old bitch." I stumbled around my office, vision hazy, filled with acute grief and suffocating anger.

"Whatever you need, boss. Which one? Riza...shit. We can't keep going like this."

"Shut up and listen, Falcone," I'd slurred.

"You got it. Next call?"

"Angelica. Angelica Saliano. Kill her. She shops at Tony's deli. I know because they pay monthly tax. They're on our payroll. I let that bitch live and didn't touch her, but now since they wanna take the only blood sibling I've got, they've got to fucking suffer like me," I raged. *"Kill her. Shoot her right in the back of the head, just like they did Riza. Don't stop until you get her. Tell the owner to call her there. Get her in there! Do it. Call me when it's done. She's gotta go. They killed my fucking sister. Riza."*

Sobs wracked my body as I dropped to the ground, struggling for breath.

"Consider it done, boss. I never liked that phony bitch no ways. RIP Riza."

I looked at that exact moment to a crow flying overhead as my mother's blood-red nails dug into my forearm. "Son, please, fix it. We can't do this anymore. Fix this. We won't have anyone left if we keep going like this."

I coughed, my throat like rough sandpaper. "I'm gonna fix it. I'm going to make it right."

***

My hand was forced, and there was nothing I could do about it. Lupo, my consigliere, Falcone, and three of my heaviest foot soldiers flanked me as we sat out back of Frankie's Pizza, discussing a peace treaty, two weeks after I had buried my twin sister.

Angelica Saliano's death had been the final nail on the coffin a few days after burying Riza.

A light misty rain pattered on the tin roof as I sat opposite lifelong family enemies. Frankie Saliano slid the paperwork in front of me as three other men peered back at me, their guns on the table. My men had theirs lying flat on the table as well, but if something went left, all of us would be dead.

The air conditioner whirled in the background as a solemn cloud of darkness, underpinned by violence, enveloped the grimy back room.

"I trust you've had time to review the preliminary documents, Saint. Here's the official one. If you so choose to accept it, you'll be asked to sign and utter a peace treaty oath, as will we. It must be sealed in blood by both Dons."

I watched Frankie's lips speaking as I considered my prize. Mira Saliano. Smart. We'd already consummated our taboo union—only it would be for life this time. I put on a good front, nerves of steel, but deep in my soul, Mira's betrayal rocked my core and had triggered hell amongst both families.

I nodded my head once. "Agreed. Let's do it." I cleared my throat, side-eyeing Lupo. He also nodded in acknowledgment. I'd already reread the preliminary documents so many times that my eyes had turned bloodshot.

I signed my name at the bottom of the document, sealing the fate of two mob families. Lupo slid an ebony velvet box in front of me. I opened it, gulping down my apprehension, sorrow, and anger. Riza's face shone in my mind.

"For Riza," Lupo reiterated, reading my thoughts.

"Yes, for Riza," I replied numbly.

Lupo pulled out the same knife that pricked my finger when I was a soldier cementing my position in the Riccini mob. Lupo did the honors of drawing blood. I squeezed my index finger together, a dot of crimson ripe for sealing. A similar box was presented to Frankie Saliano as he followed suit. I rolled my blood-tipped index finger over the paper, changing the game for us both.

Frankie placed his bloodied thumbprint over mine, making it official. I reached over the table, shaking his hand, repelled by the monster who'd fucked over my family.

"From this day forth, a peace treaty is in order between both the Riccini and Saliano families. No gun warfare and all territories will be respected. Any turf wars will be negotiated in sit-down meetings. There will be no more bloodshed on the streets of Chicago at our hands. *Capice?*" Antonio Salemme, Saliano's consigliere, advised.

"*Capice*," I replied, relieved that no more of my family members would be slain.

"I trust that all soldier and gang members on the Saliano side will be duly informed, and we won't have to enforce any additional physical contact on our side? Am I right?" Lupo brought our concerns to the table.

"Correct. We won't let that happen. I trust that will also be the case on your side?" Antonio cut back.

"Mercy for us on both sides. We can't go on like this, and we both have significant portions of the labor market in Chicago in our pocket. It's best for both families that things end amicably. Offering Mira is the most viable solution, especially since..." Antonio paused, glancing quickly at Frankie, whose face remained neutral, "...especially since their prior dealings years ago."

"I couldn't agree more." I hated that Mira, and our tryst, was being talked about in such an open light. I'd wanted to forget her for so long, and now we were to be bound in an entanglement that would forever change the course of our destiny. Grinding my back teeth, I swirled the ice block in my Scotch, wondering how the handover would go.

Light flooded through the back door as the light mist of Chicago rain brought in the source of my greatest pain. Mira Saliano. Older, even more sophisticated, she pulled down her silk black hood, revealing the face of a traitor.

A pounding tick drilled at the side of my temple, which I couldn't attend to. I flexed my body, trying to relax my shoulders. She moved forward, graceful like a gazelle, just like I remembered. Her body had filled out. Her breasts were fuller now, rounder. She was still petite, but her hips were more prominent. She was fresh-faced, wearing a black slip dress with her silver cross dangling. Oh, the motherfucking irony.

My God, you are a beautiful mistake I wish I never made.

Her father met her gaze briefly, gesturing her forward to me. Lupo moved one seat down as Mira's signature Chanel scent broke me, my leg bouncing under the table.

"Hello, Mira."

"Hello, Saint. I'm sorry about everything," she gushed in a low voice, her eyes needy for my forgiveness.

I pulled out her chair, my eyes piercing through hers as the strings of my heart tugged like a harpist in concert. No woman charged me up like she did. "Are you? You tried to run, but everybody knows you can't outrun a Riccini. So here we are with unfinished business. Is it Mira, or is it fucking Claudia? You're a good actress, I'll give you that, but not good enough."

"I guess not." She narrowed her eyes, talking out the side of her mouth.

Her pretty bow-shaped mouth irked me. The same mouth I'd savored all those years ago and would be available to me anytime I wanted now. It was going to be a long and rocky road for Mira and me, but underneath the pain was the bubbling of excitement that she was now mine.

"I adjourn the meeting. The peace treaty is effective immediately. Only reinforced by you both signing your marriage license in a few days. Let there be peace," Antonio declared.

I went into the meeting with nothing, and came out with the daughter of my enemy as a wife.

Chapter 4

Mira

I had always dreamed about a white wedding, a joyous celebration with my friends and family, laughter, dancing, and drinks. White waist-hugging, flowy dress. Sparkling diamond on my left hand. And a husband by my side. Not a rushed courthouse wedding and a dull wedding band. But I can't complain much now, can I?

I'd made my bed. And I was lucky things weren't worse.

One month passed, and living with Saint had me on a tightrope of tension every day. I brushed my wavy champagne locks, combing out the extra shedding. I didn't have the same bone-straight, sunflower-blonde hair as my mother. I often wondered why her hooked nose didn't resemble mine. I was smaller than my mother and father, figuring the tall gene skipped a generation.

"You have to sign the paper, Mira. You have to accept responsibility for what you've done."

I will never forget the day after my mother's funeral. My father had shoved the marriage license papers into my hand as I wept. I'd stared back at him through red-rimmed eyes, not uttering a word. It was my cross to bear, and I accepted it. Saint and I made it to the courthouse a few days after the peace treaty was signed.

I brought my mind back around to Saint. I couldn't predict what type of mood he would be in, but between the sheets, all I felt was his passion for me. However, as soon as it was over, he would roll over, turning cold.

A gloomy storm covered my face. I wanted to make it right with him, but I'd caused so much pain already. I sensed a presence looming in the doorway as I continued to brush out hidden knots. Saint stood in the doorway, sending a wild beating sensation through my heart space. The man was deliciously sexy. He was bare from the waist up, his stomach muscles rippling as he shifted from one foot to the other. His ocean-blue eyes penetrated the back of my head as I turned towards him, seeing his reflection in the mirror.

"Good morning. Big day ahead?" I offered a watery smile, and in return, he gave a tight one back.

I observed the prominent veins running like a river down the middle of his biceps to his sinewy forearms. Every time I saw him, my pussy tingled. He'd been working out more, probably because of the frustration of being married to me and wanting to keep sane. Peace treaty, my ass.

"Always. What are you getting up to?"

"I'm meeting with Clara for coffee this morning then heading to the library after."

He stood motionless for a moment, standing ramrod straight in the door, his hands firmly entrenched in his pockets, with bare feet. His bottom lip jutted out, the tight knot in my stomach bunching even harder. He gave me his back, turning to leave.

"Saint. Wait."

"Yes, Mira?"

"Are you ever going to forgive me?" I wouldn't beg, but I wanted to know what was in Saint's heart now.

"Probably not, Mira. Claudia was a good cover for you, though. Cute. So, I guess I was fucking another woman."

The truth pounded on the doors of my broken heart. Yes, I'd used a fake name, but everything else was real to me.

Saint's ocean-blue eyes scanned my face, unmoving. "Get the driver to take you where you want to go. I want you safe. Things are still in the early stages of the peace treaty, and I don't want you caught in any crossfires."

Does he love me? Does he love me not?

His backhanded comments led me to believe Saint cared about me more than he wanted to admit.

I faced the mirror, done with brushing my hair. I gulped down my repressed feelings. Therein lay the answer, causing a heart-sick pain to flow through my heart. Floorboards creaked as Saint exited down the hallway.

"I did what I thought was right," I murmured under my breath, standing up and assessing my physique. Clearly, I was good enough in the shadows of the night because most evenings, Saint reached for me, and I didn't deny him. It was then that I felt like we could be something.

I positioned my cross in the middle of my low-cut V-neck top. I would never take it off. My father had gifted it to me when I turned eighteen. I gathered my things, blew out a breath, and was thankful that I was meeting my childhood friend Clara. She always brought me comfort.

I called the driver to the front of Saint's apartment building, feeling resentful that I needed a driver to go everywhere. I used to drive myself, but Saint would throw death stares at me when I picked up my keys.

As soon as I saw my old friend, I hugged her so tightly, I practically squeezed her in half.

"Easy, Mira. Are you okay?" Clara also came from an Italian family, but unlike the Salianos, they were normal working-class people. When I listened to the normalcy of her life with birthday parties, christenings, and family dinners, I longed to know what it was like.

"I don't think I'll ever be good. My mother's dead, and I'm married to a man who hates me."

Clara rubbed my shoulder as my mouth watered at the macaroons in the cake display. "That bad? Sex good?" she asked, her eyes wide with excitement. In many ways, Clara wished for my life, but I doubted she wanted to deal with the immense pain of being part of a mob family.

"Incredible. I can't complain about that department. Maybe that's his way of punishing me, but if it is, I'll take my penance," I said dryly, ribbing my friend as she chuckled.

"He's in love with you. He has to be. The way you described him in Paris..." She leaned forward, her hand tucked under her chin and a romantic gaze in her eyes. "Just give it time. Have you spoken to your father?"

"Barely since he handed me over like a prize, but I report in like a good little daddy's girl, so he knows his peace treaty is secure. I hate being in some gilded cage with Saint." It was hard for me not to bite back with sarcasm. My life was not mine anymore, and I'd made a huge mistake.

Remorse overtook me most days, enmeshed with the grief of losing my mother.

Clara squeezed my hand across the table in support, but I

couldn't feel it. My soul had numbed and grown a little colder as each day passed.

The blanket of dusk filtered through the penthouse apartment by the time I arrived back from being with Clara, stopping by the library for a few hours, and running simple errands for Saint. Sighing with a heavy heart, I closed the Venetians, keys jingling in the door. My stomach still tensed up every time, even though our apartment security was second to none. I stilled my breath as the dark, brilliant storm that was Saint entered.

"How was your day?"

"Fine." He skidded his keys on the marble bench countertop, letting me know everything wasn't fine.

"Tough day?" I coaxed, moving away from the blinds and closer to him. If we were going to be married, we'd have to learn to get along, no matter how hard it was.

His chest rose, puffing out as he exhaled, his eyes slicing into me as if it was intensely painful to acknowledge my presence. "I said it was fine." His terse tone failed to stop the beads of sultry heat rising inside me. His raw, innate power spoke to me in ways I did not understand. I stopped my slow walk to him, opting to make him a Scotch.

Maybe it will loosen him up, and we can talk properly.

I walked over to the minibar, selected a Cristal glass, and started pouring. An aura of delicious heat sent my pulse into overdrive. Saint. Close by. I shut my eyes as my heart pitter-pattered in my chest. The glass tippled to the side, and with janky nerves, I stood it upright.

"Shit." Closing my eyes, Saint closed the gap, his hard-on sitting above my ass.

"Keep pouring the drink," he growled in my ear, his large

hands tracing sinful lines along my frame.

Fuck.

There was little room to turn around, but no need. Saint dipped his head to my open collarbone, dropping a kiss on it. I wondered if he knew the effect he had on me. Shots of white-hot electricity zapped through my body, but I didn't move, waiting for him. His other hand grazed down the side of my arm, sending a wave of shivers through it.

Goddamn you, Saint. Taunting me like this.

Trembling with the drink in hand, I found the courage to turn around with only a hair's breadth between us. Up close, the sheer depth of his icy blue eyes was evident, but still, I tilted my chin to him. I was a Saliano, after all. I wouldn't let him win completely. His hands closed over my damp ones, his tongue rolling around in his merciless mouth, resting for a minute around mine.

"I'll take that. Thanks." The rich bass in his voice sent a straight shot of heat to my pussy, and I quickly sidestepped him while he gulped down the amber liquid. Saint was having none of it. He caught me with a splayed hand over my stomach. "Where are you going?"

"I thought you wanted a drink since..."

He shook his head, scoffing as his head tipped back, draining the drink. "You thought wrong, Mira." He lassoed me into his arms. As I inhaled a sharp breath, our heads practically bumped into one another. Tendrils of my loose hair flew forward, grazing his face. He held one of my wrists close to his chest, but the other went roaming down my skirt and lifting it. All my senses were alive as I craved his wicked touch. It was the only way he'd let me in.

"Saint," I breathed. "Don't you think we should talk about things?" I tried to reason as he dropped my wrist, holding my bare ass for leverage, pulling the edge of my panties to the side. His two digits slid gently between my slickened folds, his palm flattening, pushing, and caressing.

My breath quickened as I whimpered in desire. "Remember this, Mira, remember this in Paris," he prodded through gritted teeth. "Come on, Mira, remember? Is it okay for you now, baby?" he teased. "Do you want me to stop so we can talk about it?"

"No, I don't want you to stop. Keep going, Saint." I'd never yearned for a man's touch as much as I did for Saint's. It made the pain drift away, where it was only him and me and nothing else. Only our passion, our everlasting fire. It was badly toxic between us. It felt dangerously good. Saint pulled his fingers out abruptly, sucking on them, his eyes on me.

"Better than I remember." His hand slid down between my fingers as he led me to the bedroom, my heart beating like a wild woman's. A light breeze filtered through our love den, tickling my face, but I didn't have time to close the window. I stood before him as he slid my skirt down, and I stepped out of them. No talking. Only jagged promises left undone.

I ran my hands to the top of his shirt, wanting to unbutton him, but he pushed my hand away with a command. "No, this one's for you, Mira." His hot mouth covered mine, sucking on my bottom lip as liquid fire pooled between my legs.

I laid back, sinking into our comfortable bed and opening my legs for him. He dragged my silk panties off, discarding them on the side of the bed, his open possessiveness clear in his eyes.

His tongue, a combination of roughness and slick saliva, glided up my inner thigh, my body shuddering in response. He blew cool breath over my pussy as my fingers curled amongst the sheets. His mouth danced lightly at first over my swollen nub, pushing, pulling, and sucking.

I relaxed, letting the moment take me. If this is where Saint and I were, I wanted to take it in. I could taste the fire in his mouth as his tongue searched inside me. His pace quickened, my blood afire as I opened my legs wider, his pace relentless. A peak of energy was building in the heart of my pussy, and I was close to the edge, dying to fly. I thrust my hips up to meet Saint's mouth, desperate to come, but he pushed me down with his hand. He softened, drawing back as I writhed, wanting to claim my orgasm. He denied me as I whimpered in exquisite torture, withdrawing his mouth from me.

Shocked, my eyes flew open as he wiped the remnants of me off his mouth with a smirk.

"Saint..." I cried out, feeling cheated, my pussy throbbing for attention.

He turned his well-cut back, walking out of the room.

Chapter 5

Saint

I wanted her to suffer like I had all these years, but the truth was I needed and wanted Mira as much as she wanted me. The love between us was still there. I felt it every time I touched her, and it killed me even more.

I wanted to bring her to climax and hear her cry out my name, but my pride and memories of what she'd done to destroy my family overtook the moment. I jerked off in the office with her in my mind to relieve the tension of my hardened cock.

Dissatisfying as it was, images of Mira reaching her French-tipped nails down to her pussy and finishing made the blood rush hard to my cock again. I finished quickly and cleaned up before returning to my chair.

Frustrated, I skimmed a hand through my dark hair with a growl. Thankfully, we were at different ends of the penthouse, so I had time to think about our marriage and what we'd become. She was right. We had to talk, but I'd chosen to delay us hashing it out a little longer.

Distracting myself from the deep-seated pain, I touched the edge of an old photo of me and Riza together in happier times.

Things were simpler back then in my teens.

I was a foot soldier, but more so an earner as I brought the cash in for my famiglia. Even then, I was enterprising with neighborhood schemes going on.

Riza believed in me back then, too. *"You're gonna take Dad's place on the throne. I hate to break it to the old man, but you've got what it takes. One day you'll be the Chi-town's kingpin, bro."*

I'd known it, too. I was a cocky shit. Riza and I would sit on a dirty Chicago industrial rooftop where we'd eat pizza and talk shit about the schemes we'd produced.

"Yeah, but you're gonna be right there with me. We're gonna rule these streets from the cops to the politicians to the mom-and-pops. It's happening, and when people hear the name Riccini, they're gonna respect it or pay up otherwise..."

I raised my arm, outstretching and pointing with a squint in my eye. *"Bang, bang."* Riza and I had laughed, and she'd thrown a French fry in my face.

That's the relationship we'd had, and if I had been there on the day they shot her, I would have taken the bullet instead.

I kissed my two fingers and touched them to her face. "Love you, sister. I'm gonna make good on my promise—restore the Riccini name. I hope you're resting up there." I stopped myself before I turned into a bumbling fool. I was waiting for Falcone to come through.

Minutes later, two raps at the door pulled me out of my misery.

"Aye, it's me."

Falcone's gravelly voice was distinguishable enough that I knew it was him.

"Come in."

He entered, bringing the fresh, crispness of the Chicago air with him. Shrugging out of the charcoal trench coat, I got up to offer him a drink. I noticed he had his satchel bag slung over his shoulder. I eyed him cautiously, not wanting any more bad news.

"What's so urgent you had to come and see me in person?"

"You might want to pour yourself one while you're over there. By the time I'm done telling you what I have to say, it's ah...gonna fuck you up a bit. Not gonna lie."

Frowning, I poured myself and Falcone a scotch on the rocks. I handed it to him, surveying the graveness on his bristly face. "Sit. Rip the band aid off and tell me. I got enough shit to deal with right now. I'm fucking over it. Can't be any worse than it already is."

"Right now, I agree with you." His eyes homed in on the picture of Riza and I. "Fuck boss, you still got her picture right there now?" Falcone sat in front of me cross-legged, his satchel on my office desk.

"Yeah," I sighed, letting the fire of the Scotch burn my throat. "Glutton for punishment. I don't want to forget her. Riza was everything to me. We were twins. We had a special connection that can't be..." I stopped, not wanting to hear myself say Riza's name anymore. "Anyway, look, forget about it. I don't want to think right now. Tell me what's going on."

Falcone sipped, sliding the drink on the table. "Alright, I'm gonna just knock you on your ass. Ain't no other way to say it. Mira Saliano is not a Saliano. She's a De Luca. She was born to a baker from South Naples."

The spinning. The same spinning I'd experienced when I found out Mira betrayed me, when my father died, when Riza died, was back, making me see stars. I pinched the skin between my temples together. "Come again, Falcone? Are you fucking telling me that

Mira's adopted? Wh-what are you saying right now? Explain it because this shit doesn't make fucking sense." I kept my voice low, not knowing where in the house Mira was.

"It's true. I got firsthand knowledge about it, and you're not gonna like it. First off, I wanna say this was back in the early days. Nearly three decades now. She ain't adopted, though...more like stolen." Falcone twisted his hand over like a seesaw, dropping the bombshell on me as my heart hammered through my chest. "Me and your father were having a few head butts, and I didn't really know if I could trust him. So I had some side gigs going and I was taking a few odd clean-up jobs here and there, if you know what I mean."

I nodded slowly, sitting back in my seat, my mind racing in a million different directions.

Mira adopted? Not a Saliano? Who the fuck am I married to?

Falcone's voice forced me back to the present. "Boss..."

"I think I know what you mean. Go on."

Falcone coughed, looking me dead in the eye. "Angelica Saliano hired me right after she lost her baby. She was in a lot of grief. She'd lost another one before that, another girl, and she'd...ya know, heard about my work through the grapevine." Falcone measured my responses, my heart threatening to burst out of my ribcage.

"What the fuck has she got to do with this? You mean Mira's mother?" I hissed, trying to make heads and tails of what Falcone was telling me.

"Yeah, yeah, her. The real b-i-t-c-h is her. She paid me half a million to off Mira's family and switch the hospital records, so she could keep her. She was a real psycho. A dumb one. Frankie wanted a girl so bad. His little princessa. Mrs. Saliano was desperate to keep Frankie. That guy runs his dick all over

Chicago, so I don't know what for." Falcone sat back, thumping his hands against the seat chair in nonchalance. "So, you know I did what I had to do. I slit Mr. and Mrs. De Lucas' throats, called it a day, and took the money."

I gulped down the hard knot lodged in my throat, staring at the family portrait behind Falcone's head. My family had been a pillar of the Chicago community since the 1930s, right back to the bootlegging era, and had made good on American soil. Mira had been robbed of a family name and thrust into our sordid family rivalry without her permission. A wave of empathy and pain for her circumstance flooded me in waves. I blinked it away, getting up to pour another Scotch.

I didn't expect Falcone to care. He was a hardened criminal, starting young when he'd been sent to war in Russia. "You got something in that bag, don't you?"

"Yeah, proof. Documents I kept to extort the Salianos in the future."

Seething anger replaced my sorrow for Mira as the liquid hit the glass. "Falcone, you're bringing me these documents now? After all this fucking time? You could have saved my sister with them!" I smashed my hand down on the bar cabinet, the glass jumping along with the bottles.

"I know, but your father told me to hold off until time was right. Said I needed to keep them close. The Don's orders. I can't go against him, even now when he is gone. He knew what I did. He approved."

My shoulders tensed when I put my hands down on each side of the bar. "The fuck! My father knew about this?" I shrieked.

"Yeah, yeah, he knew. Keep your voice down if you don't want your lady to hear."

"The fuck!" I roared at a midrange level. "Dammit, Falcone!"

"Hey, this is how the game goes. I had to do what I had to do. If I had my way, Nick should have put the Salianos on blast a long time ago. It would have saved many people. I don't know why he didn't. Maybe he was waiting to get a bigger payday out of them. Maybe the Boston deal. I don't know. You know, Nick sometimes kept things under wraps until the last minute." A tic popped up in my jaw, and I rubbed it out, pacing the office. My father and his hidden schemes. A lot of the time, they panned out, but every now and then, they backfired. Whatever plan he had going, he didn't have time to execute it.

"I dropped their bodies off in the Nightvale Woods out of town. Nick made sure the evidence was botched, so the case remains unsolved. Cops on payrolls in the District Attorney's office. It's never going to be a cold case. It's dead and buried, excuse the pun," Falcone said matter-of-factly. I understood his stoniness. Falcone didn't have a heart; inside his chest was a ball of dark hate.

"Why the fuck didn't you tell me before I made the deal with Frankie? You could have told me."

"Yeah, I guess I could have, but in my wisdom, I figure we needed this peace treaty. It's the truth. I thought I would tell you once everything settled a little. I think everything's worked out for the best."

I rubbed the crick out of my neck, adjusting it. "Yeah, yeah, too many dead bodies in Chicago. Tell nobody about this. Show me." I marched back to Falcone, and he handed the manilla folder to me as I flopped back down into my chair. Graphic photos of dead bodies contorted into different positions latched onto my eyeballs, not letting go. Mira's whole family slain. Her real family, at the hands of one of my own. My lips pinched together as I flicked through the photos in disgust, including official hospital records and a newborn wrapped tight in a blanket.

"What do you wanna do?"

"You're not getting these back, Falcone. Mira is the glue to this thing. If Frankie catches a whiff that she isn't even his daughter..." I blew out air. "We can't say shit. It's going to re-engage a street war. Keep it under wraps."

Falcone got up to leave, knowing he'd worn out his welcome in my office with the dirt he'd dredged up. But he shot one last dagger at me. "My loyalty lies with the Riccinis and always has, despite my and your father's rumbles. I could have gone with the Salianos after that. Angelica asked me to, but I said no. You need to know that." He flexed and balled up his fingers as I stared at Riza's photo again.

"Okay. It's done. I have to protect Mira now. I'm her family, and I must keep the streets in harmony, so...my father's decision stands. We keep it silent. It's between you and me, Falcone. I know you're loyal. You've proven it too many times to count." I let the shards of pain cut through me with the news. "Go."

"You got it. Things are steady on the street. The peace treaty is gonna work out."

I dropped into my chair, drinking two more glasses of Scotch before I emerged. Mira was curled on the couch watching Netflix. So innocent, so unassuming, regardless of the cold vixen she had to play.

"You okay in here?"

"Fine, watching movies. Are you?" she asked, her voice like music to my soul.

"I'm doing alright. How about I join you?"

A dumbfounded look of confusion played over her face. One minute I was torturing her, the next wanting to hold her in my arms.

"You want to join me now, Saint? You left me hanging earlier."

A long pause hung in the air as I kneaded the knots out of my neck. "I know. Cruel of me. I'll make it up to you, I promise. Let me make some popcorn, and I can get the chef to make your favorite dish. Alright, darling?"

Chapter 6

Mira

Saint and I were tiptoeing around one another, and after him leaving me wound up tight, he made up for it tenfold during the next few nights in the week. His movements were more fluid, even tenderhearted, and the way he spooned me after sex gave me hope we might make it.

Slowly, I peeled his hand off my hip but turned to face him as sunlight flooded our bedroom. His body heat turned the bed into a furnace. I stroked the side of his sleeping face, noticing he looked like he was in pain in his dreamworld. I hated that Riza and my mother had been caught in the maelstrom of chaos I'd unknowingly created.

"Take care, Mira. I love you more than you'll ever know. I risked everything to have you in my arms."

Those were the last words spoken before my mother slipped away in her hospital bed. A vomity feeling rose in my stomach when I recalled the words drifting out of her lifeless lips.

She hadn't lied about doing anything to have me.

I looked over at the man who was like a distant stranger to me during the day, but we were fiercely passionate lovers by night, reminding me of our Paris rendezvous all over again.

Saint must have felt my eyes burning onto him as they opened, his breathtaking baby blues staring at me. His fingers locked with mine under the covers.

"Morning, Saint. Sleep well?" I asked gingerly, not sure what version of wrath I would receive.

"I did. I felt you move about all night. Could you not sleep?"

"Something like that. A little restless, thinking of my mother." I snuck it in quietly, but I didn't want to sweep my grief under the carpet for Saint. As much as he was giving me the hot and cold treatment, I at least wanted to be myself in our home.

Saint shot me a pitiful expression, propping up his head with his arm. "I'm sorry about your mother in more ways than one." He leaned in, kissing the top of my head, leaving me confused.

"What do you mean, in more ways than one?"

Probing Saint when he didn't want to provide information was difficult at the best of times, but cracks appeared occasionally.

"I just mean, did you really know her, Mira?"

A spine numbing feeling came over me as I regarded him.

"I knew her as best as she let me," I confessed. "I don't think I know any of my family, especially after what Marco manipulated me to do, but it's my cross to bear." I kept it to a mumble, but Saint ignored my victimhood, pulling the covers back as if the conversation was becoming too intimate for him.

Saint understood Marco had coerced me to gather trade secrets, but it didn't warm the cockles of his closed heart to me. If anything, it widened the gap between us.

The Don of the Riccini family rose, and I admired all of him. Battle scars and all.

"We all make our choices, Mira. We must live and die by the sword. I miss Riza every day, but we both understood—and I still understand—that any day on these Chicago streets can be my last. That's the oath of the Omerta."

Saint cracked his knuckles, avoiding my gaze and leaving me frigid from his chill. His scratchy voice illustrated his grief. All I wanted was to lay my head on his shoulder. The words were on the tip of my tongue, but my mouth opened and closed just as quickly, shutting down what I truly wished to express.

No. You can't tell him. You haven't gotten that far yet. Keep it to yourself.

"You're still standing, Saint, and you made the right decision with the peace treaty. I can't apologize enough for the pain I caused our famiglias. If you're still angry with me, and that's why..." I let the words trail off, not sure it was helping us.

For a man so full of savageness, he moved with an eloquent power that captivated me. Every muscle, a masterpiece of its own design.

"Leave it, Mira. I've got a meeting all day on the south side of Chicago for a duplex acquisition. Can you keep yourself occupied?"

"I'll be fine. There are some calls that I have to make." I dropped my head back to the pillow, feeling lost and alone.

"Okay." Saint surprised me by leaning forward, his lips sinking into mine. I kissed him back, opening my mouth willingly. He darted his tongue in, lightly taking control of my face with his warm hands.

My breath hitched, hoping for more, but he ended the passion with a few light kisses, retiring to the shower.

Staring at the ceiling, I promised myself that I would make it right between us. I'd given him false hope in Paris, and now we were married by force.

Shuddering, I thought about how lucky I was that it was Saint. It would be a hellish existence if it were any other mob boss. Sighing, I wished for the best; at least we were getting along. Love? Now that was a word that left me clueless. It was too soon to call it.

Once Saint left, it gave me the freedom to speak to Ella. She'd been the only person I'd wanted to travel with as my minder five years ago. The entire trip had centered on Saint and me wanting to prove I belonged as a mobster's daughter. What a fucking crock it had turned out to be. I willed my thoughts back to what truly mattered. Ella was more than a dear friend; she was holding a secret that would cost me dearly if ever it saw the light of day before I was ready.

I basked in the sunlight on our couch, letting it warm me up. Hunkering down into the couch, I glanced over my shoulder towards the kitchen. Sometimes the house cleaner lingered around, restocking the fridge, so I had to be careful. The walls talked. As soon as I punched in the number to Ella, an extreme wave of anxiety flooded me.

Would she be there?

I scrolled through my messages, hitting the phone icon on FaceTime. The melodic tone of the phone ringing killed me for a few seconds before Ella's bright face showed up.

"Hi! How are you?" she asked with a chirp in her voice, but her expression quickly shifted to worry. "You look stressed. Everything is running super smooth. You don't need to worry about anything, Mira."

I rubbed my heart, letting go of the pent-up sigh I harbored. "Good, good. Is he..." before I got the chance to finish, she interjected.

"He's fine. Sleeping as we speak. I will not let you down. It's what I agreed to."

"Listen, I can't talk long. I'm terrified I'll be caught. I wanted to check-in, is all. Are you okay?" I questioned, palpitations racing in my chest as I looked around the room, paranoid.

"I'm perfect. Paris is busy, hustle, hustle, but nothing like Chicago. I've got my hands full, and Champs Elysees is our favorite place to visit."

Groaning, I floated back to Paris. Oh, if I could turn back the clock...would I? Saint had left an imprint on my soul, and the worst of it was that I'd let him.

"That's so great," I replied with fake enthusiasm. "Kisses and hugs to you both. Look, I gotta go. I'm...I can't talk long." I stuttered, stumbling over my own fragile emotions. If I spoke to her any longer, the pain would only spiral me into depression.

"Mira, are you going to be alright? Have you told him?"

Exhaling a jittery breath, I dug my thumb into my palm to stop myself from crying. "No. I haven't, but I must. Time isn't right, but listen...I have to go. Kisses to you both, okay?" I choked out.

"Okay, Mira. Take care, and don't beat yourself up too much. Everything is going to work out."

I gulped down the ache, burying my invisible tears. "I'll send money tomorrow. Bye, Ella, be well."

"You too, Mira."

My phone slipped from my fingers onto the couch as my head spun in disorientation.

My life is a mess. How do I cope with this?

I sat momentarily, closing my eyes, but I recovered, deciding to visit my mother's grave to pay my respects, even though thinking of her that way made goosebumps pop out on my skin.

Picking up my phone, I rang the driver. "Yes...Ricardo, can you take me to Woodfern Cemetery? I want to visit my mother. She liked red roses, so I have to stop by the florist first."

"Sure thing, Mira. I'll swing the car around now."

I quickly jumped into the shower, put on makeup after, coated my lips red, and sprayed my Chanel No. 5. I did a small twirl in front of the mirror to make sure everything was in place as I clutched onto my cross. Angelica had never cared for slovenliness and taught me the art of being a sophisticated woman.

"A Saliano woman must always play her part. Gather yourself, Mira, for we are the anchors to these childish Saliano men."

I'd watched the light go out in my mother's eyes years ago, but still, she had endured, rewarded with guilt presents such as cars, jewelry, and expensive overseas trips, but still a lack of love from my father to her.

"Why don't you leave him?" I asked her one day when she cried for the umpteenth time.

She'd looked at me as if I'd stuck a knife in her back. *"My father was a mobster, and so was my grandfather. Your father has taken care of me. I don't have the strength to leave him now. Besides, what would become of my life? I would be poor."*

Reining in my thoughts, I headed downstairs to find Ricardo waiting for me at the front. We took the short ride to the public cemetery, stopping over at a nearby florist to pick up the roses.

I picked up the twelve blood-red roses and covered my head in a shawl as the wind kicked up. Chicago wasn't called the Windy City for no reason. Ricardo waited by the side of the cemetery while I bent down at my mother's grave. I picked up the crumples of prior red roses, sweeping them away from the speckled gray stone.

"I don't understand you, and I don't like to speak ill of the dead, but what you've done to me is unforgivable." My voice cracked as a caustic tear trickled down my cheek. "You brought me into a cold, dark world. You created an illusion." My words traveled to the underworld where she surely lay, my heart and my mind broken through grief and exhaustion. "But still, I loved you. You were the only mother I knew," I remarked bitterly, cupping my hands, infusing them with breath. I'd been absent-minded enough to forget my gloves. Timidly, I skimmed my fingers over her headstone, wishing things—so many things—were different. "I love you, Angelica. Mother. I love you." Sniffing, I placed a hand over my mouth, silencing the wailing my soul wanted to partake in.

Besides, Ricardo waited curbside, and I didn't want to be seen as a nervous wreck. Salianos were never meant to break.

"We Salianos don't wear our hearts on our sleeves. That shit is for bitches. You buck up and do what has to be done. You're a Saliano, and I expect you to act like one at all times."

A sentiment my father lived and one he'd instilled when I'd cried on my thirteenth birthday. Ever since then, I thought twice before shedding a tear.

I couldn't do what Angelica did.

I wouldn't keep secrets until my deathbed.

The truth could hurt, but I couldn't deny Saint this truth.

"I have to tell Saint. It will set him free. Isn't that how the saying goes?" I whispered softly, hoping the harsh wind of Chicago would answer my prayers.

Chapter 7

Saint

I'd finished alive for another night. To the average man, that was a given, but not for a man like me. It was a privilege to be above ground.

Mira immediately entered my brain as I gripped the wheel, pressing the remote to my apartment's garage.

I still love you, from Paris to Chicago. You had a hold on my heart in the first week I spent with you. I tried to fuck you out of my brain with the others, but it didn't work. No one compares...you did what you had to do, but fuck, it hurts. I get it...here you are again, stealing my heart. The closer I get to you, the more I love you. But still, how can I trust you, Mira?

The car clock ticked over to 12:30. Standard operating hours for me. In fact, it would have been later if not for her. She had a tether to my heart, and I always wanted to return to her when it came time.

I switched off the radio, cutting the engine, satisfied with the new business expansion talks into Boston territory. The Stanton brothers ran a good game through the nightclubs and bars, and I wanted the Riccinis to tap in. There was some tap dancing between us, but we were making progress.

Rolling my tight shoulders back, I entered our apartment, leaving my shoes off at the door, not wanting to wake Mira. I padded down the dark hallway. Peace filled me as I watched the sleeping beauty from the doorway. Under the layers of pain, she brought a serenity I'd never found until the first time I had seen her. Pride wouldn't let me tell her that, but I felt it when I was inside her.

I walked through to the ensuite, stripping down and showering the grime of the day off me. Fifteen minutes later, I lay on my back, slipping beneath the covers, but I wanted to touch her so badly.

Shutting my feelings off, I breathed deeply, rolling to the other side, but a whimper from Mira's lips woke me. Shifting, I turned back, laying a hand on her bare shoulder.

"Mira?" She convulsed, wriggling and twisting as if lost in a nightmare.

"No! Stop!" she called out. I tugged at her shoulder more urgently.

"Mira, honey, you're having a nightmare. Wake up. Come on," I coaxed, talking into her ear. Her body was damp with a light sheen of sweat. I turned her towards me. "Mira."

Her doe eyes flung open, rattled from her dream state, and my heart jump-started. All I wanted to do at that moment was soothe her. This life wasn't etched in her soul like mine, but she'd more than held her own. A feature I secretly admired.

"Uh...what happened? Did you just get in?" Her cheeks were flush, and she was warm to the touch.

"You were dreaming. What were you thinking about?"

"I don't know. I can't remember." She licked her lips, but the doubt in her voice made me believe she remembered the dream. I slid my leg in between her hot thighs, drawing her closer.

My mouth found hers in the darkness, inducing relaxation. Her lips were like a tranquilizer drug to me. Sucking on her top lip, her hands eased around my back, her hips inching forward. Fingers traveled up the nape of my neck and into the damp tendrils of my hair. Briefly, I disentangled from her, drawing a line over her bottom lip.

"Better now?" I asked in a hoarse voice.

"Yes. I'm glad you're here. I was worried about you. I know I shouldn't be, but I get scared sometimes." Her vulnerability and sweet heart melted away any deep-seated pain we both caused one another.

"Fuck the worry. I'm not going anywhere."

I trapped her provocative, swollen lips under mine. I wanted to hear her call my name before I told her the ugly truth. Reaching under her silk night slip, I discovered she was bare downtown, her ass fitting neatly in my greedy hands.

I chuckled, my carnal instincts rising along with my engorged cock. "Fuck, Mira, you're not wearing any underwear. Are you trying to kill a man?" I wanted entry straight away. This wasn't a night for tenderness, but for devouring, and my raw eroticism wanted to run wild.

"I don't want you to die, but I want you inside me," she declared confidently, up for the challenge.

Her hypnotizing sweetness tempered my flame, but still, I scorched with ferocity for every inch of her tight flesh. "It's not going to be sweet tonight, Mira. I fucking need you. You're gonna have to be okay with that."

"Yes," she blinked back at me. "Fuck me, Saint. Let's forget."

Her command invoked a feverish groan, enough to send me over. I roughly flipped her on her back, but she bucked up against me, licking her tongue. "No, I want to ride you."

Growling, the throbbing of my cock blurring my vision, I slid under her, smacking her tight ass. "Get on top."

She lifted her silk gown off, her hair flowing like a waterfall around her shoulders. A wanton imp was now straddling me, raging a river through my hot veins. I tweaked my fingers over her erect nipples, tugging lightly, my cock super-hard.

If she didn't hurry, I planned to grab her hips and drop her onto my fat cock myself. She went one better, sliding her body down my thighs, bending her head forward, and slurping on me like a lollipop.

Me, Saint Riccini, was powerless against a woman who'd started a family war, and she was all I ever wanted. Her hot, saucy mouth opened wide to take all of me. My eyes widened as she dragged me deep toward the back of her throat. I pushed my head back into the pillow, my cock primed for the explosion.

Not like this. No. No.

Shaking my head, I lifted her petite shoulders as she wiped my sex from her lips. "No, Mira. Ride."

Her legs split, her eyes trained on me as she eased herself onto my cock, spreading her fingers over my chest. "Ahh, Saint," she moaned, her champagne locks falling forward, stroking my ego.

"Say my name again, Mira," I instructed, smacking an open palm against her hot little ass as her greedy pussy gobbled up my thirsty cock.

"Saint," she mouthed, pushing down harder, grinding her wet goodness on me. I loved watching the sway of her hips circling desperately, like I was needy for her.

My hands steadied around her shapely waist as I gave her all of me. If I couldn't say it to her because of pride, I could at least show my love to her. Her round pert breasts bounced in tempo with her thrusts as I kneaded them like dough in my hands.

Her ass slapped against the top part of my thighs, sweat glistening as I thumbed her clit. Her pussy vibrated around my length. "Come for me, Mira," I urged.

It didn't take long for her release, enticing my cock to do the same. She uttered a long-drawn-out groan, her legs shaking in orgasmic aftermath.

"My God, Saint!" A line of sweat drizzled down my temple, banks of unhinged passion breaking loose.

"You don't know what you do to me, Mira. Honestly."

I flipped her over, spooning her from the back, slick sweat covering me. I pumped into her, the position tighter, holding her waist close, gushing hot breath into her ear. It felt good to possess her this way.

Her breathing labored as my cock swelled until I burst free, emptying inside her.

"Fucking yes, Mira!" I cried out in jagged rasps. "You're mine, all mine."

"I'm yours, Saint, and always have been," she confessed. "There was never a man before or after you. Only you."

Now that was music to my ears. She'd said it. Paris made me wonder if she really cared about our connection, but she'd said it. Eased the pain a little.

My heart raced as I released my grip on her, falling back onto bed sheets of lathered-up sweat. After coming down and my heart relaxing, I lay facing Mira in the night.

"Is that enough to forget, Mira?" I skimmed my hands around the edge of her plump breasts, admiring her feminine form, grateful she was in my bed.

"For now. You helped with that." She giggled, inducing a smile from me, but probably after the truth I revealed, it wouldn't last.

I raised her fingers to my lips, kissing them. "Mira...you said we should talk, so let's talk. I have something to tell you, but it's not pleasant. I don't want secrets between us. You're my wife."

She slid her top lip over her bottom one, rousing my cock again, but what I had to say was too important for a round two. "Tell me, Saint. I'm not as fragile as you think. I can handle it."

A stab in my stomach told me otherwise. I paused for a beat, thinking of the right words, but there were none. "You're not a Saliano." I let the revelation sink in before I took the conversation further.

"Yes, I'm aware."

My heart skipped a beat, jarred by her response. "You knew?"

"De Luca is my surname. My mother told me on her deathbed. I went to pay my respects today." Her mouth curled into a lopsided smile.

That beat skip escalated to shutter speed in my chest. "I don't fucking think you should have visited her with what she's done to you. She changed the whole course of your life."

Mira scratched at the bottom of my chin affectionately, placating me. "I met you, though, didn't I?"

"How much do you know, Mira? Have you ever tried to look for your parents?"

"Umm, no, my mother didn't tell me the rest. Let's not talk about this, Saint." Mira turned her face from me, drawing her hand back.

"No, Mira. You have to know the full truth," I pressed, pulling her close. "Falcone. He slit the throats of your entire family, murdering them, just after you were born. We covered it up. Angelica paid my capo to do it because she miscarried." I punched out the last parts of the sentence, my heart tearing in two as I told Mira the gritty truth.

She shook her head exactly like when she emerged from her nightmare. "You are cruel! Why would you say something like this? Saint," she sobbed. "Saint, please, tell me it's not true. Angelica," she gasped. "She wouldn't do that to me." Her bottom lip quivered, tears glittering in her eyes, and all the love I harbored for her, I wanted to give.

"Mira, *bella*, I'm sorry. I didn't want to tell you, but I had to tell you the truth. We can't build on lies." Tears flowed like an overflowing dam, my arm wet from her tears. I'd never seen her break down. Her emotions were normally locked down. I cocooned her in my arms, wanting to absorb the pain for her.

"Saint! I can't...I can't..." I let her be, holding her through the night, and stroking her hair. I was the bad guy this time, and I hated myself for it. I kissed her hair as we both eventually drifted off to sleep.

I woke up late, with Mira dead asleep. She needed to rest. The streets of Chicago didn't sleep, and my phone was angrily waiting for me to answer. I left her a note and returned with her favorite take-away to cheer her up.

Sullen for the next few days, I didn't know how to make it right. Mira's whole life had been a lie, and she'd been betrayed on so many levels. "You have a family, Mira. Your father loves you. Don't think he doesn't. You have a family here with me, too."

She broke me as she looked up from her curled-up position on the couch. "What is my life, Saint? I don't think I fucking care anymore."

I stared at the beautiful, broken mess in front of me, vowing to love and protect her for as long as I had breath inside my lungs.

Chapter 8

Mira

Once again, I was being used as a bargaining chip. Facing sideways, I slid a hairpin into the side of the sleek updo, putting on my game face. Saint's raised voice traveled all the way to me in the bathroom.

"That's not their territory! Maywood, Forest Park, and Oak Park are ours. Fix it, Falcone." I winced from his barking because in the underbelly of Saint was a certified killer. He redirected his tension toward me. "Mira, we have to go. The meeting is in fifteen minutes, and traffic is a bitch this time of night."

"Coming!" I emerged, my nerves close to snapping. Trade negotiations between the families were stalling, and the promise of warfare hung in the balance. "Okay, I'm ready." Saint's irritation eased when he set eyes on me.

"Sorry," he grumbled, handsome in his sky-blue collared shirt matching his eyes and black slacks. The bulge of his bicep was evident as he raked a hand through his midnight locks. He was perched on the edge of our chaise lounge, buttoning up. "I didn't mean to snap." His eyebrow arched as he beckoned to me. I walked in between his legs, touching the side of his face. It seemed to settle his temper. He rested on it, closing his eyes. "Mira, Mira,

Mira. Fucking losing my mind."

"No, you're not, Saint. You've come this far, and you're a master of this game."

Saint nodded, standing up and interlocking his fingers with mine, but a shaky feeling still sat within me.

Tell him, Mira. You can't let this go. The anxiety must have shown outwardly as Saint opened the front door.

"Are you worried about the meeting or something else?" Concern laced his voice.

"No." I smiled weakly. "Just recovering from the news about my mother, and I have to face my two-faced snake of a brother. I haven't seen him since my mother's funeral."

Saint's eyes changed colors. "He's a dirty rat, but hey, what do you expect from a Saliano? No offense."

Partly, I worried about seeing my ratfink brother, but mostly, I was nervous about telling Saint the unbearable truth. Once I did, it would rock everything between us that was good.

We arrived at the secret location, howling winds blasting through the city. A deep-rooted sense of dread lined the pit of my stomach as my stilettos hit the ground. If I was going to be embroiled in a mob crossfire, I would at least be buried looking every inch the Saliano I was. Even Chi-town's skies were burdened with the gloom of rain.

Saint's murderous expression caused my stomach to bubble as he clutched my hand, joined in flank by Falcone, Lupo, and three other men I didn't recognize.

I don't like this. Not one little bit. Shit. What have I done?

The wind continued pummeling, swaying me as Saint dragged me in front of him, a whiff of his Tom Ford cologne reminding me of his sex appeal. Everyone was dressed in black except for me, dressed in virginal white with my fake purity.

A searing heat drew my eyes left before we walked into the dingy air hangar on the outskirts of South Chicago.

My father and brother walked in step, two sides of the same filthy coin. Narrowing my eyes in contempt, I death-stared them both. Fuck. They had more men than the Riccinis. It was a surreal feeling to be on the other side of the fence, looking at monsters I now considered my enemies. My loyalties were now with Saint. I was a Riccini, and that's how my father ordered it. In this mafia game, loyalty is the difference between being dead or alive.

A large U-shaped table was set up in front of us, with one desk at the end with a gavel. On the table was alcohol, and in each back corner, security guards manned the spot stoically. I let my eyes cover as much ground as possible, the tension thick in the air. These men had AK47s strapped over their chests.

"Sit by me. Right side." Saint dipped his mouth to my ear, and I followed his lead.

"Okay," I replied, as my father acknowledged my presence.

"Hello, Mira. Nice to see you. You look good."

"Thanks," I replied succinctly. Seeing my father tormented my soul in ways I wasn't ready for.

"Mira. How's it going?"

Brother, how casual you are. You fucking pig.

I kept my cool, holding my chin high, and squinting at him. "Fine, and you?"

He was getting fatter and looking more and more like my father every day, so that was a minor victory.

"Life's good. Can't complain. Few nuts and bolts to sort out, but I'm sure we'll get everything squared away tonight." He rocked back and forth on his heels, jutting out his bottom lip, his barren eyes devoid of any genuine emotion. He was the worst, and even though he was a Saliano, my father shouldn't have trusted him.

"Maybe," I replied defiantly. "If you're involved, probably not. You'd throw your own flesh and blood under the bus," I retorted with a curl of my lip. "Oh wait, you already did that."

Silence governed as Saint touched my palm, restraining me as both families filtered into the main entry point.

Lupo stepped to the gavel, cleared his throat, and stared everyone down. Serious kingpin heavy hitters were in the building, and my nerves were scrambled.

"Okay, you know the drill. Note that the peace treaty is in full effect. All hardware is on the table where I can see it. No funny business. This is a negotiation meeting to iron out the details for the regions of Oak Park, Forest Park, and Maywood. Is that clear?"

"Clear," Frankie Saliano grunted. My breaths were shallow pants. I kept my eyes trained on the back of the space, shivering from the breeze running through it and nail-biting fear. I glanced at my husband, his glacial blue eyes clear, his face fixated on my brother. *Oh shit. A silent war.* I gripped one hand tightly in the other, praying for the meeting to go well.

"Understood," Antonio piped up.

"Let's start. The Riccini family has been successfully covering those three territories for the better part of two decades. You've got Lower West Side and Little Village. What more do you want?" Lupo stated, using his hands the Italian way.

My father held up a fat finger. "Not entirely true. By the last account, you shot my whole crew in 1985, swamping our territory.

We had three laundromats over there. You've got a whole lotta nerve, Lupo."

"All's fair in love and war, isn't it?" Lupo concluded with a wry chuckle.

"No, it's not, Lupo. Part of South Austin is our base operations and we've been there for the same amount of time you have. Where's the boundary outliers?" Antonio argued tersely.

"Agree, plus your bitch-ass foot soldiers play both sides," Marco slammed his fist down.

"You're one to talk about playing both sides," Saint replied in a deadly tone, the room dropping in silence. A stare-off ensued as Marco's eerie chuckle pierced the space.

My eyes darted to the security. All had their hands ready on their triggers.

"Shut up, Marco," I launched a torpedo, frustrated with him getting away with everything.

"Ah, the peace token speaks," Antonio taunted, tapping his fingers together in a temple. A vice-like grip on my leg from Saint under the table reined me in, and I clamped my mouth shut, not wanting to escalate matters on his behalf.

"I think you should direct the conversation away from Mira before I have to shut your mouth for you, Antonio," Saint warned, his eyes darkening and my father smirking.

What was that about?

"Just remember who made this deal happen, Saint," my father spoke. I opened my mouth to protest them talking about me in the third person, but thought better of it. Tears pricked my eyes, wondering if my father had any clue about me. Surely, he did. My nose looked nothing like either of theirs. I had an aquiline nose while my father's was bulbous and my mother's was hooked. The edge of my mouth curled in irony. Now it was all so crystal-clear. All the evidence had been right there in front of me the whole time.

I'm not theirs.

"Fuck you, Frankie. It's not your territory. You already fucked up Englewood. You're not getting anything else from us. You took my sister." Saint's temper got the best of him as he picked up his gun, pointing it at my father's temple.

The whole table moved into action, the security closing in and jogging forward. Panic took over my chest as I touched my hand to the silver cross and did the only thing I could think. I prayed.

Heavenly father...

I didn't get far as Lupo stepped in between the pointed guns, his arms outstretched. "No gun fire. What did I say? Security, take the guns. Take 'em now! Everybody can get them back at the end of the meeting. Let's settle this like classy Chicago mobsters."

Saint kept the grip on his gun until the security guards wrangled it out of his fingers. He death-stared at my father and brother but reluctantly released his fingers digging into my thigh. I rubbed a hand over his in reassurance. Seconds later, he released me as talks resumed.

My father pulled the lapels of his suit jacket together. "I think we all need a drink to loosen up a little. Let's just say we need to talk about a boundary for the region and also a kickback to us on Bucktown on account of you shooting every one of my men over there. How about that?"

Lupo stroked his chin. "That can be discussed, and the drink is a good idea. Ten minutes, and we cut through the bull and work this new agreement out."

Saint sprung up, marching to the table, and returning with

two drinks. Hushed whispers echoed through the draughty concrete shell of a building. At any moment, things could have gone left.

"Here you go." Saint pushed the gin and tonic into my fingers, and I made quick work of knocking it back. Marco kept staring at me, but I wanted no connection to him.

"Thanks. Were you really going to shoot, Saint?"

I'd lost him. He was far away, locked in his own head. "No. I wouldn't risk your life or my famiglia's like that. You were safe and still are. Your brother, however, is a class A prick."

"You won't hear any arguments from me about that."

"Didn't think so," Saint murmured, downing his drink.

Ten minutes later, a heated debate rose again—minus the guns—but fresh agreements were signed.

As the night passed, the sooty skyline cloaked us in darkness as each mob family left in separate directions. Marco caught up, striding beside me as we squeezed through the steel back door. "I hope it was worth it, Mira."

A sinking wave of nausea covered me. It was hard to put my finger on why my brother had evil lurking in his soul. Saint strategically moved me in front of him, away from Marco, reviewing him.

I yanked Saint's hand to focus on me. He had a ticking time-bomb energy, and the peace treaty needed to stand.

Chapter 9

Saint

Days after the negotiations, Mira's obvious allegiance to the Riccinis became apparent. She wasn't really a Saliano, but I'd seen the hope in her father's eyes at the meeting. Mira might have missed it, but I didn't.

Chicago's brand of sunlight had come out to play, capturing the highlights of Mira's cascading waves. No matter how she tried to cover up her innocence, I saw the light in her eyes every day, but now, after the news of her mother's betrayal, it had dimmed. I leaned on the doorjamb as she sat at the kitchen table.

"Yes, is that what he normally eats? Can't you change it?"

I'd caught her the last few days on the phone with a mysterious person I assumed was a childhood friend. Jealousy wasn't part of my core, but our shaky beginning fueled turbulent emotions inside me. Quietly, I entered the kitchen and let her keep talking. She was too engrossed in conversation to notice me.

"Okay. Please make sure next time. Please." She held the back of her neck in distress, and I frowned, not liking the pitch of her voice.

"Mira?" I enquired quizzically. "You alright?"

Her eyes widened and her shoulders visibly tensed.

"Fine, fine," she answered, her tone shaky. She slumped the phone down, no goodbye to whoever she was talking to. My gut instinct was on high alert. She abruptly jumped up from her seat. Suspicion crept into my psyche.

Claudia, isn't that what you called yourself? Why do you lie?

"Who was that?" I cut at her.

"Ah, nobody. I mean, of course, it was somebody. It was Clara. I can call her back later."

"Why didn't you say goodbye to her? You rushed her off the phone. Don't stop talking to your friends because I'm here, Mira. I'm not your captor. I'm your husband."

She'd reached me in record time, fresh-faced like the day she'd been handed over to me at the meeting. She was wearing sweats and a tight sleeveless singlet. It took everything not to spread her out on the cooking bench and lap at her essence for breakfast, but I had to go. Her manicured fingers ran their course up to my neck, my blood firing with lust for her. "Morning, captor," she joked, lifting the bottom of my shirt and pressing her hands onto my flesh.

"Don't start anything you can't finish, Mira," I warned, my cock instantly at half-mast as her parted lips locked with mine. I pushed her lightly with her back to the bench, my legs straddling around hers, trapping her in the middle.

Damn you with those doe eyes. How can I fucking hate you, Mira? How?

Both my arms kept the cage around her as her hands roamed over my chest. "I plan to finish plenty, Mr. Riccini. Think about me during the day. What I want to do to you," she said silkily, reaching down to unzip my pants. Her spicy mouth dissolved any suspicions I had as I panted into her mouth.

"You want a quickie, Mira? I wanna bend you over this table, but I've got to be on the Lower West side in half an hour. It takes half an hour for me to get there."

"Kay."

I scattered kisses on her mouth, not wanting to leave.

"Dress up tonight. I want to take you out. We've been stuck in these trade wars and haven't had time to process being together. Let me show you a good time, Riccini style." I smiled, seeing a little of the old glimmer in her eyes.

"I would love to dress up."

I rested my hands on her ass, tapping it, sucking on her bottom lip. Her breasts crushed against my chest, tempting me.

"Be ready at eight. I'm driving. I'm going to give Ricardo the night off." Her mouth brightened into a wide smile. "There's that smile I like."

She kissed me faintly, and I broke free of her.

"Have a great day. I'll be ready when you get home."

I left for the day to hit the streets, thrown off-balance by my growing feelings for Mira. Every day I loved her a little more, and I didn't think it was possible. In the past, I'd kept a rotation of women and not given a fuck when it was over, but with Mira, all I wanted to do was to love and protect her.

I drove to the other side, calling the finest ladies' boutique in Chicago, wanting to show Mira not all mob perks were bad.

I clicked on my Bluetooth. "Janice, hi, yeah, it's Saint. I need a favor."

"Hi, Saint. Of course. What can I do for you?"

"I need you to send one of your stylists to my apartment for a private viewing. I want you to give my wife whatever she wants. Deck her out. You've got my black card details."

"*Ooo la la*, special occasion, Saint? This sounds extravagant," Janice cooed, drooling over the sales she was about to make.

"No. She is special, though, and I want her to feel that way. We have dinner and a couple of city events, if that helps. She's got style already, but I want her to feel good."

"Good man. Already on it."

"Great. Follow the same instructions when you head through to my apartment. Ricardo will be there."

"Awesome. Pleasure working with you, Saint."

"You too, Janice." Smiling, I drove into the heart of Chicago, ready to move and shake the streets up.

***

When I got home, it was after six, and the house smelled of Chanel No. 5. I loved the scent on her. I inhaled, not remembering what life was like before Mira, nor did I want to find out what it would be like without her.

God, if anything happens to you, Mira, I will carve their hearts out of their fucking chests.

A memory of Riza and me on a road trip filled my mind, blowing sadness through, but also a fierce resolve to keep my famiglia safe, including Mira.

"When you've got the love of a woman, Saint, keep that close to your chest. She can bring you life and death in equal measure. Remember that."

My twin could always see into the future better than I could.

It was only a few weeks later that I met Mira in Paris.

Speaking of...

I could hear Mira on the phone when I stepped further into the apartment. "I want to. It's not the right time. There's so much going on, but I'm working on it."

Hesitating, I waited to overhear more, but by the time I entered our bedroom, Mira had finished the call with whomever she was talking to.

When I set eyes on her, my heart damn near exploded through my chest. Her deft fingers were clasping together a set of pearls around her neck. I stood, awestruck by her beauty. Her full lips were smothered in a beautiful bronze lipstick, and her hair in a gorgeous updo.

The top half of her was covered in intricate, tight black lace patterns accentuating her full breasts, while the bottom half flared out in a black silk skirt. The woman set my blood afire, and it almost tempted me to revoke the dinner invitation and bed her.

She looked up, smiling at me through the mirror.

"You're struggling with those pearls. Here, let me help you." Words failed me for a minute until I got myself together. "You look stunning, Mira. I trust Janice helped you pick out what you wanted?" My hands massaged the top of her shoulders as I dislodged the knots in them, watching her shoulders drop.

"Thank you. She was so wonderful; it was a lovely surprise. Do you like the dress I picked out?" I let my eyes do the talking for me with a cocked eyebrow.

"I don't want to take you out of this house. That's how much I like the outfit, but your beauty's not just skin deep. You're so much more to me, Mira."

Bashfully, she looked down as I pinned her pearl clasp

together, kissing her open shoulder as I so often did. She fingered her pearls, her silver cross taking a rest for the night.

Between our famiglias, her prayers and purity were very much needed.

"I'm not sure what I am, Saint, but I am happy to be here with you. It's not so much the curse I thought it would be."

Chuckling, I fingered one of her waves, letting it run through my fingers. "You are always unpredictable, Mira. That's one thing I can count on. Let's have a good time tonight. Business is running well, and the peace treaty has been a blessing to both families."

"Yes it has, and well, my life has been unpredictable for quite some time now. We only have today."

I said nothing, kissing the top of her head. Her forlorn sadness lingered, and I wanted to take her out of it, at least for the night.

I headed for the shower. With the hot shards of water hitting my back, I began thinking about Mira bearing my child. It was inevitable. We were already family, and healing the pain of losing hers could stem part of the hurt.

After stepping out of the shower, I watched again as Mira's fingers typed on her phone. I dressed quickly, but the phone tumbled out of her fingers in nervousness as soon as I saw it.

Something was wrong... "Mira, you've had that phone attached to your hand for the last few days. Is there a problem?" I asked casually.

The rouge on her cheeks couldn't cover up the deep flush on them. "Ah, no, no. I'm sorry, Saint. It's Clara. She's...she's h-having trouble."

"Hmm, we should invite her here. I want to meet your friends. I want you to be comfortable. Live your life."

"I know you do. I will. You'll like her."

"If she's part of your life and important to you, I'm sure I will."

We arrived at the restaurant an hour later, the ambiance intimate and chilled. It had taken a month to secure a reservation at La Merde, but I had priority, given that they paid us street tax every quarter. Keeping a hand on the small of Mira's back, I led her through the restaurant's side door. Sure, we had priority entry rights, but still, my shoulders tensed as I checked that the host and servers weren't potential enemies.

Given my position, I could never fully relax, but my gun stayed full of enough bullets in its chamber to handle things if it came to it.

"Wow. I've never been here. I've always wanted to...couldn't for obvious reasons." Her face lit up as she sat down at a candle-lit table. The vintage décor and elegance of the place suited Mira.

"This is only the beginning, Mira. I have whole worlds I want to experience with you."

Her eyes landed on me, and I could feel the warmth of her love radiating. "I bet, Saint, and I can't wait."

In the following weeks after the dinner, I gave her insights into what the Riccini empire could bring. Boat cruises, pampering, weekend road trips, and whatever she wanted. But I couldn't shake the feeling that Mira had hidden parts of herself she didn't want to tell me about.

Yet.

Chapter 10

Mira

Every day, my soul crumbled a little more. Keeping secrets from Saint and talking in code on the phone drove me nuts.

I must protect what's mine. He can't be used like a pawn. Not like they've done to me. It's too risky.

My mind was constantly playing tricks on me, but I held steady. His capo had robbed me of my whole identity as a De Luca, but trust was budding between us.

I wiped the excess sauce I had prepared on my apron.

Almost ready.

I stirred the homemade pumpkin sauce on the stove with a wooden ladle, blowing on it to cool it. My fake mother had at least taught me to cook a few dishes in her short life.

Hmm, more pepper.

I sprinkled in a little, tasting again, but my mind was elsewhere.

Saint was being the kindest, most gracious man to me, and he'd suffered as much as I had. Sometimes I saw him staring at Riza's picture for too long, a tortured expression cloaking his rugged face.

Should I tell him? Should I tell him he has a protégé that's looking more like him every day?

Trust was growing between us, and Saint's borders were open, but mine still had a gate or two closed. Alessandro was growing so fast, and it broke my heart not being able to hold him in my arms. Every day, I struggled to know if I was doing the right thing. I always kept my phone close to me, just in case. It pinged three times as I turned down the bubbling liquid. A photo of my beloved popped up with a smile emoji from Ella. Quickly, I scrolled through the snapshots of our love child, my stomach churning.

Oh, Alessandro, Mommy loves you. Oh, how I love you. I'm doing this for you.

I kissed the screen, gulping down the pain of not seeing him. I turned over the phone so as not to let the tears fall and kept cooking. Before I could beat myself up in my own thoughts anymore, Saint's passionate voice vibrated through the kitchen manifold doors.

"Lupo, I'm telling you this can work. Just listen to me. Yes, it's gonna take some feeling out, but it can work. We've got all the regions tight. The Salianos are expanding into Boston, and we need more of a labor force. The Callahan brothers are interested, as are the Zig Zag crew, Murdoch Industries, and the Prentice family, too. They've got their tentacles in the arms dealer market...we need to consider if we really wanna take over Chicago's underworld." My ears perked up, hearing the Saliano name.

I turned off the stove, satisfied with the sauce, only needing the pasta to finish the dish. I scuttled closer to the partially open living room door, which divided the kitchen from it.

"Working with my father and brother?" I said aloud to myself. This I had to hear.

"No, we're not involving the Salianos. It's too fucking risky, and they've jacked enough of our trade. Fuck the hell out of them. We do this on the low. Slow talks with each family, and all of them have something to offer. We can start our own cartel."

My father's face dropped into my mind. I wrenched the doors open, and Saint looked up, smiling.

"Can I talk to you a minute, Saint?" He eased the phone down to his lap. Damn, why did he have to look so good when I wanted to fight with him? He was bare from the neck down. Only his black slacks were on, his athletic, well-cut physique spreading the length of the couch. Shots of white electric heat circuited through my body, but I ignored it, concentrating on why I wanted to talk to him.

He lifted the phone back up after realizing he was still on it, staring at me, mesmerized.

"Ah, Lupo. I gotta go. My wife wants me for something. Looks urgent, plus whatever she's cooking smells too good." Saint dropped the phone after a chuckle, his mouth salivating in open desire, directing his full attention to me.

"Hi, you look fucking sexy in that apron. I'm glad you let the chef take the night off. What's up, baby?"

Hard to be mad at the man, but I controlled my body's reaction to him, speaking my mind. "What was that about the Salianos and keeping them in the dark?"

"You were listening in?" Mild interest lined his face as he sat up, the fibers of his shoulder and biceps twitching as he leaned forward.

"You were talking so loudly, it was hard not to overhear you.

Yes, I was listening, Saint. I heard Salianos in there. A cartel, Saint? Is that a smart idea? It's going to ruffle feathers and land us in hot water. Frankie Saliano is a ruthless man. He's not going to let you start a cartel without his say-so."

Saint's wolfish eyes homed in on me as he got up to stand at full height, stepping towards me. Pussy tingles were all I could feel. He had some sort of hold on me, but I wanted him, too.

"Is that right? Like you're not married to a ruthless man. How quickly you've forgotten Mira, but fuck, do I love you in that apron."

I put up a hand to stop him from getting closer, the heat flaming through my soul. I had to finish what I had to say. "No. You're asking for trouble. There's a peace treaty in place. Did you forget that? Find another way, Saint!" I shot at him passionately, fire emblazoning my eyes. There was no way I wanted to lose him or my father. The stakes were too high. If Saint did this, Alessandro might be forced into the middle of this. Worse yet, my sweet little *figlio* might lose his father to the street war.

He can't grow up like me. He can't.

"Damn, I like you this involved in the business. Caring," he replied smoothly, a dirty smirk riding over his sinful mouth. "I won't do anything to rock the boat just yet. Talk is all. I'm the Don of the Riccini famiglia, and this is how I handle business. My father built this town, and I plan to uphold our legacy. Besides, your brother and father have done enough damage in both our lives, don't you think? You don't have a family because of them, Mira."

Saint's swagger and dominance dripped from his every syllable, his musky scent intoxicating me out of breath. We were inches apart, my defenses breaking apart piece by piece. His words about being unintentionally orphaned stabbed me right in the chest.

I tilted my chin high, like every time we fought. "They might not be my birth family, but I know what's right. If you go through with this, it's war."

Saint's hot breath covered my face, his hands gliding over my arms, locking with my fingers. "Mira Riccini, I will do whatever I want, but I will let nothing happen to you. Do you trust me?" he hissed, electricity dancing through the tips of my fingers. His malicious mouth moved over mine, caressing the fire with a brand all his own. I resisted, not parting my lips right away.

"Maybe I do, maybe I don't," I stated, as he drew back, our fingers still intertwined. A magnetic pull pulsed between us, his pupils dancing with carnal lust.

"Then what can I do to show you that you're safe with me?" His fleshy lips kissed my neck, sending shots of fire to my hot pussy.

"Time." His lips crushed mine, caving me in as Saint possessively took both sides of my face, his tongue plundering into the crevice I left open for it.

"Time is what I have for you, but I'm going to do this, Mira. I will go to my grave protecting you. That's the one thing you can rely on. Now, how about we form a peace treaty, and you get naked for me?"

I hated and loved how quickly my body unconsciously responded to his sexual demands. I said nothing because my torrid flesh had already won out.

Saint dropped my fingers, untying my apron, balled it up, and threw it to the side.

"Here?" I squeaked, excited by his spontaneity.

"Yes, every fucking room is where I'm going to have you eventually," he growled. I loved the way he craved me. He lifted my top overhead, our breaths fusing together. I dropped to my knees, unbuckling his pants—I was so wet and feeling like a wild woman. Dropping his pants to his ankles, his stiff cock stood at full mast, ready for attention.

I surrendered my mouth to him, gripping the base with two hands, suckling and opening my mouth to receive the man I called my husband. Groans rang out as Saint tugged at my hair, guiding my mouth. "That's it, baby. Feel that cock in your mouth a little quicker, Mira. I'm your king. Worship me. Fucking feel this."

Fire bloomed through my body, taking me over. I was somebody else now, rebirthed into a woman who wanted her husband every which way. Saint was the only man to christen my body and the only one I ever wanted to claim it. Since Saint, there had been no one else. Before he swelled anymore, Saint stopped as I stretched out my jaw.

"I want more," I breathed, my chest expanding, in and out.

"You're gonna get more. Get on all fours for me. Face the couch." My sensory circuit was on overload, my hair everywhere. I stared at Saint's cock, my pussy dripping hard.

Vulnerable with my ass in the air, Saint reached to unsnap my bra, my breasts hanging freely. I was wild for him, panting, desperate, waiting. A warm hand steadied my lower back as my walls stretched and Saint penetrated from behind.

I almost screamed upon his entry, it felt so damn good. He glided with such ease, in and out of my velvet pouch.

I bucked forward, reaching for my clit to stimulate myself as my pussy rumbled, clutching around his sizeable girth.

"Saint, all I want is us. You. Me," I sang out. He made me feel confident in myself. If this is what the aftermath of a fight felt like, then I wanted it all the time.

"You've got all of me, Mira. Every fucking thing. You can have it all, but will you give me all of you?" He pushed harder as I arched my spine, a volcano building in my pussy.

"Yes," I breathed, our flesh slapping together as my head barely grazed the carpet from his power. "Yes, I will, Saint."

"Then stop questioning me, Mira," he grunted. "Come with me, baby. Together. Us. Now." I dropped deep into my body, Saint's cock growing. He was close. I was dangerously close but wanted to be in sync with him.

Yes, Saint. Yes.

Inhaling a deep breath, I let go when my internal walls expanded a little more. My pussy erupted as all the nerve endings sparked into orgasm, ricocheting waves of pleasure through my body. I cried out, a tear plummeting to the carpet. Saint had taken me all the way to heaven. I kneaded my own breasts as Saint growled.

"Mira!" he breathed, gasping. "Mira. What are you doing to me?" We both keeled over, sated and drenched in love sweat, catching our breath. Saint ran a hand over my belly. "I would die for you, Mira. I swear I would."

And that was the part that scared me...

Chapter 11

Saint

Three days later, I defied Mira. Every morning, I touched Riza's picture, hurting like hell that I couldn't ring her and shoot the breeze with her. I hurt for Mira and what her deceased mother had done to her, but the irony of our twisted union caused my head to shake. If my capo hadn't annihilated her whole family, she wouldn't be a Riccini—the white flag between bloodthirsty mob famiglias.

I slipped through the plastic strips of one of Chicago's oldest pizzerias for a hash-out meeting. As I walked in, I stopped to check behind the garbage bags and on the side street for cars that might have been following. Coast clear. I rubbed the stainless steel of my Glock, ready to pull it if needed. The streets might have appeared harmonious, but one wrong move by drug mules under the capos, and a war could break out. Falcone and Antonio had a lot of bricks stacked on their backs, and crews had to be handled appropriately so street violence didn't spill over.

A thunder of beats ramped through my heart, but there wasn't a single car parked. Another green light. I waited a minute, spitting on the pavement, listening for danger. There was none on the outside, but on the inside was another matter. If I'd gotten my hunches wrong with any of my gang lord picks, it could set the wheels of a ride to hell in motion.

One dim industrial light overhung a couple of chipped vinyl wood tables, but the good thing was the place smelled like my favorite Chicago slice. Two bulky African-American males from the Zig Zag crew sat at the table chewing gum. I shook both their hands.

"Fellas, glad you could make it."

"Aye, if we get a chance to join the conversation with the Don, then we do it."

I nodded at them, where a very different cut of a man sat. Tommy Mathers from Murdoch Industries, one of the city's most sought-after real estate developers, was a man I wanted in my back pocket. I had a separate meeting with the Prentice family planned, but one step at a time.

"Hey, Tommy, nice to see you."

"You too. Always a pleasure, Saint. I'm really excited about this venture. I wanna hear all about it."

Mira's impassioned face found a slip lane into my mind. She did that way too often. All the decisions I made included a future with her in mind.

"You're going to start a revolt. Don't do it, Saint. It hurts. I get it, but this isn't the way."

I let the memory of our morning conversation disintegrate.

"Me too. Note these are only preliminary talks. Before we get started, let's eat."

I called Marlotta so as not to draw attention to myself. "Hey, can you bring us a menu? I want a large pizza back here."

"No problem, coming up, Saint." The server dropped a menu,

and the rest of the men ordered. Half an hour later, bellies full and slightly less tension, we dug into the particulars. Treading carefully, I sized up everyone in the room.

"The reason you're here, Tommy, is you have a nice slice of the pie in the urban housing market, and Reuben here has a street run in Aurora, Rockford, and New York. Small fry, it looks like, but listen up." I directed a finger at Reuben. "What is it you bring in per month, Reuben?" I nodded to prompt him.

"A hundred thousand bands. We run shit. We're about to hit up Naperville, but there are a few small-time jitterbugs we need to run out of town first."

Tommy raised his eyebrows. "Impressive. So, what's that—one million before or after taxes?"

We all bust out laughing because there was no way in hell the Zig Zag brothers paid taxes.

"You're funny, my guy. Why's he here again?" Reuben asked, his face settling to a sour disposition.

"Tommy's here because he's about to start a development project for public housing in Aurora. This will give you more coverage. If we link, we can make a lot of money. I'm in talks with the Prentice family, and if we get them involved, they have political affiliations that would prove beneficial." I made sure Reuben understood where I was going. The greed in his eyes made me believe I was on track.

"Ah, I see. We're forming a revolt. A union of sorts working together."

"Exactly. I want further reach outside of Chi-town, and I can offer guns via Prentice, provided they're on board and have deep police networks. I'm also in cahoots with a few people for Boston nightclubs, and if you act right, I can let you in on it."

Reuben drank from his water bottle, and I could visibly see his mind cogs turning.

"What do you want from the deal?"

"A little kickback, of course, and, I need more foot soldiers. You have a strong gang network that could be useful to the Riccinis." Reuben gave his partner a look, and Mira's subtle persuasion haunted my thoughts again.

"It's a bad idea, Saint." My guilty conscience kicked in, and soon enough, I wanted to finish the meeting.

"Look, think it over. Nothing is concrete. My kickback rates are fifteen percent, including access to my connects, and I'm sure you can appreciate how valuable those could be to your organization," I coaxed.

"Yes. Very. I have to say you've thrown me off-guard because there are many other ways you could have gone. Why this route?"

Revenge and power. What else, my friend?

I stared at Reuben as if he were glass. "It's a solution where everyone benefits and a smart future investment. You've got a stellar street reputation that speaks for itself, and I like to nurture new talent. The seat is open, but it's up to you if you want to take it."

"Yes, it's lucrative, and we could use the firepower in Aurora," Reuben stated.

Tommy didn't say a word.

"Tommy?"

"It's an easy decision for me. We work together already, Saint, and it's been a positive experience. I'm down."

Grinning, I shook Tommy's hand, hearing Reuben and his counterpart Street Butcher receiving phone calls.

Reuben's face turned grim. "Duty calls. Thanks, fellas, for the meeting. We'll be in touch, but I like where you're going with this, Saint. I really do. I wonder what the Salianos think about this with the peace treaty you have. Will it put the deal in danger?"

In a bald-faced lie, my lips widened into a Joker-like smile. "Nope. The deal is untouchable. This is between you, me, and other potential cartel members."

"Excellent, excellent. Good to hear because I would hate to have my dealers put at risk because of bad blood between partners." Reuben's onyx pupils bored into mine as I stared right back at him.

"Correct. We're good." I watched both men walk out with Tommy still in place, staring after me as I rechecked the outside.

Tommy was standing by the time I got back. "Tell me you're not on some war path right now, Saint. You can't bring Riza back, and breaking this peace treaty will kill anything you have going. You're on a roll right now." He slapped my back as pure flashes of anger rampaged through me.

"That's not what this is, Tommy. It's a good deal, that's all. I'm glad you're in. I have a meeting in a couple of days with the others. It has the potential to bring in another two to three million a year and open international gun trafficking, including military operations contacts."

Tommy sighed, throwing his head back. "You're gonna need those guns if you plan on stepping into military and government networks. This is a whole other level, buddy, and you know what they say—new levels, new fucking devils. I urge you to sleep on it."

"Thanks, Tommy." I bit down on my teeth, my jaw locking, thinking about Riza and Mira. All I cared about was them now.

***

A week later, at Saint's apartment...

"Fuck it to hell!" I threw the Chicago Chronicle down, rain pelting against the window. I reread the headline to make sure I wasn't going blind or crazy.

TWO DEAD IN GANGLAND WAR. A DRIVE-BY SHOOTING IN AURORA HAS THE TOWN SHAKEN.

Late in the afternoon, and already my plans were backfiring. I didn't read the rest; I didn't need or want to. My phone was on silent but vibrating from a phone call. Stretching out over the table, I picked it up.

Private number. I bit the bullet, taking the call, my mind thinking about Reuben and how to cover the fact that I'd gotten his gang members murdered. Did Tommy have something to do with it? He was the only one I'd been in talks with. I picked up the call, my office door open, but my temper had flared to a point beyond, so I became careless.

"Saint," I barked down the line. "Who the fuck is calling my private number?

A throaty chuckle was the imminent response. "Ah, you still haven't learned a thing, have you, Saint? You're too impulsive. In your feelings too much. Don't you know these streets are cold and don't give a motherfucking damn about you?"

Instant recognition. Frankie Saliano. "What do you want, Frankie?"

"I'm sure you know I have eyes and ears all over Chi-town. You thought you were gonna punk me and start a cartel in my city.

Stupid jerk-off. You really wanna die, don't cha?"

Rage kicked in as my hand white-knuckled the phone. "You fucking asshole. You've got your shitty Boston deals. This has nothing to do with you."

"I would say it's got everything to do with me. We're in bed together, and you're married to my daughter. You're my son-in-law, and that's no way to treat famiglia. On the contrary, you've got a blood oath to uphold. Not only to the Omerta but our peace treaty."

"You should think about what you've done to Mira. Her life, and taking your wife's life was child's play," I lashed out in anger. I had no idea if Frankie knew his daughter wasn't his. He had to know. Frankie Saliano was one of the most conniving carnivores in the city. Nothing went past him. And yet...

"Temper, temper. See what I mean? Mira's where she wanted to be in the first place. It's working out, isn't it?"

I let my rage die down to get to the answer. "What did you do?"

"What I always do. A little birdy got back to me about your whereabouts and the talks being had, so I organized a nice little night-night shooting. Nothing major, but let that be a lesson for you. Don't pull rank again, Saint. You're still wet behind the ears. I've been Don of these streets long before you could say your ABCs. You're no match for me. Best remember that before you do something stupid like this again."

The dial tone clicked dead, and I hesitated before sending the phone flying across the other side of the room.

"Saint!" Mira's calm voice forced me out of anger as she walked in. "Was that my father just now? What have you done?" Her nerve to sound irate irked me, but the sweet balm of her voice was one I listened to.

"Ah, Mira. I'm losing it, that's what. I went ahead with the meeting like I said."

Mira stared at me in horror. "Saint. Stop now. It's going to get worse. My father..." She stared at me as if relieving the past. "He's going to kill you. He will ruin you. This can't go any further, and I'm your wife. You promised to keep me safe, Saint!"

"You don't have the full story."

Mira seemed to deem her outrage Oscar-worthy, but didn't understand its origins. "I read the paper, Saint. I put two and two together. I'm not stupid."

I grabbed her hand, her long hair flying wildly around her as she twisted away from me to leave. "Sorry, Mira. You're right. Don't leave like that. Come over here."

Chapter 12

Mira

Saint's overstep maddened me. "I warned you, Saint. You could have prevented this whole thing. Whoever you're talking to...now you have another enemy. Don't you see?" I pleaded, wanting the violence to stop, but all Saint was doing was snickering at me, further infuriating me.

"I love it when you're like this. An intelligent woman taking care of her husband. Doesn't get better than this, and I can think of nobody else I'd rather fight with more."

"Shut up, Saint! You drive me nuts, and why don't you put a shirt on around the house?" I hated fighting when he had his own brand of secret weapon.

His eyes were gloating with victory, diverting away from what really mattered. I wanted him to listen to me. He rounded the table as he took in a deep breath, sweeping all the papers off the desk, including the picture of Riza. "Saint? What are you doing?" I breathed, wondering if I married a psycho.

"You have no idea what you do to me, and the only way I can show you, is well, by showing you..." he ticked his head to the side, his long tongue skimming over his lips, "...right here." He tapped a finger on the table. "I heard what you said. You're right—I lost it for a minute, but I'm back. All I want is to protect you. I don't wanna forget about Riza, either..." He raised his hands behind his head, opening his chest as he paced.

I crossed my arms over mine. "The way you're going about it, Saint, isn't the right way. You can't defeat my father like that. Peace treaty. Hello, white flag. Remember what that means?"

He came out of his dark world only to smile at me. "You've got a sassy mouth. Did I tell you that? I still want you to get on the table."

"Come and make me Saint." I tapped my foot, tilting my chin haughtily, sick of Saint's shit but turned on by his enticing command.

Shouldn't have done that...

I watched Saint's expression change from an amused smirk to a wolf ready to devour his prey. It took him mere seconds before he crossed the bridge of space dividing us to get to me. He did something then I wasn't prepared for.

"Don't resist since your pretty mouth likes to talk so much. I know just the thing to shut you up," he warned. The angry tension gathered in my belly turned to laughter. I couldn't help myself.

Saint Riccini hauled me over his shoulder, uprooting my legs like a tree trunk.

"Saint," I giggled, mortified as his muscular frame elevated me with ease. I had no choice but to comply. "What are you doing?"

"What do you think I'm doing? Come on," he replied simply, as if it were the most normal thing in the world. "I'm carrying you to the table. You said to make you, so here I am, making you."

I cracked up into laughter, but still let go of resistance, swinging my legs in the air as Saint smacked my ass while still grinning.

"Saint, you are..."

"What am I, Mira? Huh, what am I? Tell your husband. Don't keep secrets."

He reached his large office desk in a few strides. I slapped his bare back with my hands.

"Insufferable!" I called out, finding the words.

"Insufferable? Is that what you said?" He gently dropped me on the table on my back. "That's a big word. So smart, Mira," he taunted.

"Yes, that's what I said." I'd stopped giggling now, staring at the man who oozed sexiness from his pores as if he were born into sexual prowess. He joined me on the table as I slid upward on the smooth mahogany hardwood. His hard, toned body overshadowed mine, his arm muscles straining inside their skin on either side of my body.

Oxygen was scarce because Saint was driving all of it out of the room. He made room for himself between my legs, sliding his palm up my body-hugging tank top and onto my cool flesh. It was no longer cool—I was burning up inside from his touch. His icy blue eyes were like laser beams of heat, his hand reaching for a handful of my breast, kneading, cupping, and tugging. His fingers pulled the top and bra down in one hard yank.

"Silent now. Hmm, Mira." His hoarse-coated tone added more sizzle to the heat vacuum we were forming in the room. I hadn't forgotten what he'd done, but Saint's hand exploring my inflamed breasts was a welcome distraction.

Arching my back, I sank into the rush of euphoria flooding through my hot veins. Saint's touch stoked every fire within, drawing the heat to the surface. I never actualized my own carnal desire until he taught me what lay beneath.

Saint stretched my top out, lifting it above my head, balling it up, and throwing it on the side of the table. I hooked a leg around his back, digging a foot into him. A sadistic smirk cloaked his fleshy lips as his head dipped, kissing all over my stomach. He stole a glance up at me, his eyes unfocused as he cupped my hip, his tempestuous lips sinking into my hipbone. His mouth traveled back to my chest as he unhooked my bra and threw it on the floor with the other pile of clothes. My round, full breasts were free. Saint's greedy hands couldn't stay away from them.

He bent forward, licking, sucking, and teasing me until I wriggled under him, unable to take anymore without him touching me elsewhere.

"Saint, stop teasing me. You're driving me nuts," I pleaded, the wildness in me coming out.

"Now you know how I feel," he reasoned, his voice thick and low, his ocean eyes dragging me to his underworld.

I let the waves of our union carry me. Could it be love? Could we make it work despite all the obstacles standing in our way? I didn't have the answers, but every time Saint touched me, it felt as if we were a little closer to the answer. He peeled down my satin night shorts, the coolness of the air feeling exquisite on my naked body. Saint still had his slacks on but didn't make a move to get out of them.

His mouth continued its deadly assault, claiming every open spot on my body. My legs opened wide, ready for his hot mouth. Once he traveled south, he didn't waste time teasing me. His tongue wedged between my slick folds, the pressure mounting as we both let the anger turn into an overflow of searing passion. Unable to control myself under his relentless command over my body, my pussy clenched tight, bursting free of orgasm.

Now, Saint rose while my body jolted in the aftershock of pleasure rippling through me. He slid his belt off its loops, my sex glistening on his mouth. I watched as his chest expanded, in and out, dying for him to be inside me. He dropped his pants, his cock always a welcome sight, solid as a rod.

Saint dipped for a minute, sucking my big toe, my nerve endings lighting up as he gauged my reaction. I flexed my feet as he licked the insole of the other one, igniting me. Saint dragged my body down the table as my back squelched against it.

He entered my slick wetness with a powerful thrust. Once again, he had control over my body, slowly creeping into my heart. My breasts bounced in time with his strokes. I bit my bottom lip.

Damn. So good, Saint.

It was my turn to drive him to the brink. I tightened my legs around his back as he thrusted, the rawness of our lovemaking on display. Saint eased his thumb over my clit, knowing how much pressure to apply.

Drowning in all my senses, a tsunami of energy built, funneling through to my pussy. I could tell he was lost in me, like I was in him, his forehead pinched together in a contorted frown. The desk shook under our weight as Saint buried himself inside me.

I spread my arms out, holding on to the edges, but there was no use. His cock swelled, pushing against my walls as I cried out excitedly, watching his abs flex.

He dug his fingers into my thigh, gushing as an orgasm washed over him, the strain showing through the veins in his neck.

Both of us relaxed, limp and panting from the intensity of fever-pitch sex.

Saint stilled, planting kisses on my stomach, my hands rifling through his hair.

"Saint, you undo me every time."

"And you do the same to me, Mira. But I know you're not telling me something. I can feel it. Don't betray me again, Mira. I'm warning you."

Pounding rushed through my ears as I lay stiff, tensing up.

Tell him, Mira. Tell him. You can't keep it a secret forever.

We lay together on the table, two hearts battered by the dirty world we lived in, but what was between us felt pure, so very real. I turned sideways to kiss his cheek in fake reassurance.

"I won't. I promise." Saint's iceberg eyes stared into mine as he dragged my hand to his mouth, kissing it.

"Okay," was all he said, making things worse.

As the day broke through the next morning, I arranged a catch-up with my girlfriends, Monica and Clara, wanting to escape the guilt gnawing away at my insides.

"Are you alright today, Mira? You seem distant. Is everything okay with you and Saint?" Clara probed after telling me about her work schedule and recent drama with her boss. Monica had chimed in with what was going on in her life. I had sat, silent, eating macaroons and sipping my coffee, unsure where to start, let alone whether I should open up to them. My life was a mess.

Would they understand?

Blinking rapidly with a contrite smile, I answered. "Fine, it's fine. We're getting along great, in fact." On the surface, things were fine between us—as fine as it could be for a fated tryst like ours.

"Then why do you look like you're somewhere else?"

I ignored her question, Saint's warning ringing in my ears. A man could only survive so much before he snapped, and Saint wasn't to be underestimated.

"I'm sorry, but I have to go." It had barely been half an hour since I sat down. "I have a lot on my mind. I shouldn't have come out. It's not Saint. I have other things to deal with, but I'll be in touch soon, I promise." I squeezed Clara's hand as Monica looked at me, befuddled by my departure. I had too many stomach churns, and a yearning to call Ella. She was the one I really wanted to speak to.

"Okay, love you. Call me if you need anything. Don't be a stranger." Monica stood to hug me along with Clara, and I left, alone with my bag of heavy guilt.

In that guilt, something flourished.

I needed to suck it up and do what I was supposed to do. As a mother. The only way to keep me sane while making sure my Alessandro was safe was to do the one thing I feared the most.

In the coming days, the streets calmed. What I feared most didn't come to fruition, but Saint was watching my every move. Every day became a little harder for me to hide, but I had to find the right time.

Chapter 13

Saint

She'd lied to me. I'd felt it, her body doing the talking. I was so attuned to every part of her that I knew when she was lying to me. She'd stiffened when I told her she was hiding something from me, and the phone calls were driving me nuts.

Why do you defy me, Mira? Don't you know who the fuck you're dealing with? I've taken too many losses, and I'm not taking any more.

I wanted to tap her phone and put a tracker in the vehicle I'd purchased for her, but I decided I would do one better. Things were running like a well-oiled machine, only minor squabbles between territories and a few things to clear up relating to cartel talks. I figured I had enough time on my hands.

We ate breakfast together like normal, but when I kissed her cheek as a greeting, she balked. I let my eyes linger, worried I might have said or done something wrong.

"What's your plan for today? I've got a half day off. Movie or a day trip?" I wanted to spend time with her to bridge the invisible gap between us.

"Umm, I can't, Saint," she said, her lashes covering the deceit in her caramel eyes. "I've got a full day. I'm going to the gym and running errands."

I leaned against the bench, my legs crossed with a bowl of cereal in my hand.

"Are the errands going to take you all day to finish up?"

She sliced the apple she had in her grip on the cutting board, a thick cord of tension running from her to me. The knife slipped, nipping a piece of her skin. "Shit!" The knife toppled out of her hand, and I took it.

"Let me get you a Band-Aid." I kissed the nape of her neck, dropping her hand as blood trickled to the floor.

"Uh, thanks. I have to clean this up. Shit."

"It's not a big deal, Mira. Give me a second."

She's lying to you, Saint. Are you going to make good on your promise? You can't allow her to betray you again.

I found the Band-Aids in the medicine cabinet, pulling one out and smoothing it over her slender finger. "Thanks." She withdrew her hand as if recoiling from a predator as I caressed it.

"You're welcome. I can get someone to run the errands for you so that we can have the day together. What do you need, Mira?"

She resumed chopping up the apple, sprinkling the slices into the fruit salad as if I didn't exist while I asked the questions in my mind.

Are you seeing someone else, Mira? Or is it Claudia I'm talking to now?

"No. I prefer to run them myself."

"Rain's coming down."

"Doesn't matter. I like to be productive, Saint. Let me run the errands."

"Okay, I'll back off. Have a great day."

The kiss of death was one I was familiar with. My father used to give it to his enemies in the old days. Now I planted the same kiss on Mira's face with force. She pulled her head up cautiously with a tight line across her lips.

Parting from her, I decided I would track her every move personally. I had to. I wanted to find out why she would keep things from me.

As soon as I heard the door click and her say goodbye, I grabbed my keys, my mind obsessing over what she was doing behind my back.

Chicago was gloomy, like my heart, with its gray skies and clouds full of rain. I waited in the shadows for her to drive out from our parking lot, carefully staying two cars back.

I ducked and weaved in and out of traffic congestion as she drove southbound towards the freeway, sliding through Chicago's suburbs with ease.

Where are you going, Mira? Is this where your new lover lives? If it is, he's a dead man. Do you think I won't shoot the fucker in the face and send his head to his mother? Oh, Mira, you don't know who the fuck I am.

The devil was taking hold of me, my fingers digging into my leather wheel, my eyes never leaving her license plate. I grit my teeth, wanting to call her to tell her I was following her, but my street instincts kicked in, wanting to see her unravel and whatever this was play out to the bitter end.

I peered through the windscreen, wanting Mira to be careful on the roads, and almost missed the turnoff. We were traveling four lanes deep now, and it was tough to keep up.

Looking down at my speed-o-meter, I saw we were over the

speed limit.

She's in a hurry to get to her lover. How can you do this to us, Mira? Am I not enough for you?

Venomous thoughts broke free in my head. My hands turned clammy.

"Mira, I'm a fucking Riccini. You can't get one over on me," I said out loud, convincing myself, the irony being that Mira had already duped me once before changing our family's fate.

I put a hand to my beating heart, thinking of Riza, praying she was somewhere nice and out of this hell-bound world. A call filtered through from Falcone, throwing me off.

"Falcone, make it quick."

"Bad time, boss?"

"Very. What can I do you for?"

"Ah, it ain't that serious, just mouthy talk from the cartel talks you engaged in."

My ears perked up, but my main concern lay with Mira. She hit the off-shoot lane to the airport, and now I was 100% sure she was picking up a lover from there. Slamming my hand against the steering wheel, I closed the three-car gap, the rain falling harder now, making my line of sight to her even murkier.

"Listen, it's raining hard out here right now. I got some things I gotta take care of. Let's talk about it tonight. Thanks, Falcone."

"No problem at all. You good?"

"Never better." Scoffing, my eyeballs were burning from lack of blinking and monitoring Mira's vehicle. "I'm out."

"Later, Saint." I ended the call on the Bluetooth as Mira led me to the arrival's terminal. I couldn't stay there with her. I would have to time it and drive by. I watched people get out of their vehicles and kiss their loved ones while their luggage was being hauled out of trunks at the departure terminal. Airport staff were moving people on and keeping the line mobile.

"Fuck!" A burst of anger ejected out of me, but I contained it, slicing a hand through my hair. Mira's car sat in the arrival's bay longer than I could stay idling, but I was a man who knew how to remain in the shadows until the right time.

Seething, and jumping forward to a solution of how to handle Mira circled my brain, but the scene I saw in front of me didn't match up. A woman with dark hair was shielding something. I craned my neck forward over the wheel, visibility poor, staring at the woman.

A friend of Mira's? Why wouldn't she tell me?

The fire in my belly died down, determined to find out why she'd kept this from me. The woman was with a kid—hers, I assumed. He didn't look older than five, and Mira held an umbrella over the woman's head.

Mira wasn't oblivious to keeping watch. Her eyes scanned the airport taxi rank and the cars immediately behind her. If she looked further down the rank, she would have made out my vehicle. I watched her slide into the driver's seat and drive off.

Following her for another fifteen minutes, she pulled off the road to a diner. Thankfully the rain had eased considerably. Getting out of the car with the woman and child, I watched them walk into the diner together with her arm around the kid.

I had so many questions, but a phone call interrupted my stalking.

"Saint."

"Aye, you missed the meeting." Lupo was in my ear about a meeting for real estate property in Boston.

"Sorry. I've got bigger things to worry about. Reschedule for tomorrow morning same time."

"Sure. It can get done. Might not be tomorrow, though." I'd checked out of the conversation, slowly easing into the diner's parking lot and looking through the dingy window. Mira's expression had changed. Her facial features were lively, and her hands were animated while speaking. The woman clasped her hand over the top of Mira's, firing up my system. Who the fuck was this woman?

The kid had a head full of dark unruly curls, and Mira was incredibly affectionate with him. She was running her hands through his hair, doting eyes, staring at him with love.

Do you want a child, Mira? We can have one. Together, we can make a family. Why didn't you tell me you wanted a child?

I felt a twinge of stupidity at jumping the gun, thinking she was cheating on me, but my gut told me it was wrong.

"Hello, earth to Saint. You still there?"

I jerked back to the call I was still on with Lupo. "Hey, sorry. Preoccupied. What did you say?" A hard lump collected in my throat.

"I said tomorrow is better timing, anyway. There's some paperwork I wanna check into about the properties. I'm gonna send the details to you tonight."

"Sounds good," I trailed off, disturbed by the child. "Gotta go, Lupo." I didn't hear Lupo say goodbye, too much blood was rushing through me. Mira was too close to the boy. I needed a closer look. Shit was off—Mira was holding onto the kid for dear life, rocking him in her lap. She was in plain view doing this.

"Mira, what game are you playing at?" The rain returned as I watched Mira put money in the pouch for payment and the boy hugged Mira tight. Was this another member of the Saliano family I hadn't heard about?

The near-black hair. The face of the kid had Mira's likeness, and it was hard to hide. His nose was like Mira's. Did Mira have a kid with someone else?

I ran a finger over my temple, trying to rub the throb away.

You can't see right. It's raining.

The rain was frustrating the fuck out of me, and the shards of pounding rain on the windscreen weren't helping me stay sane. I reversed from the parking lot, careful not to be seen. I slammed the brakes, swinging back into the street, heading for home and ready for war.

Chapter 14

Mira

"You've taken such good care of him. He's grown so much. I can't thank you enough, Ella. I don't think I'll ever be able to repay you for what you've done. He's so amazing." I had to bite down on my lower lip to stop it from trembling. I was so happy to see my baby. I squeezed him so fiercely that I was afraid I might break him.

Ella and I sat side by side at Featherstone Park, a small slice of heaven on the outskirts of Chicago. I'd covered my face with sunglasses, a black baseball cap, and a gray tracksuit. I wanted to appear like a normal civilian. It was extremely risky for me to even be out in the open with him, but I had to see Alessandro.

Less than three days ago, Ella had called to tell me her mother was in the hospital in America, and she wanted to see her. There was no one she could leave Alessandro with—not that I would trust anyone else with my precious son. Our hands were tied. Ella would have to travel with him to Wisconsin and keep my baby with her. It had been a last-minute decision for them to have a daylong layover in Chicago. I was going insane, wanting to see Alessandro badly.

Ella patted my leg, her kind face relaxing some of the strain but not all. I had Saint on my mind the whole time I looked at my blessing, Alessandro. How could I not? They were peas from the same pod. "There's no need to repay me. It's been a joy to raise him. We're family, and I've known you since you were little. I'm here for you, Mira. I know it's hard." Crow's feet crinkled at the edges of Ella's eyes. "I'm sorry about your mother, Mira. I can't imagine finding out that way." The lump in my throat was hard to swallow. The pain of everything was stabbing into my back and wearing me down.

Not telling Saint was killing me a little more on the inside. Ella knew everything. There was no need to hide anything from her. She was the minder of my son, carrying the burden of the deadliest of secrets on my behalf.

A single tear dripped on my pants as I watched the joy on Alessandro's face as he swung over the bark of the flying fox. He must have gone through a growth spurt because his feet nearly touched the ground. It was all I wanted for him. I didn't want him to be involved in mob business. But he was a Riccini, the progeny of my husband.

"I can't believe you're here. I understand the risks, but it's been too long. If I wasn't married to Saint, I would have been able to bring you over sooner. I have to keep him safe, Ella," I said in a hushed tone, clutching her hand, scared, my heart about to cave in on itself as I checked out the playground's surroundings.

A man in a trench coat invoked cold sweats, but I calmed when I saw his sausage dog peek its head out in front of him.

I can't live like this anymore, but how can it be different? Even when Saint finds out, Alessandro will have to stay hidden until it's the right time.

A smirk lifted the corner of my lips. Now I understood why my father wanted me to stay hidden, but I had to fuck it up, didn't I? I rubbed my legs. They were getting numb.

"Mommy, Mommy, *voir*! Look! I made it all the way across."

I clapped my hands together, my heart bursting with the fact my son was calling me Mommy and looking at me, not Ella. I worried about him seeing her every day and not me.

I kept my eyes trained on the man walking his dog. Was he a spy? Heart palpitations kick-started in my chest. I rubbed my chest, trying to smile for Alessandro, not wanting him to know the immense pain I'd suffered.

I'd been restless in the lead-up to going to the airport. Saint had had to turn me over in my sleep. I tried not to think of him, but there was no way I could get away from the man. He seeped into every crevice of my psyche, and it was unnerving.

I was feeling restless, wary of the trench-coated man, knowing how my father would hire hitmen who looked exactly like this guy. "Quick, grab Alessandro. What time do you fly out tomorrow evening?"

"Six pm. What should we do in the morning?"

"I'm sorry I have to ask you to go with him while you're tending to your sick mother."

"Don't worry too much about it, Mira." Ella's words did nothing to soothe my worried soul. I hadn't seen my boy face-to-face in over a year. I'd been able to travel every year for a month or two to see my precious, lying to my family that I'd had a travel bug. Each year was a different country. Being older, I hadn't needed a minder to accompany me. But that didn't mean I wasn't wary of the people around me. Each time I flew out, my heart swelled with excitement at seeing my bundle of joy, and every second after I returned to Chicago, my soul darkened a little. This time wouldn't be any different.

Sliding a hand over my throat, I rose and walked to Alessandro to collect him. His hair was growing long, and I mussed it up, the little boy responding by hugging me around the neck. His soft scent brought me such happiness, my cheeks wet with my tears. Alessandro giggled, sticking a finger in my tears.

"*Maman,* why are you crying? Are you sad?"

I chuckled, sniffling and swiping the water works from my face. "No, no. I'm fine. Are you having fun?"

"Yes. I'm hungry now. Can I have those star nuggets like at the diner? Can I? *S'il vous plaît!*"

Lips like his father's, and the same cool blue eyes. My little boy had all the markers of a heartbreaker like his father. He had my nose and chin but his father's athletic physique, and I could already spot the broadness in his shoulders.

"Yes, I'm sure the hotel has them. You just ate, Alessandro!" I pinched his nose as he crinkled it, effervescent laughter escaping his lips.

"I'm hungry!" Stubborn, too, like his father. Yes, I would defend Alessandro until the end of time. If either of the families knew about him, it wouldn't have been just me as the sacrificial lamb. I hated that I had to let him go and head home to Saint as if I'd been running errands all day. Lies were stacking up like Jenga blocks, threatening to topple over.

"I've called the Uber. It will pick us up over there, ready?" Ella asked, looking at my son.

"Okay, come on, little man." I took the little man's hand in my own, hustling him towards where the cab would pick them up. I would drive away separately to Ella and Alessandro, not wanting to take any chances. Ella threw me a pitiful look before hugging me tightly.

"Tomorrow. Call me early. We'll be ready." I glanced over to the far end of the park. The man had gone, and there was nobody left.

"Sure," I choked up and balled up my fist, stuffing it in my mouth to stop myself from crying. Ella's Uber arrived in less than a minute as I twinkled my fingers in a wave to Alessandro. I put one hand on the hood of my car as the Uber pulled off from the curb. "Fuck." I kicked the fallen leaves in the gutter, my stomach lurching from pain. It was getting harder and harder to leave him.

My only son. Saint's progeny. Life was hard.

I couldn't pull off walking in the door with puffy eyes, so I played upbeat music to counter the numb ache in my spirit. I sighed in relief when I found the house was empty. Moping to the shower, I shampooed my hair, letting the water wash over me. Stepping out, I felt a little better, but I wanted Alessandro with me. He belonged in my arms, and should know his father. The door creaked open as Saint looked in on me.

"Hello."

"Hey."

"How was your day?"

"Good. Standard. Running around. I got it all done."

"Nice." He stood for a moment longer, a smile on his face. "Take out?"

"Sounds good." The tiles were the only place left for my guilty pupils to look. I picked up stray hairs, avoiding Saint's gaze, fearing he would look at me and figure me out.

"Are you good, Mira?"

"Fine. Processing things. Do you mind if I spend some time alone tomorrow for the day? I know we had plans, but I-I just need a little space right now."

A pregnant pause stood in the way of us. "Whatever you need,

Mira." My stomach dropped, and the tension I didn't know I was holding shifted. Okay, no grief from Saint. One less thing to worry about.

As nightfall hit and I lay awake, the strike of the clock timed with the beat of my heart. Saint's body was turned away from me and the drifting between us increased. The problem was that the pool of mobster men for me to pick from was slim, and only Saint was right for a woman like me.

Tossing and turning, I'd created a groove on my side of the bed. If I didn't get up, Saint would question why I was so restless. I moved to the living room and watched TV until I fell asleep.

As the warmth of the light hit my face, I jolted awake, wiping the side of my mouth.

Alessandro. Time was ticking. I looked down to see a blanket on top of me. Saint must have gotten up in the night to cover me. Squinting, I looked around for him. I saw the corners of a note on the kitchen table.

Hey, see you tonight. Hope you feel better, love.
xxx Saint.

Nothing else. I touched the paper as if wanting to read between the lines.

I'm sorry, Saint. I have to protect him.

I dressed quickly, my stomach queasy, so I ate a muesli bar and practically inhaled my coffee. The entire way, I checked my rearview but arrived at the hotel on the outliers of Chicago in good time before eight. I wanted the maximum number of hours with my son before he and Ella left for Wisconsin and then the country. If I didn't find the right time to tell Saint about him, I didn't know when next I'd see his mini-me.

Licking my dry lips, I dropped my sunglasses down, determined to remain incognito. I was wearing a trench coat this time around. I texted Ella like we agreed to meet me in the hotel lobby. Not a run-down hotel, but not a luxury swank one either. My legs jittered along with my keys as I sat stiffly on the lobby couch. Saint being out before me and leaving me a note made me nervous.

I needn't have been. Ella emerged a couple of minutes later with Alessandro wearing his favorite soccer team's Manchester United's jersey. His innocent baby face elicited tears wanting to spill over, but I gulped down the overwhelm instead, opening my arms wide for him to run into.

"Alessandro, good morning. Come here!" I hadn't planned on saying his name out loud. I'd been careful that way, and now I was slipping. I loved him too much and wanted to be as close as possible to him. He complied, letting go of Ella's hand and jogging into my warm embrace as I kissed his soft dark curls.

My boy, how I love you. What are we going to do?

We stayed this way for a couple of minutes, and I could have cradled him there in the lobby for longer, but we had a full day planned. Only after the hug did I acknowledge Ella.

"Good morning. How are you both?"

"Sleepy from the jet lag, but good. The coffee is excellent here."

"Good, good," I rushed, showering my boy with kisses as he sat quietly beside me. I directed my attention to him. "Are you ready to have some fun today?"

"*Oui*, Mommy. Where are we going?"

"I thought we could go to the pancake factory and then to a movie. How's that sound? Would you like that?" I asked, tears sparkling in my eyes.

"I like flapjacks. I eat them all the time back home. What movie? What movie?" Alessandro jumped around on the spot, eagerly drawing laughter from me. His enthusiasm was infectious.

Caution kept me on my toes as I ushered Alessandro and Ella along the streetlights of Chicago. I swung my head to the left, rushing freeway traffic filling my eardrums.

Get him out of here. Anyone could see, Mira. Be smart.

I hated this paranoid feeling. All I wanted to do was ring Saint and tell him the hard truth about his son. I rehearsed my words, imagining his face. "Saint, you have a son...he's five years old, and he looks like us." Dissolving the idea, we scattered to the underground parking lot with Ella driving. It was for the best. I tipped the front view mirror to myself, so I could get an eye on my son.

"Whoosh, whoosh. Look, Mommy. This is what we came in on. We're going on the *avion*, we're going on the airplane," he sang in a melodic voice.

His song brought sadness to me. To hear him be so happy about leaving brought unnecessary chills to my arms. Ella's eyes shunted toward mine, understanding the feeling as she spun the wheel into the street. "We're going to have a great time, Mira, and make the most of things."

"Yes, yes, we will," was my stunted reply. Knowing this was my last day with Alessandro for a long while, my heart wanted my son more by the time it was the end of the day.

As I watched Ella pack up her suitcase, I put a gentle hand on her wrist. "Stay. I'll pay to change your flights and things. I need you to stay."

It was selfish for me to ask, but I had to try. I couldn't bear it any longer.

Ella took my shoulders, a small smile crossing her face. "I understand. I'll make some calls."

Chapter 15

Saint

It was hard to build a life with a woman who lied right to my face. The wound ran deep, afflicting me in the worst way. I wasn't about to have a second round with Mira. Bitterness topped up my soul as I watched her sit at the dresser, brushing her lustrous locks. Mira's body was in front of me, but she was nonexistent, far away.

Back-to-back meetings helped cover up the denial. The boy. Had to be Mira's friend's son. Nothing more, nothing less. Thinking about the mop of dark hair, the same color as mine, had me pulling over and cars incessantly beeping at me.

Even Falcone had something to say to me. "Boss, you're looking secondhand today. What's up with you? The missus giving you trouble?"

"Something like that, but it's going to be sorted out quick enough."

Falcone and I were standing near our vehicles post-lunch meeting and three million dollars richer with a secured nightclub deal in Boston. "Uh-oh. Keep it smooth, Saint. We've got momentum. I don't wanna give Frankie Saliano the satisfaction, but we got some rumbles with those street gang members you were talking to. It ain't good, but I trust you're gonna handle it."

"I'll handle it, Falcone. Trust me. I won't be giving Frankie Saliano shit."

"That bad, huh?"

Shaking it off, I cupped a hand on Falcone's shoulder. "Nothing a top-shelf Scotch on the rocks can't cure. Don't worry about it. I got it on lock like I always do. We just signed a three-million-dollar deal. The Salianos aren't the only ones who run these streets. We're gonna push them out, Falcone. We're gonna make it, so they ain't got no place here. Frankie's getting old, and so are his old ideas. The Riccini family runs these Chicago streets now."

My blood surged with fire. Things needed to be ironed out, but not while my marriage was on the rocks. Falcone nodded, tipping his hat to me. "It's working mostly, but don't neglect those Callahan boys or underestimate them. You keep putting them off. If you're not going through with the cartel merger, tell them. Your father would be proud of you nonetheless."

I ignored his warning flag about the smaller gangs, hearing only what I wanted to.

"Ahhh, he would be, but it's been a knock-down, drag-out fight. All of it truly started with a Saliano plant. She's not one of them by blood...we both know that." I shot him a wry look of irony.

Falcone chuckled. "Ah, boss...eh? How about that drink?"

"Yeah. Let's get one before I crack up."

I drank my Scotch with Falcone, but it only burned inside me. I stayed out as late as possible, making excuses for why I couldn't go home. Another dealer to talk to over here, one over there—

whatever I could to extinguish what I'd witnessed a couple of days ago.

Bone-tired, I made my way home deep in the night, hoping Mira was asleep. I slipped my shoes off at the door, releasing a heavy sigh when I saw the lights were off, but Mira's silhouette stood out in the shadows. A fork was scraping along a plate, a sound I hated.

"You're up."

"Yes. I tried waiting up for you, but I got sleepy. I'm not feeling the best."

Flicking on the light, I put a lid on the hate fueling inside for her. I buried my eyes on her strained face, watching her put a mouthful of pasta in her mouth. Her hair hung forward, dark rings gathered under her eyes, her pale face like I'd never seen it before.

I put my keys down on the table, taking a seat at the other end of it while she ate her food in silence.

That's what lies do to you, Mira. They eat away at the core of your soul until you don't have one left.

"Why?" A simple question. If she were a truthful woman, I would have been able to get an honest answer.

Shock registered on her face as she looked over at me, the dullness pervading her listless eyes.

"I might be coming down with something. I don't have a clue." She shrugged.

"Mira." The sink tap dripped, a brick wall standing between us. I wanted to knock it down, but what I'd seen...

"Yes, Saint?"

"Is there anything you want to tell me?" A blanketed threat, but an opportunity for the woman I loved so deeply to tell me the truth. I fingered my keys, Mira unresponsive as she slowly chewed on her food. If she was so sick in the stomach, why was she still eating?

"No, Saint. There's nothing. I'm just not feeling well, alright? I'm going back to bed. Glad you're in safe."

Her chair scraped on the marble tile as I watched her form under her nightgown turn and move to the sink, walking out on me.

You've got enough bullets. You haven't touched your Glock in a long time. One of the drug dealers skimmed from you the other week. Get your frustration out and go deal with him. Take the edge off.

"Fuck, I need a Scotch." I quickly pulled my mind from the Chicago street gutter, retreating to the office. I poured myself a drink, thinking about my life. A young man born into the streets, now thrown into the lion's den by my father. My eyes glazed as a huff left my body.

"One day, Saint, this is going to be all yours. You're going to run the streets of Chicago."

"Nah, I'll never be as good as you. You're the king." Wistfully, I jutted out my bottom lip, a painful sorrow washing over my soul as I recollected the golden light in Mira's smile.

"No, son. You won't be like me. You'll go one better. You've got that street hustle in you and the heart of a true champion."

So much for having the heart of a champion when blades were dug deeper into my back daily. I loved Mira enough to give her every out. Every. Single. Goddamn. Out. Her defiant resolve wasn't breaking, and the trapdoor to her secrets had me on the brink of destruction. I let the burn sink, swaying on my feet with the Cristal glass in my hand. Primed and ready, all I had to do was pitch it at the wall. One good time, but I couldn't even do that.

Ungraciously, I tossed the empty glass on my office table, watching it roll to a stop.

If Riza were here, she would have known how to handle her. A mop full of ebony night curls—the same hair I had when I was a kid until I'd gotten older and realized having a head full of curly hair made me a prime candidate for bullying. The kid's milky skin was the same pearlescent tone as Mira's. A cupid's bow mouth like hers.

My past clashed with my present.

Plummeting into my leather office chair, I stretched the skin back from my temple, losing it mentally. If I let my lips sink into one more drink, there was no telling what I would do. Instead, flat-footed, I dragged myself to bed, watching Mira stir with the soft sounds of Chicago outside our window.

Her hair spread out over the pillow behind, sheets bunched up around her neck. It took every ounce of strength not to spoon with her as we did most nights. I loved her warmth, and how she silently locked her hands into mine when I grooved in behind her back. Not tonight. I faced my back to hers, staring at the carpet, wishing for the death of any street soldier who mattered little, because inside me was a dormant monster knocking on the door to get out.

How hard is it for her to tell me the truth?

***

Peeling my tongue off the roof of my mouth, I woke to an empty bed. Mira was up before me, but I'd come to my conclusions. I followed the sound and smell of food from the kitchen, padding in behind her.

"For someone whose stomach is hurting, you're eating a lot."

Coffee brewed, and Mira turned sharply regarding me with pain hidden in her irises.

"I never said I had a stomachache. Just a general unwell feeling. I'm going to the doctor today to see about it. Shouldn't be out too long. Won't matter, anyway. You'll be gone."

No face-to-face, just a cold, deceitful back. "Business is excellent. We closed a deal on a Boston nightclub. I wanted to tell you last night but thought better of it since you weren't feeling the best."

"Thank you. Coffee?"

"Yes." Stilted and thick with bullshit, our conversations were sinking like quicksand. "Is this where we are now, Mira?"

I posed the question, my brain not processing before asking it.

Mira didn't answer, and her mouth stayed slack as she handed me my coffee.

"I guess it is."

Chapter 16

Mira

Ella accepted my request to stay. It had been nearly two weeks now. Thankfully, her mother was out of the woods, but the guilt of keeping her from her own kin weighed on me each day she was stuck in Chicago. But what could I do? I wouldn't survive if Alessandro wasn't here with me. He was the only anchor that I had to my sanity.

Meanwhile, I remained stuck in the jaws of the crocodile, the most unsafe position to be in. I cast my mind back to the fight Saint and I had about forming a cartel. It's why I'd been so angry with him. He had no idea of the ripple effect. My father, however, was a street hawk, and he got wind of Saint's devious plan, so the best place in my mind for my son was in my arms.

Frankie was an unhinged man, and if he already knew about Alessandro, he would take him. He'd already shot Saint's soldiers over the cartel issue, so why would he let me off?

He'd sold me to the devil, after all.

To keep Saint at arm's length wasn't working anymore—for my soul or his safety.

The façade of my sickness was crumbling, and I hated having

to deceive Saint every minute. Every morning, I raced out of the door, rugged up in my tawny cashmere jacket, desperate to see my son.

Twice, I missed putting my keys in the ignition due to nerves and wanting to put distance between me and Saint before he examined my odd behavior.

Running's not an option, Mira. Who do you think you're fooling?

Today wasn't any different. I was shaking with sweat as I made my way through Chicago's streets, checking my rearview mirror every second. Jerking my head up for the umpteenth time, my phone vibrated inside the console. I fumbled with my free hand, grimacing as it evaded my grasp between other items—one of the other items being a pistol Saint taught me how to use at a local gun range a week into our marriage. It had been one of those moments that thawed our rather tumultuous union.

I'd seen Saint order hits. I'd seen his face after he'd killed a man, and it was no different from his everyday face. He could rip a man limb from limb and sit down for dinner without a qualm. Shuddering at the thought of being next, I touched the cold steel, wondering if I would need to use it.

I bent too far, anxiety taking hold, not seeing the fast-approaching Jeep in front of me. A loud, angry driver leaned on the horn, rolling down his window, and dishing out the middle finger to me. A heart-starter for the morning. I gasped inwardly while he yelled obscenities at me. I couldn't hear him, but I had to calm my nerves if I was going to make it through the day.

Making a right on Allen Boulevard, I glimpsed a looming black truck in my mirror. A washing machine of nausea tossed in my stomach. The car was familiar to me, but I couldn't place it in my panicky state. Was it Father? Or Saint? I couldn't be sure.

Straightening my arms on the wheel, I drove straight, knowing there was an upcoming turn-off after the roundabout in three miles. The car stuck with me, and now my eyes weren't on the road. They were on the car. Four cars behind. Now a second black truck emerged like a giant ant on steroids.

Gently, so as not to cause alarm, I switched lanes. The vehicles. Who?

A lightning bolt fed through me. Shit. Saint's people. To confuse the men, I opted to stop for coffee at Denny's and sit in wait. At the upcoming stop light, I texted Ella, thinking quickly on my feet. My fingers trembled, but I let them fly over my phone's keyboard.

ME: *Wait for me. I'm being followed. Saint.*

ELLA: *OMG! Quick. Get here as fast as you can.*

ME: *I will. Promise. It will be fine.*

This time, I didn't think that casual sentiment was true. Saint was about to find out I'd been keeping a deadly secret from him for five years, and given all the family losses he'd taken, this could break him.

"Be brave, Mira. You're in this now," I talked to myself as the cars of death closed the gap, surrounding me on both sides. I stayed the course, executing my plan. Sharply, I took the next exit, pulling into Denny's and eating for twenty minutes. They wouldn't be able to hide they were tailing me. The car parking lot was sparse of vehicles. Turns out they didn't care. Both imposing vehicles parked close by, waiting for me to finish.

I could barely eat but managed a coffee and a small burger. An invasive call broke through my plans to get rid of Saint's henchmen.

"Morning, darling. You raced out of here mighty quick." Saint's sarcasm rang out loud and clear over the line.

"I-I had to...wanted to get to the doctor, just to get some bloodwork done. Check-up. I'm fine. I've been off for the last few days, but it's fine. We're fine." I licked my chapped lips, the thick neck of one of his men visible from inside the restaurant.

"You're lying to me, Mira. We need to talk. I've given you so many fucking chances. I can't believe you're doing it right in front of my face."

"Saint, you're being overbearing. I've told you everything is fine. All I have to do is get some bloodwork done, and I'll be okay. I'm sure it's stress-related."

"I hope your doctor's appointment goes well and you feel better. Why do I feel this is your alter ego Claudia back to play games? See you tonight. We should talk more. There are things to be said."

I closed down, defeated. "Yes. You're right. We have a lot to talk about. You've got cars following me?"

"I don't know what you're talking about. I wouldn't do that." A dose of my own sour medicine.

"Alright, Saint. I give up."

"Tonight, Mira. Bye." The sharp cut of his tone invoked a pulse spike as I walked to the cash register in a time warp, paying the server.

"Ma'am, your change. Don't you want it?"

Folding my jacket tightly around my body, I moved towards

the front door. "No, you keep it." I never ate at fast-food restaurants, ever. Angelica wouldn't allow it and normally would either cook or we would eat the richest of foods from five-star or Michelin-star restaurants. Not that it mattered. Not today. All that mattered was Alessandro and getting to him without these buffoons tailing me.

Boldly, I marched over to the first car, tapping the window to the glib reaction of a large, chunky meathead. "What can I do for you?" he replied in a voice like rough-grade sandpaper.

"You can stop following me. Saint has spoken to me. I assume he told you to tail me?" I looked the guy square in the eye, the whites of his eyes showing through for a moment.

"Look, I'm doing my job, lady."

"No, you're not. I'm Saint Riccini's wife, and you also take orders from me. Knock it off and stop following me. Otherwise, I'm going to send you on a wild goose chase all day. Besides, I'm pretty sure you're doing a shit job. I can see you in plain sight. How about you tell Saint that?" Tilting my chin, fire flamed in my eyes at the nameless man. The arm he had hanging out the door retracted inside, his window rolling up with him, ignoring me.

Both enraged and scared, I walked back to my vehicle, not caring anymore. If Saint wanted me harmed, it was a cross I would have to bear, but my son...

Screeching out of the parking lot in anger, I headed to Alessandro, smiling as I studied the roads behind me. The two vehicles had stopped tailing me altogether.

Two can play, Saint.

I arrived half an hour later, peak Chicago traffic in flow. Ella and Alessandro were in the lobby, my son playing and running around without a care. I feared I'd unsettled him, all the to-ing and fro-ing with his life, but he appeared to be an adaptable kid who always kept an adorable smile on his face.

"It's dangerous now." Defeated, my shoulders slumped as I laid my head on Ella's shoulder.

"Well, it's time, Mira. It's time he got to know Alessandro. He can keep him safer than you think he can. It's Saint Riccini, but it will be a matter of approaching the situation delicately. You've withheld his son from him."

Absence from Alessandro's bright face had become non-negotiable. It cut through my heart too badly. "Alessandro, come to me. Let me see you. Are you alright?" I touched his cute face, staring at his rosy cheeks, scanning his little body, committing every inch to memory. I ran my hands over his arms, furrows of worry etched on my forehead.

"I'm fine, *Maman*. Where are we going today?" Terrified, I stood up from my bent position, putting a hand on my clammy forehead. If I cried anymore, I would build a river, so I let the sparkle of Alessandro's eyes keep me grounded.

"Good question. There is someone I want you to meet. He's a very important person. Would that be okay?" Alessandro asked me once about his dad on FaceTime, but never in person.

"Yes. Is he as important as you, Mommy?" Alessandro twisted his eyelashes, fluttering back at me, melting my heart as I hugged him.

"Yes, Alessandro, he is. I think you should meet him."

"Okay, Mommy. I don't want to stay in this hotel anymore. Why can't me and Ella come with you? I want to stay with you." His bright eyes were pleading with me, and the knife ran a little deeper through my chest.

"I'm working it out, Alessandro. I want you to stay with me, too. Mommy loves you so much."

Alessandro tilted his head up at me, slapping at my knees playfully. "Yay! I like Paris, but it's better here with you and Ella."

Poor little guy. I was going to crush him more than once. Ella would have to go back to her old life after she'd seen to things at home in Wisconsin. I'd broken my own vow of fierce protection over Alessandro, but all the FaceTime connections and "vacations" weren't enough for me. I didn't want him to forget I was his mother. That he was part of me, and I was part of him.

I distracted Alessandro by taking him into the hotel restaurant and asking him to fill his plate for breakfast.

When he was out of earshot, I spoke to Ella. "What will you do once this is all said and done?"

Ella shrugged casually. "I don't know yet. Take a break, but it's going to be hard with Alessandro. I've become so attached to him. He's not my child, I understand, but I've raised him." I touched Ella's hand.

"You can come visit anytime. You can even stay and be Alessandro's minder, if Saint allows. If I tell Saint and he flips out, I'm not sure what I'm going to do, either, but I have to protect Alessandro. He must understand why I did it."

"Saint Riccini understand? Maybe you know him differently, but I would prepare to flee, though you're trapped in a way. How did you shake off his men?" Ella asked.

"I faced them. I went over to their cars and told them to stop following me. Saint already wants to talk to me tonight. I will know after tonight. I can't bring Alessandro to the apartment just yet. I can't be sure of the steps Saint will take. I must be sure." I ran a rough hand through my hair, tension in my skull nearly exploding.

"Mistrust with Saint has brewed to a peak, especially after how he rushed with the cartel deal. I don't want Alessandro in the middle of this. I have to be confident that he would protect our son." My voice might have been cool, calm, and collected, but inside, all my bones were shaking.

Chapter 17

Saint

Arriving home early from the streets, I waited for Mira. A long, painful wait. She didn't return until after dusk, sheepish guilt lining her delicate features. I opened the door, breathing in her sweet scent, but its top note was laced with poison.

Gently, I bent, kissing the side of her cheek and taking her coat.

"Cold out?"

"Yes, chilly." Her eyes wouldn't connect with mine. She was afraid to look at me, and all that did was convince me that what she was hiding in her vault was way worse than what it looked like. The flood of thoughts running through my brain stopped my mouth from opening. There was too much going on inside me. I gathered myself and spoke.

"Come inside where it's warm. The chef prepared a meal earlier, and I thought we could eat and talk together."

Mira placed a palm over the back of her neck, rubbing at it.

"Yes, that would be good. Smells delicious." We were dancing, but once she sat at the table, all bets were off. I would pull every thread of truth out of her, no matter where the night took us.

Mira losing weight on her already petite frame made her look fragile, but she was far from a frail woman. Otherwise, my soul wouldn't sing for her like it did every second of the day.

She slid onto her seat, a glass of wine already poured for her, and I sat in mine, acidic rage tucked under my hood. "Have a nice day?" I ventured, stabbing at my broccoli.

She sipped her wine. Now she looked at me, a savage fire in hers. "You had me followed, Saint."

I'd elected not to drink. I wanted a rational mind when speaking with Mira. "I did, and with good reason." Mira pushed her locks behind her ears, prodding at her mashed potatoes before looking at me. There was a sledgehammer she was about to drop, and the room spun around in orbit. Pinching my temples, I stared down at my food, not hungry anymore.

"Speak, Mira. Tell me the truth, and don't leave me out in the cold. I've been following you. I saw you with a lady at the airport a few weeks back."

Mira's eyes jerked open wide, her mouth agape. "Saint. I did it for his protection. Please understand." She was already begging, and I didn't know what for.

"Understand what, Mira? Stop with the cryptic fucking games because I'm not letting you leave this table until you tell me everything. That's all I want."

If the woman was attempting to break me, her efforts cracked me into pieces, and if she wasn't careful, I wasn't sure if I could keep the insidious monster running the streets of Chi-town suppressed.

"Yes, you deserve the truth." Her French-tipped nails gripped the wineglass, her neck muscles flexing with tightness.

"Saint, the boy you saw at the airport is your son. Alessandro."

A small sentence, but one that carried the weight of the world on its shoulders. My ears deceived me because she'd just revealed the unthinkable. I heard the words travel through my ears, but it was as if they were muffled, like I was swimming underwater. I asked again, too afraid to feel the incredible weight of the lie and betrayal.

"What did you say? Tell me again, Mira."

"I said you have a son. His name is Alessandro. He's from our time spent in Paris. Obviously, I couldn't tell you then. I-I had to do what I had to do."

I screamed uncontrollably, a reflex reaction to the pain she continued to inflict. "How can someone like you, someone so beautiful, be so bloodthirsty? How Mira?" I strained, standing up to digest the news.

"Saint, please! I wanted to appease my father and my brother. I thought it was the best way. I couldn't tell them. They would have used Alessandro—our son—in the territory war. Ella has cared for him—the lady with me. He's been raised in the best private school in Paris. He knows two languages. His hair is yours. Saint, please don't do anything rash." Frantic, the truth regurgitated out of her, spilling over. My body flamed, coupled with sorrow, wanting to touch my own blood.

"You-you," I waggled a finger at her. "You're a Saliano through and through. They taught you well, vixen. You hid my son for five years from me?"

"Yes. Saint, listen to me." She threw her napkin on the table, lunging in my direction, but I turned my shoulder to avoid her touch, moving to the other side of the room.

"Keep your hands off me, Mira. Tell me how you did it? Did you really come back to America after you duped me? Where did you have the baby? I want all the gory details. Boy, are you good." I spat out.

Anchored motionless, she continued, her fingers curled by her side. "I traveled around Europe for a while. I didn't know I was pregnant until I started having stomach pains after two months. Marco told me it was better for me to stay away from Chicago. It was because of the number of hits they were executing on your family with the information I collected. I'm sorry, Saint. I can't turn back the clock." The high-pitched timbre of her voice kept delivering death by a thousand cuts.

"Better you stayed away," I scoffed, listening to the story that read like my worst nightmare. "You're right, it was. It was about the same time we got into a turf war in the South, and they killed four of my men in a week. Congratulations, you betraying me led to the murder of many a man. You're the ultimate executioner. The fucking ultimate," I accused, firing darts back at her—every knot chasing another knot in my shoulders. "Are you sure you're not the Don with those skills?" I moved towards her now, determined to bruise my treacherous wife. To break her completely as she'd done to me.

"Saint, you've done far, far worse. You offed eight of my father's men in two weeks. Do the numbers matter? I tried to make the best of a critical situation. I didn't realize the repercussions of my actions. Surely, you've done the same when you were younger. You can't tell me you got it all right."

"Maybe not, but tell you what I didn't do. I didn't have a rival mobster's baby and hide their son. Where did you have him?" I kept my voice low. I wanted as many details as possible. By now, my mouth was dry. I drained my glass of water, some spilling over and running down my chin. Mira didn't look away. Her eyes were locked in with mine with no signs of remorse.

Worse than I thought.

"Milan. A brilliant hospital with the best healthcare. I stayed there for another six months, recovering and working out a plan with Ella to mind him. Nearly a year and a half away from Chicago. Through my father and my brother, they told me how bad the street violence was, so it was the decision I made."

"Huh." Reasoning flew out the window as the gut punches kept hammering at me. "A son. I've got a fucking son. Where is he staying?" I barked.

"He's safe with Ella. I've done the right thing for once in my life, and I will not let you screw him up. I heard you talking to Falcone. Things aren't so good, are they? You keep telling me about the nightclub deals, glossing over how you were trying to start a cartel right under my father's nose. Did those gangs just go away, Saint?" She huffed, her bow-shaped lips drawn in a snarl.

"All you had to do was keep to the peace treaty, create a safe environment for Alessandro to come into...but, but...you couldn't help yourself. You know what? I'm out of here, and I'm taking my son. I will protect him with every ounce of strength I have. You can't stop me."

Mira headed for the bedroom. My head rocked with confusion and pain as I followed her. She was right, and I hated it. Falcone had downplayed the street niggles. Smaller gangs were making noise, upset the cartel hadn't eventuated.

"Saint, you might have problems at home, but you got residual problems out here. You have to clean up. You promised a couple of very important people about this cartel, and they're not happy about it. The Callahan brothers, the Prentice Family. You can't avoid them. If you don't fix it, we're gonna end up with blood on your hands."

I recounted Falcone's last conversation with me about the Prentice Family, who had heavy hitters in the right places. Their foot soldiers used brute, bone-breaking force as a tactic, and as armed dealers, they were the wrong famiglia to play tic-tac-toe with. I'd rescheduled too many times, obsessed with Mira's whereabouts.

I'd been off my game. This time, I reached for Mira as she flung open the closet doors, yanking out her suitcase and folding clothes into it neatly as if our whole deck hadn't crumbled.

"Don't leave it like this, Mira. I want to see my son. You can't keep him from me, and the streets aren't safe. You wanted to be part of this life, and now you're running?"

Her hair fell forward as coat hangers popped and the suitcase filled. "I'm doing a lot better than you, Saint. I'm not starting wars for no reason. You're the one making things harder for yourself. I've kept Alessandro safe all these years, haven't I? You call me the executioner, but what kind of Don are you?"

She flung the arrow in my direction, and I had no comeback. Business had fluctuated, but I planned to sort it out. "Mira, you can't keep my son from me."

Her fiery eyes looked up. "I don't want that. You can talk to him. I'll send photos, but you have to keep him safe, Saint. I'm moving out to an apartment. Either you find me one, or I'll have Ella do it. I need to be with my son. *Our* son."

Reality hit me like a ton of bricks.

Son. I have a son.

Chapter 18

Mira

One week later...

"I'm completely fine, and so is Alessandro. I haven't told him you're his father yet, so if you want to do that, you can. I can put you on FaceTime with him." I'd overwhelmed Saint with the information about his son, but he wanted the truth, so I hit him with it.

Alessandro was with Ella, getting washed up. I heard their intermingled laughter down the back of my new apartment Saint had organized.

"I'm not letting you organize it, Mira. Let me make a call. I know the security on the desk. They're the best, and it's a safe block of apartments."

He'd snapped into action, and within a day, an apartment for Alessandro and I had been arranged. We weren't cordial, it was transactional, and the ice queen in me surfaced. I would do anything for Alessandro.

The apartment had excellent lighting, a balcony large enough for a small group of people, fully furnished with charcoal trim, and a second bedroom for Alessandro. I kept the curtains drawn, rarely stepping out on the balcony for fear of being watched. Saint called every day to check in with us both, but any pleasantries were at a bare minimum between us.

I tied my hair up high in a messy bun, slipping into a black long-sleeved maxi dress. I skimmed a finger over my protruding collarbones and examined my sunken cheekbones. Stress had taken its toll on me. But now I'd told Saint about his son, certain pressures had eased, though others flared. One of those was with my own estranged family members. I could not rest.

I sliced sandwiches for Alessandro's lunch, enjoying being able to fully step into my motherly role with him. My phone buzzed on the counter and I picked it up, annoyed that Saint was calling me again.

"Saint. I told you to stop calling me. Everything is fine here." Immediately, the dulcet sound of my father's chuckle filtered down the line. He'd been calling more. A lot more, and I'd been holding off seeing him.

"You should check your caller ID before you answer your phone, Mira. This is not Saint, that's for sure. It's your father. How are you this fine Chicago morning, Mira?" My father sounded as if he were in high spirits.

"I'm doing well," I said to him cautiously.

Does he know? Please, don't let him find out about Alessandro.

"Mira! We're almost ready," Ella called out, a flush of heat firing through me.

"Give me a minute, Dad," I asked, placing him on mute.

"Sure, sure. Do what you have to do, Mira."

I rushed down the hall with the shh symbol on my lips, shaking my head at Ella. "Can you keep it down just a little? Frankie is on the line."

Ella put a hand on my shoulder, with Alessandro standing underneath her. I mussed with his hair, kissing the top of his head. "Who's Frankie, Mom?" Cringing, I hoped his inquisitive voice didn't travel the distance to my cell phone even though it was on mute.

Returning to the phone, I picked it up timidly. "Hi, sorry about that."

"Ah, don't worry about it. Nice hold music you got there."

I picked at the lettuce from the sandwich, knowing there was not a chance in hell I could hide from Frankie Saliano. "Thanks. We haven't caught up recently, but Saint and I have been busy with interior decorations."

"Ah, so that's what it is. Antonio said he waved to you on Saltwater Street. Not your usual spot. What business do you have over there? You wanna be careful. That's Callahan territory, and it might not end well if they get eyes on you. Don't go over there again."

Awkwardly, a stilted half-chuckle escaped my lips. "I must have missed him. I can't remember why I was there. When was that?" My head had been frazzled since Ella and Alessandro had arrived a few weeks back. I'd sought alternative routes, trying to shake off any tails.

"Last week. Your husband knows this. I sent you over to him so you could be safe, but apparently Mr. Riccini missed the memo."

"Don't give Saint a hard time. He doesn't know where I travel to Chicago every day. I am afforded certain freedoms. I'm not a prisoner," I said in an annoyed voice, Alessandro's bright laughter trickling through to the kitchen. I moved swiftly to the balcony, hoping my father's hearing was dying off.

"It has nothing to do with being a prisoner, Mira. Now you can see the method to my madness when I tried to keep you shielded during your younger years." I could almost hear him grinning through the phone. "But hey, you're a curious one, and it's led you into some dark places. Marco sends his well wishes."

Anger bloomed as soon as my father uttered the snake's name. I hated my bastard brother for life and vowed never to forgive him. "Then I'm in alignment with my mobster family. The darkness is where all of us live. Isn't that right, father?"

"Ah, Mira. You're a delight. I won't keep you, but I'll be in touch soon."

"Send my death wishes...I mean well wishes to Marco as well." I drove the nails in where I could.

"Don't be like that, Mira. Your brother loves you."

Alessandro peeped his head around the corner, Ella unable to contain him anymore.

"Dad, I have to go," I said hastily, not taking chances.

"Speak soon, my love." I clicked the end call button, embracing my son.

"Good morning! How about breakfast?"

"Yummo. Frosty Flakes?"

"No, no. You can't eat all that sugar. It will rot your teeth. Avocado on toast and eggs."

"Eww, that green stuff I've seen you eating?"

"Yes, that green stuff that you love eating." I scooped Alessandro up, planting numerous kisses on his cherub cheeks, not wanting to let him go.

"Mommy, too many! Too many kisses. *Arrête ça.* Stop it." Alessandro wriggled hard out of my grasp to the ground, giggling and being rambunctious. Sighing, I smoothed down my maxi dress, Ella rubbing the top of my shoulder in comfort. It was going to be a major challenge to keep Alessandro cooped up inside a tiny apartment. He was a boy who required space and movement to play. If I had my way, he would have been in school right away and on the soccer team.

I smiled, thinking of his speedy feet at the playground. Soccer would have been the first sport I would have placed him in. "I hate goodbyes. I don't want to tell him I won't see him for a while, but I don't want to lie, either." Ella tucked her hair behind her ear, laying her head on my shoulder.

"Ah, Ella. This is total shit. I don't want you to leave." What I didn't want to admit to her is that without her, I felt naked and fearful I wouldn't be able to cope as a mafia wife. But she had to go see her mother and family. Now that Saint knew about Alessandro, I didn't see a reason for my son to leave with Ella. Alessandro's place was with me. I wasn't letting him go this time around. "I could use a true ally in my corner, but I've disrupted enough of your life, and I hate that I've even done that."

"I don't. It's been the best disruption ever—better than babysitting your father's goons. As a matter of fact, it's a miracle he let me resign. We both know the only way out of the mob is in a body bag or..." Ella sucked in a hot sigh with a woeful glance, my stomach like a washing machine of turbulent emotions. "You know the rest."

"Yeah, I know the rest." A confused frown got me thinking about why he let Ella resign due to her fake pregnancy. My father was a kill-first-questions-later type of man. Secretly, it's why I considered renaming Alessandro to Amara—one who is blessed without end or death, but I figured Alessandro, meaning defender of men, was good enough.

The conversation had turned dark, so I chuckled to shift my emotions, my phone ringing again. "Hang on, let me answer this.

Ella, can you make sure he doesn't go out on the balcony? I don't want to risk him being seen publicly. My father has too many street spies. Maybe play in the bedroom for a minute."

"Okay," she gushed as I picked up the phone to see that it was my brother, Marco, calling. I braced myself, my teeth automatically wanting to grind together, but I did my best to stay relaxed.

"What can I do for you, brother?"

"It's a friendly call, wanting to see how things with you and Saint are. Check up on my little sis. He's treating you well, I hope." The fake care irritated me to no end. For all my father's street spying, the veil cloaked his eyes when it came to his own flesh and blood. Marco, to me, was a snake right under his feet, ready to inject its poison.

"What do you care?" I pulled no punches with my brother; he wasn't mine by blood, anyway.

"Aww, come on, Mira. You can't be salty after all these years, can you? I love you. Truly, I do." No part of his fraudulent claims spoke of love, only sly behavior.

"If you say so. I can't talk long. I have things to take care of."

"Huh. I heard you're redecorating over there. Good luck with it. Take care, sister."

I didn't offer him a goodbye...he deserved no airtime with me. I clicked off the call, just hoping to get through the day with Alessandro and Ella.

As dusk skated into the night, I locked the doors, checked twice, and listened for any unwarranted sounds from the front door to Alessandro's bedroom.

It took me the better half of three hours to fall asleep because of my increased paranoia, but better safe than sorry.

Days passed with Ella's departure looming. Going to the airport with her was a no-no, but I had a duty of care to make sure she arrived there safely.

"I want you to call me as soon as you hit the freeway if there's anything funky. I mean, one thing off with the driver, Ella, I want you to text 8 to me, and I'll get Saint to take care of it."

"Wow, you think something will happen?"

"I do not wish for it, but you're important to me. You're part of Alessandro's life as well. Text me when you get to the airport and before you get on the plane. Before you ask if it's necessary..."

Ella shook her head. "I know the protocol. Remember, I worked for your father. I know what to do, but thanks."

Blowing out a labored sigh, I hugged Ella tight. "Sorry, I forget sometimes. Thank you so much. I love you like a sister. Give your mother and family my apologies and love."

"Love you, too. You're great with him. He's going to be good, Mira. You've got this." Ella squeezed my fingers as she and Alessandro said their goodbyes.

Alessandro rubbed his hand over the back of his skull with a curious yet confused look on his adorable face.

"Wait, you're not coming back? *Au revoir?*" he asked, his timid voice breaking my heart.

"Not quite, but it's going to be a little while. You can talk to me just like you used to with Mommy on FaceTime if you want." Alessandro threw his arms around Ella's legs as I saw the tears well in her eyes.

"Ah, this is too hard. I gotta go. The Uber's here." She looked down at her phone as I watched her leave, my heart stomping through my chest as she descended on the elevator. By the time she got to the bottom of the elevator, my phone rang.

Frankie Saliano...the bile in my stomach began rising. "Alessandro, go and watch some TV, I'll be right there with a snack."

Once Alessandro made a move towards the TV, I answered the call.

"Hi, D-Dad," I said. It didn't get lost on me that I hesitated to call him dad.

"Morning, my love. Can we catch up this week? I feel like I haven't seen you all year."

"Dramatic as always, Dad. No, I have a few more things to finish, and then I'll be free."

I craned my neck back to the ceiling, happy that Alessandro was watching cartoons on the couch.

"Why do I feel like you're avoiding me?"

"It's not like that," I pressed back, wanting to dry-heave, praying and hoping Alessandro would remain quiet.

"Sure seems like it, but I'm not going to pressure you. Talk soon."

"Talk soon, Dad." Cautiously, I put my cell phone down. "Phew." I touched a hand to my heart, relieved I'd endured the brief conversation, but the reprieve lasted all but a few seconds.

My phone pinged, and a photo message streamed through. I frowned, my forehead creasing together. A photo from my father with Ella holding Alessandro's hand, directing him into my car at the Chicago O'Hare airport.

Gasping, my pulse thudded in my eardrums. "Mommy, what is it?" Alessandro's head turned my way.

"Nothing, baby. Keep watching TV, Mommy's fine. I just saw something on my phone."

"Okay."

I read the text to go with the picture.

DAD: *Is this why you don't want to meet with me?*

Shivering, and not from the cold, I wrapped my hands around myself as my phone blew up again. Once my father smelled blood in the water, he was relentless.

One ring. No answer.

Two rings, no answer.

Four, and my phone would go to voicemail.

Breathing deeply, I finally answered. "Yes?"

"Thought so. So, whose kid is it?"

I heaved. There was no point in keeping this from him.

"Mine and Saint's from five years ago."

"There we go. Finally, the truth. My daughter's a mother now. Would ya look at that?"

Chapter 19

Saint

Alessandro, my flesh and blood, not in my house along with my ferociously protective and sexy wife, wore thin on my mentals. I reached over for her during the night, only to clutch empty bed sheets, not her supple, warm, sweet-scented body. I missed nuzzling into her neck, hearing her cat-like murmuring in her sleep.

My son, whom I'd never set eyes on, was in Chicago, right in the middle of a cartel mix-up and a deep web of crime syndicate territory. A compelling urge coursed through my veins to call and see his face, hear his voice, and find out if he was really my son. My fucking son. I'd loved and lost so many loved ones. I'd cracked a thousand times inside, and hated the feeling.

It was 6 am. I sat at my office desk, the same one I'd laid Mira on. A slow smile drifted over my lips, reminiscing over her beautiful moans and captivating slender curves. I returned from the memory, preparing for a long overdue meeting.

It included the Zig Zag crew—whose two soldiers had been offed by the Salianos as retaliation—the Prentice Family, Murdoch Industries, and the Callahan crew. If I didn't angle it right, pure street destruction would erupt. I had a backup plan to purchase hardware from the Callahans to smooth over the loss of the cartel deal, even though I lied about it going full steam ahead.

Once I got the paperwork together, I strolled to the bathroom. Shaving, Mira's shampoo bottle caught my eye. I reached for it, popping the top open, and inhaling her long-lost scent. I wanted her so badly to come home, for us to work it out, but a Riccini man has a certain level of pride that's hard to break down.

Huffing, I placed my phone in the holder next to the mirror, calling Mira. She would be awake. She had a boy in her care, so I assumed he would have plenty of energy to spare if he was anything like his father. Mira's face popped up in my mind, tugging at my heartstrings as I grooved my razor upward toward my chin.

"Morning, Mira. How are you?" She looked brighter now that she was away from me. I never wanted to add stress to her life. I only wanted us to be together and love one another. Difficult for a Chicago kingpin like me to admit.

"Morning, Saint," she yawned, sleepily stunning. "Getting Alessandro ready. He's a handful." I loved seeing her in motherly form. Her champagne locks were mussed up, her eyes dreamy, but she looked like a weight had been taken from her shoulders now that I knew she was with my child.

"I bet. Mira, I want to see my son. You can't keep him from me." My command was loud and clear but unnecessary.

"Sure. Saint. I told you I don't want to keep you from him. I only want to keep him safe from this mob bullshit. I don't want him being used."

Deep down, I recognized that the best option for Alessandro was the one she'd chosen. The streets were sizzling, and I had to set records straight before several misunderstandings blew the gates of Chi-town street hell wide open.

"I would never use my child, Mira. You think so lowly of me. I'm not your father." We were estranged, and the hurt from her actions killed my soul. But living without her and my son did far worse.

"Saint, I don't want to argue. I'm sleep-deprived. It's been a rough week. Yes, you can see him. I haven't told him you're his father. I thought you could do that. Once you tell him, he'll want to meet you. I guarantee it."

I wasn't a man to get nervous, but I was now. My progeny and the boy who would take over the Riccini empire once it was all said and done. Mira springing the brutal truth on me the way she did hadn't given me the time to think about what I wanted for my son.

"Fine by me. I can secure the venue. It will be up to you, Mira. Whatever's going to make the situation comfortable for everyone."

"Glad we agree for once," she quipped, dipping off-screen for a moment as I heard the little man's voice and her soft whispers to him.

"*Oui*, Mommy," he replied, showing off his Parisian schooling. My pulse beat in strange places around my body as a boy with a bright, innocent face, a full head of dark hair, and a cute toothy smile filled the screen.

I rinsed under my chin, wiping away the excess shaving cream.

"Hi, Alessandro?"

"Hi. What are you doing to your face?" he asked, Mira coming back on screen. He must have been sitting on her lap. Picture perfect.

"I'm shaving up. One day, I'll teach you how to do it when you get hair."

"Hehe. I don't have hair like that. No, no," he said.

I grinned, lighting up from the inside with pride. "Sassy, like your mother. Why did I expect anything else?" I quirked an eyebrow, leaning forward over the sink. My boy looked good. Cared for. "Do you know who I am?"

He fumbled around with his fingers, tilting his head to the side. "*Non.* Who are you?"

Exhaling a sigh, I glanced at Mira for a moment, expectations in her wheat-colored eyes.

"I'm your father, Alessandro. I'm the one who gave you all that dark hair on top of your head."

The boy's mouth opened as he pulled up strands of his bouncy curls. "You? You did? You're my *père*? My father?" he squealed as Mira broke into a grin. My kid's energy was infectious.

"Yes, I am. Saint Riccini, and your name is Alessandro Riccini. Your mother is my wife. We're a family—together." I made a circle to emphasize my point to not only my boy but also to remind Mira she belonged to me, and that I looked after my possessions very well. She and I would forever be tied, no matter what.

"Wow! Daddy. So cool. Will you come and see us?"

"Yes, when I can, I will. I have to sort a few things out first." Floundering in the moment, I caught myself being lost for words. What did I say to a five-year-old boy who I only recently learned was mine? I noted some of his mannerisms were like mine, and it did me in a little.

How could this little being pick up on them already without knowing me?

I unstuck my hands from the basin, taking my attention off the screen to my face, and checking for any missed spots.

"Okay. Nice to meet you. What's your name?"

I chuckled, arching my eyebrow as Mira tucked the little boy closer into her. "It's Dad to you, but my friends call me Saint." Alessandro looked preoccupied with what he was doing and wanted to scramble off his mother's lap. He almost wrenched her arm out of her socket, bringing a grin out of me. "He's strong. A real Riccini boy. Are you coping over there? You could use my help." I had no intention of being a hands-off father. I wanted to be at his first sporting events, christenings, birthdays, and wherever else I needed to be. Seeing him gave me a renewed purpose for the street meetings ahead.

"No. You do what you have to do, Saint. Have things settled?"

"Truthfully, no...but I'm on my way to settle them right now. Trust me."

Mira pursed her lips together, brushing her hair back from her face. "If you say so." Her eyes slanted sideways, inciting anger in me. She had the nerve to be irritated with me after the pit of suffering she'd dumped me into.

"Mira..."

"It's fine, Saint. I've done my dirt, too. It's what it is between us. I need some space right now. Please sort it out." She licked her lips, making me readjust my cock; her lips had that effect on me. "I have something else to tell you. I don't want to keep anything hidden from you anymore—and it sounds hypocritical, I'm sure— but he's going to call you. My father, I mean, he knows about Alessandro. Be warned."

"Fuck! How did he find out, Mira?" I hissed, my hands gripping the porcelain basin.

"I told you—my father has eyes and ears all over Chicago."

A text blinked through from Lupo, ending the strained

conversation.

"Mira, I gotta go. Street duty calls. Call you later."

"Bye, Saint."

Switching into game mode, I slipped my black collar shirt on, splashed on my cologne, checked the bullets in my Glock, and texted Falcone and the three sharp-shooting snipers I secretly had in place atop the opposite building for our meeting.

Frankie Saliano and his peeping Toms. Fuck me.

I drove to Cortlandt Street, a warehouse with no occupants and the perfect place for a street meeting. One of Murdoch Industries buildings was a drug warehouse for us to set up for our new Boston customers. Learning to compartmentalize wasn't my forte. Mira and Alessandro were woven into every action.

I let the cogs of my mind tick over to the possibilities, but the treble of my phone chiseled through my mental fogginess. "Saint," I snapped.

"Saint, Frankie here."

"Ah, long time no hear. This time I got the heads up. I know why you're calling."

"Good, so this shouldn't take long." Pent-up animosity festered with the knowledge that this man would be my father-in-law for life, but I couldn't have it both ways. "I want to set up a meeting to see my grandson. We can meet on neutral ground. Do you think this can be arranged?"

I paused, sliding my hands over the wheel as I thought about what Mira would say. I cared about her opinion. Even if I failed to voice it out loud, I liked how she protected our son.

"If Mira is okay with the meeting, then I'm down, but if she isn't, it's a no. So, the call is hers." Me surrendering to anyone, especially a woman, was unheard of. But here I was, doing it. I crossed the back streets to my destination.

"Understood. I'll make sure it's cleared with Mira. Keep out of trouble, Saint."

As Frankie signed off, I understood his last sentence to contain a warning. I would have to tread lightly on the streets.

My wheels crunched over gravel as I slowed to a halt in the parking lot of the terracotta warehouse, drawing my gun from my hip holster. I confirmed the number of bullets in the chamber. One for every person in the meeting, if need be, but hopefully, it wouldn't come to a bloody end...

Chapter 20

Mira

Two days later...

"Are you sure you're ready? Do you want me to come in with you?"

"Bring two cars, Saint. I want extra protection with Falcone and his soldiers in the car behind us. Can you do that? My father is unpredictable. It's for your safety, too."

I'd been dry-heaving all morning, but I kept this insignificant fact hidden from Saint. If he knew, he would have jumped into crisis mode, asking me a bunch of questions, and all I wanted to do was get the meeting over and done with.

"Why the hell did you agree to this? Look at how stressed out you are. Tell Frankie to take a short trip to hell. He's got one foot in it already, anyway."

My hair was irritating me. Everything was. I blew it back out of my face, searching for a spare hair tie, but not finding one. "You think I wanna go, Saint? Nope. Like hell I do. My father is a bull. He will charge at you until he impales you. If I do it this way under these conditions, it's better," I exhaled. "My way."

"Fuck me. I hate this. Frankie Saliano." He huffed out. "Okay, don't worry, the car will be there. Do you have the gun I trained you to use? Do you think you have what it takes to use it, Mira?"

"How can I know that, Saint? I've never had to shoot anyone," I jabbed, not wanting Alessandro to hear the gory details and my blood pressure rising like flood waters the more Saint pressed me.

"He doesn't know you're not his daughter biologically. There's no telling how that man will react. I'm going to be strapped, and so will Falcone and the boys. This is one reason I don't want you to go."

"Saint. Please don't make this harder." Saint was hard of hearing and kept going.

"He has to know. She told you on her deathbed. Where was Frankie then, since he's such a KGB spy? He needs to get a new profession."

"I don't know! Stop, Saint," I struck at him in a low hiss.

"Don't get testy, Mira. If you were here, all that tension would go. I know what to do to get you to calm down."

Saint looked every inch a Riccini in his tailored navy-blue suit, with the deep groove of his chest muscles peeping through his unbuttoned shirt. His face was clean-shaven, his ocean eyes appreciatively staring back at me via FaceTime.

I wanted a piece of him. My body remembered him, and it seemed silly we weren't together. But in our distance, I didn't know how to lock us back in together.

"Saint, can you focus for a minute?" I told him, wanting to secure the two cars to show presence.

"How Mira? Look at you. You're sexy as fuck with that right-out-of-the-shower hair, and that dress...that fucking dress you're wearing. I want to rip it right off you. I miss you, okay? My son, I want him here with us, Mira. I don't care how far you are from me in that condo. You're the woman for me. We're a family, whether or not you like it."

Saint speaking with such passion lit the fire in my soul. "Saint," I whispered gently, watching Alessandro fitting puzzle pieces together. His face appeared so enthralled with what he was doing, and Saint's baritone voice brought out my horniness in a way I hadn't felt for the last couple of weeks.

Now that I had Alessandro under my watchful eye, my stress level had decreased. I folded my bottom lip inside my mouth, peeking at Alessandro to see if he was looking my way.

Saint's sky-blue eyes drilled into mine. I knew what those beautiful full lips could do in so many ways. Saint groaned, his face altering to one of feverish passion. "Can you go to the bedroom? I wanna try something with you. You game, baby?"

I giggled. Saint had a way of leaving me speechless. "Saint, Alessandro is here..." my voice trailed off, but I was more than game and already moving from the stool at the kitchen counter.

"Well, how did he get here? Come on. I want you. I've got time. Come on, Mira, give me something to dream about tonight. Let me see you." His silky bedroom tone turned on every sensual code in my body. He had the key to breaking down all my defenses.

"Wait till I get to the bedroom, Saint." I turned to my son. "Alessandro, I'm going to the...the toilet, okay? Stay here. Don't open the door. Yell if you need anything. Okay, baby?"

"*Oui, Maman*," he said, not even looking up at me as I kissed the top of his head.

"Keep going with your puzzle. I want it finished when I come out."

I kept the phone up as I walked through the lit-up hallway to my bedroom. I would have to close the door so Alessandro didn't know what I was up to.

I smothered a giggle and felt naughty with Saint. He brought my soul alive to the fullest level. I tucked a finger under the shoestring strap of my tight dress, dropping it off my shoulder.

Saint's eyes turned lucid. I wanted to make him drool, so I bit my lip again, scuttling into my bedroom, closing the door behind me, and locking it. "What are you going to do next, Mira?" he breathed heavily as I scooted up the bed, keeping my phone upright so he could see me. I'd have to keep my moaning low.

"I'm going to blow your mind, Saint, and remind you just what you've been missing."

Saint shook his head, driving a hand through his longer locks, parting them down the middle. "Fuck, I already know what I've been missing, but show me anyway. I can't wait. I have to see. Let me see your pussy. I want you to come while I'm watching."

His raw demand blazed white, sweltering heat through my cells, my skin prickling with microscopic beads of sweat.

"You want that, Saint?" I replied, sliding down the other strap so the top of my bosom showed. "What are you going to do for me? I want a peep show, too."

Saint wasted no time unbuttoning his shirt, and pulling it overhead. "Oh, baby, I'm ready. You don't have to tell me twice." I admired the smooth cut of his chiseled chest, wanting to rub baby oil all over him and slip-slide. But for now, all we could do was play out our little fantasy.

"My God, you're hot. Your hair's getting long. I wanna run my fingers through it. Something for me to tug on when you put that sexy mouth on me." I was becoming more confident talking dirty to Saint, and nothing was out-of-bounds with him in the bedroom. He made me feel safe enough to express myself sexually.

"I was thinking about cutting it, but now I won't if that's why." Saint put the phone on the headboard as he slipped out of his pants. My eyes bugged out at the sight of his thick hard-on through his underwear. He teased, dropping a side of them down, thrusting his hips at the camera.

I laughed, feeling free with him but still flooded with unfulfilled desire. The dull ache of pleasure rose between my legs as I wriggled my dress down further underneath my breasts, displaying my red lace bra.

"God, that looks downright sinful." His eyes ogled me, and I nodded.

"Wanna see more?" Saint positioned himself on the bed, and this time, I placed my phone on the headboard, dropping my dress all the way down, revealing a red lace G-string. I turned my ass to the camera so he saw all of me.

"Fuck Mira! Why don't I drive there and just put you to sleep with this cock? Seriously, I can't take it. How do you get sexier every time I see you?" he growled, panting. I liked his violent darkness; he added that kerosene to flame my fire. In my short time trying to date after Paris, all the other men had been lukewarm at best. No one had sparked my fire enough for me to fully give in to them.

I didn't answer but took the phone, letting my eyes soak in the man feast in front of me. That deep V near his groin, the ripple of his abs as he inhaled, his rugged face. I slipped my panties down my hips and opened up my legs, dropping the phone there, so he got the close up.

"Uh-huh, like this Saint?" I gushed, my fingers gliding between the hot goodness between my legs. I dipped two fingers in, making sure he had a front-row seat to the show.

"Goddamn it. Fuck, yes. Keep going. Keep those fingers

moving. Imagine it's my tongue there, Mira. Do it. Do it for me," he commanded hotly.

I struggled to keep my eyes open to Saint's mesmerizing voice. I wanted to because he had a firm hold on the base of his cock, gliding his hand up and down his engorged shaft, his wrist pumping, and the ache deepening in my pussy.

I wanted him inside me. It was a waste, but we had to make do. I tried not to let my head drift to Alessandro and into Mommy's world as my cheeks bloomed from excess heat.

Luckily, I'd left the bedroom window open a crack to catch the breeze. Wafts of the cool breeze tempered the sizzle, but Saint's hand moved quicker, the veins of his hands straining from taking hold of himself. I picked up my pace, alternating circles and sliding digits inside my gooey wetness.

"Oh, yes, Mira. So wet, fuck. Why am I not there? Tell me?" He groaned.

I got more comfortable, leaning my head back as I brought the phone back up top to my breasts, pulling one out for him to see as I played with my erect nipple.

"If you were here, this would be in your mouth. Taste it," I beckoned. I checked the temperature at Saint's end, his penis dribbling with pre-cum. Our dirty fever ran extended through the phone line, both of us driving ourselves to the precipice.

"I would do more than that. Push those fingers deeper, Mira. Feel my cock. See how hard it is for you. I want you to come. Do it with me, we're good at this. Can you feel me, Mira? Can you feel how much I want you?"

"Yes, Saint, I can feel you," I pressed, circling, teasing, and coaxing my clit. Saint grunting into the phone was the catalyst as my pussy clamped together in a tight, nerve-ending orgasm. I suppressed a moan, eyes glazed over as I looked into Saint's ocean blues. His body went stiff. Saint ejaculated, his hand shaky, sweat dribbling down the side of his dewy skin.

"Mira, fuck!" His chest expanded in and out as I dropped the phone for a minute, flushed and enjoying the waves of pleasures sweeping through me. "Mira?"

"I'm here," I replied drowsily. "Wow, I needed that."

"I think we both did. Mira, I will not let anything happen to you tomorrow. I will lay down my life for you and Alessandro."

"I believe you, but I don't want you to. I want you alive."

D-Day arrived way too soon, but Saint did as I asked downstairs out front. Two all-black tinted Jeeps were outside, Saint waiting for us in the first one. I reached into the inside of my jacket, feeling around for my gun, Alessandro holding my other hand.

"Where are we going, Mommy?"

"To meet your grandfather. It should be interesting, and now you get to meet your father in person."

"Wow! Dad's inside there?" He pointed to the black vehicle in front of him.

"Yes, he is."

My hand slid up to my tucked-in silver cross as the door opened to the first car. It was now or never.

Chapter 21

Saint

As soon as I saw Alessandro climb into the truck, there was no doubt he was my kid.

"Hi, Dad," he said casually, as if he'd been calling me it his whole life.

"Son," I replied croakily, kissing Mira on the cheek as she settled beside me. "Good to see you. You look like a sharp young man, like your father," I grinned, unable to stop myself from connecting with him.

Alessandro didn't understand how important the moment was, but Mira did, tears welling up in her eyes. I covered her hand with mine.

"Hello, my love. You look wonderful. Elegant and poised. My Riccini woman." I didn't want to hold back. I needed to tell her how I felt about her. If things fell apart today, when would I let her know? We'd been through hell and back, and here we were, still glued together.

"Thanks, Saint. I don't feel like it." Yesterday, when I'd spoken to her, she didn't let me in on her fears about her father. But now as I sat beside her, the trepidation was hard to miss.

Locking my fingers into hers, Alessandro watched us together as if he was seeing us for the first time. He smiled but turned to look out the window. "I miss Ella. When will I see her, Mommy?" Alessandro climbed on his knees, but Mira pulled him back protectively.

"Alessandro, get down from there and put your seatbelt on. Ella's still with her family, honey. You can talk to her next week on the phone. She misses you, too."

Obediently, he slunk back into his seat, putting his seatbelt on. I was proud of how courteous he was. "You're doing a good job, mama," I whispered in her ear.

"Some days, I don't feel like I am, Saint." Her grip tightened, and I brought her hand to my lips to soothe her.

"Here, look at me. It's going to be okay. Falcone's behind me and my best three. Your father's not stupid. It's us now, Mira. Stop worrying. He just wants to see his grandson." I bent to her glossy lips with a light peck, wanting to do more than that. Our FaceTime sex session had me hot and bothered under my suit. She turned every light on inside me.

Alessandro giggled, pointing at us both to our amusement. "*Embrasser*, smoochy. You two. Mommy and Daddy. Ha-ha!"

I pinched his little leg lightly with a smile as we approached our destination. Frankie's pizzeria. Saliano's side. "I can't believe he picked this place. The last time I came here, I was a teenager. This is bringing back memories." A dreamy look formed on Mira's face.

"Good or bad?"

"Good. My father and his friend would play cards and dominoes. They were so loud, but I knew something was going on out back because I could hear the money counting machines. It's where he laundered money. I'm sure he still does." Mira smirked, looking at me as Ricardo stopped the car.

"I bet he does," I agreed.

"Okay, this is it. You want me to wait for a bit like you said, boss?"

"Yeah, wait for ten. I'll text if it's okay to leave. I'm sure it's gonna be fine."

"No problemo."

Mira reached for the door handle, but I splayed a hand over her stomach.

"Wait, let me clear the area and check in with Falcone. I'm in Saliano territory. I'll be back."

Mira nodded in approval, hugging Alessandro to her. He must have sensed something was wrong as he buried his head in his mother's side.

Sliding out, my jaw tightened as I looked up at the peeling sign of the forty-year-old pizzeria, which had stood the test of time. The smell of deep-pan pepperoni filled my nostrils. The side screen door opened, and Frankie's salt and pepper head poked out the side with a welcoming hand.

"Come in. No need for guns. Everybody's safe. Bring my grandson," Frankie said gruffly, a rare smile curving the old man's lips. Taken aback, I stepped backward, ushering Falcone back to his vehicle, mouthing at him to go.

Bad preliminary move, but to me, it felt good, different, and that smile on his face told the story. It didn't stop me from double-patting my gun just in case. I called Mira and Alessandro out of the vehicle as Frankie held the door open to the dimly lit back half of the pizzeria.

Two amber industrial lights hung over a trestle table with

pizzas, soda, cake, and alcohol. Frankie looked down at Alessandro, who hid behind his mother's leg, sneaking cautious glances at the older man. Frankie outstretched his hand to me.

"Saint. Thanks."

I shook it firmly, not 100% sure how this would go down, and stayed close to Mira.

"You're welcome," I replied, picking a chair and sitting down. The local Chi-town radio station played the hottest hits in the background, but I was busy staring at the back door for security purposes.

"It's secured. I got my boys out there. We're good. Ain't nobody coming down here," he said, reassuring me.

Better not be. Otherwise, I'm pulling the trigger, no questions asked.

"Hi, Mira. Take a seat. And you, little man, it's alright. I'm not gonna hurt you. I'm your *nonno*. Grandpa. I ain't got nothing but love for ya." Frankie's voice leaned on the intimidating side, so I understood why Alessandro appeared reluctant.

"Hi, Dad."

"So good to see you, sweetie. You look beautiful. A true stunner. Look at you with your *famiglia*. I'm a proud father. It's all I ever wanted for you." Frankie's adoration for his daughter shone through, and when I heard the heartfelt nature of his voice, I texted Ricardo, letting him go.

"Thanks. Is it though, Dad?"

He patted Mira's hand. "Let's get some food in the belly. It's time I told you a couple of things."

Alessandro was slowly warming up to the situation, but my hands were tight, and my hypersensitivity had me monitoring the periphery of the back door. I sat where I could see it clearly, but my belly began rumbling, embarrassing me. Frankie laughed wholeheartedly.

"See, that's why we gotta eat. You got a gremlin in there," he pointed out.

Alessandro grinned. "You're funny. Are you a grandpa?" he asked, leaning over the table. Mira sat him back in place.

"I'm your grandpa, kid, and the only thing funny about me is my looks."

Alessandro, not comprehending, grinned again. I rolled my shoulders back, seeing the sparkle coming back into Mira's eyes.

Frankie summoned the servers from the front, ordering pizza and spaghetti. Fifteen minutes later, enemy Dons were chowing down together.

"That's much, much better," Frankie advised, swiping a napkin over his mouth. "Mira, I have to apologize to you. I've made many mistakes, but raising you as my daughter wasn't one of them."

He cradled her hand as Mira stared at him, dumbfounded. Crinkles formed around his mouth as it formed a thin line.

"It's time you knew. Maybe you even know." Frankie's face tightened. "I knew about what your mother did. She told me a few years later after bringing you home. I asked questions when your blood type didn't match up after you were in the hospital for a stint."

Frankie stared at the tablecloth for a minute while Mira shook her head in disbelief.

"We fought for a long time after that, but the truth is I loved you the moment I saw you, and I never wanted you to feel you weren't mine. I know it must have hurt you to your core to find out. I begged her not to tell you." Frankie coughed as a melancholic expression drifted over Mira's face.

"I know. Mom...Angelica told me when she was on her deathbed." Mira flicked a look towards me, keeping to herself that Falcone had been the hired hitman. Though, I wouldn't be entirely shocked if Frankie already knew. "I can't relive this again. I don't think I'll ever be over it, but I never once thought growing up that I wasn't yours unless you shut me out of family business."

I sat silently, letting them have their moments of healing together. Alessandro was aloof, slurping on his spaghetti with a slice of celebratory cake next to him. I kept my eyes trained on him.

"I was doing my best as a father to protect you," Frankie explained.

Mira bobbed her head up and down slowly. "I get that now. History repeats itself. It's the same thing I've wanted to do for my son. I didn't want you to use him as a pawn in your turf wars."

I glanced over to gauge Frankie's reaction. "Hmph," he rubbed his stubbled chin. "I wouldn't do that. Not to my grandson, regardless of the father. I knew about Saint, too."

"What? How could you know?" Mira's voice went up an octave, shocked by the admission.

"I have my sources, Mira. I'm a Saliano, and nothing slips by my radar. To find your way with your son, I wanted you to stand on your own two feet. I didn't want to interfere. Why do you think I let Ella resign? I knew she was taking care of Alessandro. Smart choice. I hired her. I should know. I knew she'd be loyal to you. If she screwed it up, I would have had her chopped and bagged up with the remains sent to her mother express mail."

I barely avoided choking on my own saliva, immune to my own father's death threats when he was still alive. I'd overheard so many of them in my life. "This is nuts, but how?"

"Ahhh." Frankie stopped speaking as Mira and I exchanged

looks, and I mouthed "I love you" to her.

The bleary glaze over her eyes as family secrets tumbled out of the closet gave me the impression she'd not seen my silent declaration. "You didn't come home, so I had a friend of mine track you. They saw you check into a hospital in Milan and come out with a small bundle in a wheelchair. I put two and two together, plus we were in the middle of a turf war with the Riccinis. And of course, I knew where Saint was."

"You are slick, Frankie. You've got better tracking skills than I do," I chimed in.

"You got that right, bud. You're sloppy," he replied.

He sipped his vodka slowly, as if contemplating the next truth bomb to drop. "But I tell you something...this peace treaty is going to stay in place as long as I'm alive. You hear me?"

"Loud and clear," I remarked, grinning at my son, who popped up to ask his grandpa a question.

"What's a peace treatment?" Alessandro asked, Mira's eyes shooting wide in alarm.

"A peace treaty is an agreement where two groups of people decide to be kind to one another," was Frankie's succinct reply, and I couldn't have said it better.

Alessandro looked around the table at the three of us, assessing what his grandfather had told him.

"That's *bien*. People being nice to one another. I got a sticker at school for giving a girl half my sandwich. Does that count?" We all chuckled, and Frankie's eyes glittered.

"Yep, that's the right thing to do. You'll be a real hit with the ladies when you're older." Frankie gestured to me. "This is your kid, for sure. The heartbreaker."

"Your grandson, old man," I cajoled, wondering how we were all sitting at the table together, eating as if we hadn't tried to kill one another repeatedly in the past.

"True, true, well before your mother."

Mira rolled her eyes at her father, but good-naturedly as she wrangled Alessandro into place. "I'm not touching that statement with a hot iron."

"Best not to. Your brother..." Mira's eyes narrowed to suspicious slits. "I was aware of what he made you do. At the time, I thought I should keep a lid on the situation as well. I wanted you to learn from your mistakes, and since you so desperately wanted to be in on family business, I wanted you to experience the hardships of what it was really like to live this life."

Mira blinked rapidly at my father. "You did that? Why? You deliberately let him throw me under the bus like that?" Anger flashed in her eyes.

Her father stroked his bristly chin. "Yes, regretfully so. Now, I would rethink it. It was cruel of me. However, a turf war would have gone ahead, regardless. Am I right, Saint?"

"Absolutely. Nick wasn't about to let you take the Southside without war. Not in my father's ethics manual. Sorry, babe." I sighed, the talk heavy in the room, but Mira seemed to handle it with grace.

"I love you, Mira, so much. Please forgive your old man. I will make sure Alessandro is safe. No harm will come to him, ever. This has been the best day of my life, and Saint, you look after my family. I put her life in your hands for a reason."

I nodded solemnly. "You have my word.

Chapter 22

Mira

The whole scene overwhelmed me so much that I kept looking to escape outside for some air. "What is it, Mira? Is something wrong?" my father inquired, concern etched in the furrows of his leathery brow.

"I need a minute. A quick breather because this is a lot to take in. Can I go out back to where the guards are?"

My father nodded. "Take the time you need. I'll pour a drink for you."

"Please." My nerves were shot. I trudged to the back door where plastic strips hung over a dingy screen door. Two of my father's men stood on both sides of the door, making me feel claustrophobic. One of them moved to direct me back inside, but my father called them off.

"It's okay. I'm taking a breather," I told them with a smile.

"Okay. Cool."

I put my hands up behind my head, opened my chest, and sought as much air as possible, even though Chicago's air was disgustingly polluted. City smog, I called it, but I would never leave. I wasn't one for country life.

We can make it now. Me and Saint. Together, we can be a family. All the hiding is over.

I'd spent so long on the run, sneaking and keeping secrets, that my brain found the peace hard to fathom. Looking out into the back alley, flashes of cars on the main street crept by, but I paid no attention. This was my father's and my grandfather's meeting spot for all things Saliano. Nobody would dare try anything on his turf without prophesying their own deaths.

I sucked in a few deep breaths, dropped my arms, and moved back inside. My father and Saint being in the same room, chatting as if they were old friends, was the most surreal thing I'd ever seen.

What my Saliano mother had done was a hard pill to swallow and a recurring nightmare I wanted off the repeat loop. When I healed enough, I wanted to find out where and how my De Luca family lived and where in the south of Naples, but I was nowhere near ready for that.

Saint had been a rock throughout, and being out in the open with him and my father was a Godsend. It was as if me being without Saint was only a prelude to us being together.

I returned to the table and settled between the most important men in my life. Alessandro's temporary shyness faded as he ventured from under my hip over to his grandpa to playfully poke him in the ribs.

My father scooped him up, tickling him. "Look at you now. At first, you didn't want to know about your grandpa, but now you can't stay away. I knew I'd win you over." Hearing his gleeful laugh and seeing the diamond smile on my father's face was incredible.

I rounded the table and sat beside Saint.

"Hey, how are you feeling?" he asked, a small whisper in my

ear.

I lay my head on his shoulder. "Honestly?"

"Yes, honestly."

"Like this is the best and worst moment of my life. Two men connecting who are so dominant in one area of life, and at each other's throats. I'm surprised we've gotten to this place of peace."

"You and me both. I was ready to shoot him in the face when I walked in the door. No offense, he's your father, but hey, he's a sworn enemy to the Riccinis," Saint muttered out the side of his mouth. I slapped his leg playfully.

"Saint Riccini! Take it back. I wouldn't let you do that." Euphoria and a mixed bag of other emotions had shaken me. My men, together. My father loved me! He really wanted me to be part of the famiglia. I hadn't anticipated his reaction today. Frankie Saliano was not a gentle and understanding man, but I had been wrong in that assumption. So very wrong.

My father looked up from tossing Alessandro around and blowing strawberry kisses on his stomach. Alessandro kicked and wriggled, laughing the whole time, lighting up my heart. What a day. Frankie Saliano was still as strong as an ox, tossing and flipping Alessandro over easily. As he did, his puffer jacket opened, giving way to a shoulder holster, and I bet he had one clipped to his hip, too. Shivers dotted my spine, wondering what would become of Alessandro. I smiled affectionately at the complicated man who claimed the spot of my father. I saw him as this invincible man capable of world domination in many ways.

Frankie's hearing was second to none. "I heard that, Saint. Trust me, I had the same idea in my brain when you walked into my spot with that cocky swagger, but we're here for the greater good of our famiglias. All the gun warfare is kapoot. Now, we sort things out like men." He thumped his hand to the table. Alessandro mimicked him with a wide grin. "Yes, Alessandro. That's it." He nodded in approval and etched his arm over my chair, kissing my cheek lightly. "Right here. This is where we discuss things amicably and work them out. You've got my grandson, and he needs a legacy he can stand in and be proud of. Not just one side, but both sides. He is the future."

Saint locked fingers with mine, as my ears had trouble adjusting to the logical words floating from my father's mouth. "I agree. I'll hold up my end of the bargain, and I know you'll hold up yours. Alessandro's got the best of both worlds, if you ask me."

"Why do you keep saying my name?" Alessandro whined, looking between the two men, too young to comprehend the gravity of the shoes he had to fill.

"Because you're special, and you've got the world of Chicago at your feet. It will be ready for you when the time is right."

"Eh, I want to play soccer with my friends," Alessandro whined, and my fears surfaced of him not being able to have a normal life.

Saint and I resumed our semi-private conversation. "I want Alessandro to make his own choice about the mob. Can he do that?"

Saint sucked in a breath. "If you're born into this life, you can't avoid it. Besides, if he's going to take over businesses, it's all built on drug money. This is the crux of the business."

"I figured that would be your answer. I just want him to have a normal childhood. Go to school, all these things."

"He can, and he will," my father said openly.

Aghast that he was listening in, I reprimanded him. "Can you stop listening?"

"Nothing's private in here. Security cameras and sound recorders are all over the place. Careful what you say." He winked with a chuckle. "I don't wanna hear how you two are making another baby."

Laughter filled the air, completely breaking the tension between us. Even Alessandro joined in, not comprehending why exactly we were laughing. It was a moment I would never forget until...

A loud popping sound rang out from the front of the restaurant. I jolted, my eyes immediately flying over to Alessandro. Saint's reflexes were lightning-quick, withdrawing his gun from his holster—my father, a close second behind him as he released Alessandro into my arms.

"Go to your mother." Poor Alessandro's face was open, staring right at the guns drawn from Saint and Frankie as more shots sounded off.

Blood-curdling screams pierced through from the front of the restaurant to the back.

Alessandro tapped my stomach with his palm, and my heart was pumping so damn hard I thought it would catapult out of my chest. "*Maman*, mommy, what's going on? Why are the people screaming?" Chaos had broken out as walls shook, the ground vibrated at the front of the window as doors burst open and the sound of shattered glass rocked my eardrums. I glimpsed people running to their vehicles and shouting from patrons in both Italian and English. My mouth dried up, my tongue sticking to the roof of my mouth.

My worst nightmare was coming true, and my feet were planted solidly on the stained concrete.

"Mira, get under the table for me. Get down now!" Saint waved the gun, barking orders. I bobbed down automatically, trying to keep Alessandro calm, but he was wise beyond his years, his face curling into fear as he wailed.

"Mommy, why are people screaming? I'm scared." His tiny hands gripped my body while he sobbed. I held him tight, terror making my body quake as I covered his ears with my hands. I shoved his head inside my jacket, attempting to shield him from the brunt of the impending violence.

"Tommy! Anderson! Rocco! Get in here now. We got trouble around the front. Hit them from the front. It's a hit. Let's go!" My father's bellowing voice rang out as I hid under the open table, locked in fear with Alessandro. If the perpetrators burst through the door, it wouldn't be hard to spot our curled-up bodies under the table. I prayed they were stupid and would not find out we were out back.

I did the unthinkable, wanting to protect not only Alessandro, but also my husband. I'd been so determined about our son's safety that I'd put Saint and me on the back burner, but after today, I realized how important he was in my life. Equal to Alessandro. Equal to me. Snot dripped from my nose in fear as I wiped it away, drawing my gun.

Who was it? My brain worked like a processor, wondering who would have the gall to break into Frankie's pizzeria. As long as I'd been alive, Frankie's pizzeria had been a haven for all the Saliano crew. Yes, it had been hit twice, but not like this, as far as I knew.

Nervous but clear-eyed, I checked the safety and the bullets, carefully making sure I had everything lined up.

Stay calm, Mira. If you have to shoot, do it. Aim and shoot like Saint taught you that time at the gun range.

Forceful, aggressive thuds against the back door splintered, eventually loosening from its hinges. "Mommy, please. Make it stop!" Alessandro called out, wailing. I covered his mouth quickly, speaking in his ear.

"Keep your voice down. We're just playing a game of hide and seek, okay? Hide real good for me. Ball yourself up as tight as you can. Can you do that?"

"Yes, I think so." His cries muffled into broken-up sobs. We were about to see who had it out for us, whether we wanted to or not.

"Mira! Don't come out. Stay down." Saint gave the directive, and I listened, torn, not wanting Alessandro's father to be ripped away from him. Gunfire sounded as Saint shot at the door as the perps burst through. More shots fired. I doubled back, calling the police from my phone under the table.

"Who the fuck are you?" My father yelled as I studied the shoes of the men from under the table. A pair of black Tom Ford lace-ups in front of me. Two other sets of feet. I counted three. Definitely mobsters or gangs with beef. Could they not see who the men were? "Take your fucking masks off so I can see you, coward!" my father kept shouting, answering my silent question. Alessandro wriggled underneath my jacket as I willed him to be still.

This was the stuff waking nightmares were made of.

Chapter 23

Saint

I held my gun steady. Three men in ski masks stood in front of me.

"Don't come any closer. Otherwise, I'm going to shoot your face off, bitch." The street killer housed beneath my suit lapels came out to play.

"There's only two of you. You and this fat old man, you're gonna die right here on Saliano turf, you sell out," the voice punched back as I strained to listen for the inflection in his voice. It was familiar in a way, but in the heat of the moment, with guns pointed in multiple directions, my brain missed the details.

"I'm ten men rolled into one, fucker."

Less talking and more action.

The fact they were talking was enough to let me know they were scared. Men jacked their jaws when they were too scared to shoot first. "Let me do the honors." I gave Frankie the head nod to retreat. A simple nod in a hair-split second. He was part of my famiglia now, and a fire blazed, wanting to protect him, too. I shot at one of the men's feet.

"You shot me, you fucking idiot!" he yelped as the other two dropped their guard and their guns. Perfect, exactly like I wanted. Frankie read my playbook with a drop and roll to the edge of the wall, scooting a stack of cardboard boxes in front of himself as the stupid bitches argued amongst themselves.

I dropped back a few paces to gain range on them. "You're on our turf, and you thought I wouldn't do anything? Take the mask off and be a man. Who sent you?" I screamed. "Who fucking sent you?"

No answer as blood seeped from the man's shoe. He raised his gun, and the closest man to him was the one I shot square in the kneecap. The one in the middle had the answers I wanted. He was the ringleader. I knew what I was looking at. If I shot one of his, I hoped he would call out his name in shock, but he stayed tight-lipped.

Oh, this one knows the street law.

Every false move by either party was one toward the grave. I scissor-stepped backwards, my gun cocked all the way, wanting to be closer to the table where my son and beloved were. Frankie had a shield covering him, a smart old man. The one man in the middle had a stocky physique that seemed familiar.

Where do I know you from, you bastard?

My mind whirred as I concocted a plan to get Alessandro and Mira out of the building as soon as humanly possible. The two other accomplices were bumbling idiots taking directions from the one in the middle. The man I shot slumped to the ground, blood running in a small river right under the table.

"My knee, my fucking knee. Arrgghh! You blew it out." Funny how the one in the middle had an opportunity to shoot but didn't take it. I reached into my pocket with one arm, keeping a steady aim and eye on the three intruders. I used the emergency code I had in place with Falcone pressing the number through.

Cold ice filled my veins as I cocked my gun, firing another round to his good knee, sending a simple message. The other two jumped, unsure if the shot was coming from Frankie or me.

"Now it's your other knee, fucker!" I screamed as the other dropped right to the ground on all fours with no knees to balance him.

Frankie further confused them, firing off several shots, giving me good coverage to get to the back side of the table. The perps shot back as I bent down, speaking under the table but not wanting the perps to look underneath.

Frankie's shoulder leaned against the backside of the cardboard boxes as he mouthed for me to get them out of the mix.

"Mira, Falcone's waiting for you. Move out back and quick. Slide out with Alessandro," I hissed in a low tone. There was minimal time to talk and only mere seconds to ensure the safe delivery of my famiglia to the outside. I stubbornly refused to lose any more blood from my camp. Mira and Alessandro were all the family I had and ever wanted, except for Riza and my father. Fuck, I wished he was here to fight with me.

I bent over the trestle table, distracting the goons, tossing a pizza box at them. I pilfered the glass tumblers and half-empty alcohol bottles, firing the items one by one to confuse them and give my family time to slip out. They put their hands over their faces, attempting to cover their open bodies and keep their guns pointed, but they failed to do both as old man Frankie squeezed off a fresh round of bullets.

A rain of bullets hailed, and through the haze and me shooting, I didn't know who I hit. Seconds passed as Frankie squealed in pain. "I'm down, Saint. I'm down." He placed a hand over his ribcage, wet blood seeping around the hole he was covering with his hand. His body lay sprawled in the opposite direction.

I watched Mira and Alessandro scurry like mice out of my peripheral out the back side of the table, racing for the open back door. Mira saw her father down but continued like a trooper. Alessandro screamed loudly, my heart breaking. This memory would scar him, but at least he would be alive to tell the story.

This was when the real measure of street kingpin surfaced. Who had the bigger balls and the smarts to win out? Rage bloomed like a fire out of control once I knew Mira and my son were out of harm's way. Falcone would be with them any second now. I was about to annihilate these goofy fuckers, but that one in the middle...I knew him. His shoulder cut. The shoes. I'd seen them before if I could only get my brain to recall.

Time was running out, and the cops would swarm the building like ants soon enough.

Frankie gestured, putting a hand on his heart and closing his eyes, seemingly grateful that Mira and Alessandro were out safely. "Now, let's kill these fuckers," he said angrily as I nodded.

"You're not killing anybody, old man. I know your weaknesses," the ringleader sang out, his voice muffled by his ski mask. Those beady eyes. Shiny onyx death adders. Who are you?

A known enemy. My heart hammered in my chest, skipping several beats. Three bullets left in the chamber, a bullet for each.

Oh yeah, it's a good time for you to die. You live by the sword, then you can die by the sword, too.

Caught in a time warp, a memory showed itself. Riza, my sweet rough and tumble twin. So alike, but so magnificently different. A simpler time when I was a young man, beads of saltwater glistening my skin on the Amalfi shoreline. I took it for granted and whined every summer we stayed there, but now I craved those times, and to see Riza's face again.

"One day, we won't be coming here, and you'll be just like Dad."

"I wish."

"You'll be your own version, but you'll end up like him. You already are. You just can't see it yet."

I was busy flicking water at Riza with my hair, and she was hell-bent on locking me under her armpit in a headlock. Funny how she softened over time, her wisdom shining, and I became the ruthless, cunning drug lord of Chicago.

As the years rolled into one another, our individual personalities shone through, and the gritty streets of Chicago called my name.

"You think that's a good idea, Saint? It's reckless to start a turf war on Penrose. You're going to lose your whole crew if you do that. You're an underboss now. You're not some street mule. You've graduated." Riza tapped my head. "You gotta think like a Don. One day, you're gonna take that seat. Come on, twin, think!" A hint of a smile reached my lips. Riza grounded me. My silent advisor for so long, right along with my father.

When I hit the underboss role after a long time of pushing shit uphill and building street cred, my father sat me down for Scotch and a heart-to-heart in his office.

"You remind me so much of me. Young and reckless, man, I've seen and done it all, son. Nothing you can't tell me about these streets, and boy, will they ravage your soul if you don't take care of it. You know how you do that, son?"

"How, Pop?"

"One day, you'll have your own family. I want you to remember to keep them close to you. Just like we keep you grounded, so will yours. Stay anchored. These streets, eh, they're your playground, but your family..." he poked me in the chest, "...your family is everything."

His words stuck, reemerging right on time. Frankie Saliano was family to me through blood and we were on the verge of imminent death, bound by a mafia code that didn't discriminate. The expansion and revenge plot seemed stupid now. That's the cruel twist of hindsight. It's too fucking late when it hits you in the face like a hammer.

Sirens rang out, interrupting my death plan. Cops. Had to be. My phone beeped against my thigh.

No time to check it. Life and death hung in the balance for me and Frankie.

Chapter 24

Mira

"Mommy, where's Daddy? Who were those nasty men?" I ran, dragging Alessandro out the door with my lungs burning up. A black Jeep screeched, coming to an abrupt halt in the smelly back alley of the pizzeria. The door opened.

"Get in! Hurry!" Falcone ushered my son and me in, as I feared being shot in the back, but I wanted Alessandro covered first. I slammed the door shut, staring down at my shaking hands.

"Alessandro, I'm sorry, baby. Mommy is so sorry you had to see that. Are you okay?" I pulled him into my arms, wiping debris and dust out of his hair. I cradled him close as his warm, fragile body held me around the waist.

The car moved swiftly, reversing down the cobblestone back street until Falcone picked a side street to maneuver down. "Your pop is gonna be fine, kid. He's a Riccini, and so are you. You're made of the good stuff." Falcone winked while a foot soldier sat stoically in the passenger seat with an AK47 on his lap. There was no going back from this. Alessandro would forever have this memory entrenched in his developing brain, and it's not how I wanted it to go.

I kicked myself internally for being selfish and wanting Alessandro with me in Chicago, thinking I could keep him safe. What was I thinking?

"Don't scare him, please. He's seen enough today." I skimmed over my son's body, checking for wounds as cop cars passed down the main street. Tiny bloody splatters decorated the front of the sneakers I'd purchased recently for him. "I'm going to wash your sneakers when you get home." I threw the line in, wanting to create some sort of fake normalcy, but none of our lives would ever be the same again.

Frankie. Saint. Sweat popped on my skin. Are they alive or dead? Is my son an orphan?

"Sorry, sweetheart, I hate to break it to ya, but he's the progeny of a Riccini. He can't avoid the reality." Falcone's sarcasm irked me, but the man was right. So much for giving my son a normal life.

I muzzled myself, haunted by seeing my father grimace, his shirt blood-soaked. Did he make it? Tears shed from my eyes. I was powerless to stop them. Alessandro cupped his hands at the bottom of my face, catching the tears. My boy, such a sweet soul. "Mommy. Don't cry. We're safe now. These nice men are looking after us."

Upset and drowning in my emotions, the bitter truth escaped my lips. "These aren't nice men, son, but they will protect you. You might as well know the truth."

Falcone turned his palms up as we waited patiently behind the major streets. Falcone kept looking at his phone, which showed he was waiting for Saint to come through. "We can be nice people, can't we, Tony?"

Tony chuckled. "Only if you're nice to us. I'm nice to pretty ladies. That's about it."

Falcone thumped his arm. "Aye! We got Saint's kid in the car. Let's not corrupt him just yet. Settle down." Using the back of my hand, I swiped my wet cheeks, but Falcone handed me his handkerchief from his shirt. "Here, I hate to see a lady crying. You worried about Saint? Boss is gonna be fine."

"Yes and no. Dad got...hurt." I stopped myself from saying the word "shot" so it didn't affect Alessandro, but with his short attention span, his gaze was already out the window, looking at the gathering of people in the suburb.

"You mean?" Falcone made a pistol symbol with his fingers, pursing his lips together.

Stretching a gulp down, I nodded. "Yes."

"Hey, he's had a good run. He's in his seventies. He's been running this town for the longest. It's a shame it happened when we were patching things up with the Salianos. Who knows, it might have turned into good business."

"Falcone!" I shouted, upset he showed no remorse, but why would a capo who sent men into battle to kill care about my father? A ping came through on his phone, and he moved once more, the route familiar as I realized we were headed for home.

Soon after, I got the same ping. A text from Saint distracted me momentarily from Falcone's thoughtless comment.

SAINT: *I'm good. Falcone is taking you home. Stay there. I'll come for you.*

ME: *Is dad ok? Please tell me he is.*

Seconds turned to minutes. "Falcone, turn this car around." I had to go back.

I knew Falcone and his man were taking me home to my apartment, but I had other plans. I wouldn't be able to sit still. I texted Clara to see if she was free to watch Alessandro. I had to go back to the restaurant and find out what had happened to my father and Saint.

"What?" He shrugged, cutting through my racing mind. No matter what, I had to go back. "No way. We are following Saint's instructions. This is mob business, and as I recall, you so badly wanted to be a part of it. Gets me to thinking though...who's the underboss of the Saliano family?"

A lightbulb flashed in my head as the suburban houses passed us by, Falcone's question settling in my mind. "Marco." The words stung as they hit my tongue, a wishy-washy feeling swimming in my belly. "Marco would be the Don. He's not good enough to be a Don. He doesn't have the expertise."

Falcone's sharp, barren eyes looked through the rearview at me. His eyebrow arched in question. Blood pumped thick and fast through my body at his insinuation. I cut my eyes over to my son, pulling him back from the window, wanting to feel him as Clara confirmed her availability. One small step.

Once we reached our condo apartment, Falcone and the beefy soldier cleared the apartment, torturing me with their prolonged presence. Time was precious, and if I wanted to get down to the restaurant, I had to press forward.

I scrubbed Alessandro clean, putting him in fresh clothes and washing off every trace of the day's events. Clara walked in soon after.

I bobbed down to kiss his forehead.

"Mommy has to go for a little while. Clara is going to stay with you."

He tugged at my shirt, scared out of his wits. "Mommy, don't leave!" he cried.

"I have to. I'm going to pick up Daddy, okay? I'm coming back home with him. You'll like Auntie Clara. You haven't met her yet."

"Noooo, Mommy!" Alessandro pouted, with Clara soothing him.

I tore my pinched shirt from Alessandro's hands, my keys in hand. "Take care of him. I'll explain everything when I get back. He's a little upset."

"Go, go. It's fine. Quick! Falcone's at the back," Clara urged. "Hurry before they catch you! Be careful, please. I love you."

Falcone and security were at the back end of my apartment, but neither one of them would stop me from getting to the men I cherished the most. I took the fire escape, pumping my legs like pistons down it, wrenching the door open leading to the parking lot. I jogged to my car, no gun in hand, blindly wanting to race to the scene. I entered my car and pulled out seconds later.

Gritting my teeth, I raced through the back streets of congested traffic, slicing and dicing in angst behind cars. I did everything possible to reduce time, fearing I was too late to figure anything out. I didn't even know what I was looking for.

As my vehicle approached the pizzeria, I zoomed through the T-junction, the three-story underground parking lot for the downtown Chicago mall to my left. A large silver pickup truck passed me, all my preceptors on sensory overload working in slow motion. The car was moving at breakneck speed, heading straight into the mall parking lot, and my red flag alert went off. A flash of a face. Marco. Skittish and guilty.

That's how you look when you've done something wrong. The same look when you took a dump in Mrs. Hurley's garden because she gave you a D on your math test.

Falcone's face, when he pointed out who was next in line for the Saliano throne, came to mind. Holy shit. Bile rose in my throat as I breathed hard to keep my meal down.

I had to stop. Marco hadn't seen me, I was sure of it. I jerked the car left, barely missing the entrance, scraping against the metal dividing pole, my eyes following the silver truck.

My chest was beating, but I couldn't feel it anymore anyway. I pulled over on the lowest level, killing the engine, my legs operating like Jell-O sticks, my ankle crunching as it hit the ground.

"Fuck!" I screamed quietly, biting down on my bottom lip, breaking the skin, and tasting the metallic blood. I reached down, rubbing it as it throbbed from the unplanned ankle roll. I kept going, knowing time was extremely limited. Falcone would be after me soon enough. I bent over, creeping forward with light feet, jogging behind the thick, concrete pylon, hoping to catch a glimpse. I peeped from around the pole and stared upwards to the second level where the silver truck had stopped.

The first thing I saw was the Tom Ford shoes. My eyes widened in horror. I put nothing past Marco, but to witness what I thought I saw right in front of my eyes was nuts. His fingers casually held onto a black ski mask in his right hand. Shit. They were two other men who remained in the car, talking in low, animated voices, and I had to fucking go before I got shot.

Who were those other guys? Why did they seem like men I'd seen before? Who would be so dumb as to team up with my ratfink brother? Tears pricked my eyes as I lay my back flat against the cold concrete pylon.

Get back to the car. Get back to the fucking car, Mira.

I dropped, hobbling from the ankle crunch to the front seat, a combination of fire and ice infiltrating my being. I reversed fast, praying my tires wouldn't screech and give me away, hightailing it out of the parking lot.

I knew my brother was a sociopath, and not trustworthy. But killing Frankie Saliano, our father, was putting an instant street bounty on your head.

Chapter 25

Saint

Metallic skyscrapers to my left and the Chicago River to my right. Standing smack bang on the streets I'd inflicted years of war on, I looked up to the heavens, questioning what it was all for.

I stood with my feet shoulder-width apart, anguish written on my face. I knew the jig was up. Sweat patches soaked my armpits, and blood splashes crusted my Italian leather shoes. A film of dirty sweat covered my face. A reconciliation gone wrong in a matter of minutes. I knew a peace treaty was too good to be true. It reminded me of The Joker card in the card deck, except the joke was on me this time.

The world seemed like a fuzzy place, discombobulated. A deranged number of ideas ran the gauntlet through my head.

Hazy figures of Chicago authority passed in front and behind me, with people eyeballing me from the safety of the police barricade, but they weren't on my mind. Mira, Alessandro, and Frankie were.

My gun sat in its holster, but if my mind got a hold of my physical being, I would have been rapidly firing at everyone in sight. I'd lost everything dear to me, and I refused to lose Mira and Alessandro with every molecule of air circulating in my lungs.

The middle of the asphalt outside the restaurant was the only place I could think to stand. The only place to catch my breath. Grimy sweat trickled from my brow, what was left of my heart ka-booming in my chest.

Come back, bitches, and face me like men without your masks.

One of the officers figured my middle-of-the-road meltdown wasn't the best idea. He walked over to me with caution. "Yo, you good Saint? Need some water? You gotta get out of here, and especially out of the middle of the street. We don't need any more fatalities today."

"I need more than fucking water. I need a Scotch. Can you get me one of those?" I replied, hysteria pumping through my veins.

The well-seasoned officer, whose name I didn't know, managed a chuckle. He'd likely seen it all. "O'Reilly's is a block away. I don't advise you go in there. It's a rough day for Chicago. Come on. You gotta move, Saint. Now."

The forensics team was already inside the restaurant, blue plastic gloves on, doing what they did best. Cops swarmed the streets like bees, pushing the crowd back from the barricade that had blocked off the back half of one of Chicago's most prominent downtown locales. I looked past the crowd seeking clues, anything they might have missed, but my eyeballs were stinging, so I stopped.

I didn't answer the cop. My mouth was too dry, and the pain burrowed too deep to worry about him.

Frankie's limp body had been put in the ambulance already.

Why didn't I have time to get to him? How did it go down again?

I put a shaky hand on my brow, feeling lost.

Over. Over. Over. No peace treaty for you. Only war.

The Riccinis were back to square one, and the violence of the past wouldn't work in either famiglias favor. Shakily, I put one foot in front of the other as the cop ushered me to my vehicle the back way. The same way I'd entered to meet Frankie.

Falcone's shadow greeted me, and instantly, I jumped forward, snatching up the fabric of his shirt. "What are you doing? Where's Mira?! You're supposed to be taking care of her. What are you doing here?"

Falcone closed his eyes, putting his hands up while the cop looked on at my animalistic display. I would have put the gun to Falcone's temple if he wasn't standing so close to me.

"Thought you might be mad," he said calmly. "She's here somewhere. She came back for you. Your wife is crafty. I gotta give it to her."

Red-hot rage torched through my soul. "Where's Alessandro?"

"At home with Clara, her bestie. I got three on guard. Two out front of the apartment. I didn't leave it bare. She's here, I'm sure of it."

The officer left us to our conversation, Falcone marching in step with me as I sifted through the crowd, looking for Mira behind the police barrier. She wasn't always the best at following instructions. "I can't lose them, Falcone. I can't," I gasped, struggling for life force, broken after all the deaths.

"Your family is your anchor." Nick's words broke the pain barrier, sinking into my subconscious.

"Listen, I got wind of some news on the street. There's talk." Falcone kept his voice low, given the vicinity of all the cops slithering around.

People scattered away from the barriers as cops enforced

movement from the scene, but Mira's worried face and cascading halo of hair stood out. Her hands were on the barrier, the cop blocking her from jumping over it.

"Saint!" she cried out. "Saint!"

"I'm coming, Mira." Over forty paces away, I spoke to Falcone who kept pace.

"Talk quick."

"Callahan brothers and Marco. That's the word. Percy, who runs the block on Albion Avenue, got the word to me when I put out the message. They've been bragging about the plan since a few hours ago."

"And when I'm done with them, I'm going to brag about cutting their balls off and feeding them to the lions at the Chicago Zoo. I want a meeting called. This is war."

"No doubt about it. Headquarters?"

"Yes. Mobilize every force we have. Find out if Prentice, Murdoch, and the others I spoke to are banded together on this."

I didn't have time to feel guilt over the decision I made. Marco capitalized on my weak emotions, and I had nobody to blame but myself.

"Already done. Keep your phone on. I'm out." Falcone's voice faded out. The only one I wanted to hear was Mira's and my son's. I was her only hope, the one to protect her. The one man who truly loved her was the only one she could count on now. I wished Frankie alive for Mira's sake, for my sake, but in my heart of hearts, when I saw the bullet fly and dig a hole in his rib, I knew it was the beginning of the end.

"Mira baby!" I found my legs through adrenaline, jumping over the barrier.

"Hey, Saint!"

"It's my wife. Do your job and find out who shot this place up." I threw daggers back at the young cop guarding the barriers. Cops feared us. We weren't scared of them. Prosecutors, the Chicago mayor, and high-ranking government officials sat on both sides of the Riccini and Saliano families. Chicago was our town, and we ran it.

The officer said nothing as I pulled Mira inside my embrace, wanting to absorb the pain, violence, and grief. Her body shook with gut-wrenching sobs. "Saint. My father! Saint, no, please. Tell me what happened." Mira's hysterical tone peaked as she fought to disengage from my arms to learn a truth I didn't have the answer to.

"They put him in the ambulance. Chicago Memorial, I'm guessing," I replied hoarsely. Mira's red-rimmed eyes and puffy cheeks stared back at me for solace. Goddammit, Mira was so freaking beautiful to me at her worst.

"Saint," her lip quivered, her face caving in. "Saint," she said my name again, losing breath. I wanted to save her from the breakdown, but knew I couldn't.

"Come on, let's get out of here. Can you walk? Mira, it's you and me now. We are forever, and I love you so much. Let's get home to Alessandro."

"I'm sorry, I-I..."

"Forget it. I don't care. I'm glad you're here." I slid my hand in hers, jogging to the back. We ran to my black Jeep, numb and wanting to see my boy.

Mira's tears continued to run, the Chicago air burning my lungs. "Tell you in the car. The longer we're out in the open, the more vulnerable we are," I cautioned, my eyes covering as much ground as possible, even with the cops covering my back to the car.

Both of us slipped into the car, devastated by the catastrophic turn of events, but I sensed it was only the beginning and events were about to amp up.

"Now can you tell me?" Mira asked, her caramel browns begging me for information.

A flicker of recall replayed the scene in my head like a movie.

"You shot my man. You're gonna pay for that!" the ringleader had called out. Now I knew it was Marco, the arrogant bastard. He'd fired shots in my direction, but apparently, he'd been rusty at the shooting range. The Parabellum bullet had whizzed past my right ear. I'd shifted my body weight left, electing to fall back further. "Shooting, that's what happened. Bullets flying in your father's direction, and I was too late to get to him because we were outnumbered."

"Saint...Saint," she began crying uncontrollably, dropping her head into her hands. My automatic reaction was to soothe her. I reached out, putting a hand on her thigh. "I know the truth. I know who shot my father..." She fought to get the words out, and I kept looking forward, navigating the road blocks and the Chicago afternoon traffic.

"You do?" Licking my chapped lips, I listened intently.

Mira nodded. "Yes, when I was on my way here, I saw a silver Jeep pull into the parking lot for the Chicago mall right before the pizzeria. You know the one," she spat the information as best she could.

My Mira. You're so brave. This world isn't for you, but you're a ride-or-die.

"Keep going. You got it," I encouraged, feeling her choking up.

"I saw him. Him and two others. He had a ski mask in his hand

and those shoes. He had on Tom Ford shoes. I only know that because I'd looked at a pair, thinking they'd look good on you."

"Fuck, I love you," I jerked out, wanting to kiss her mouth badly.

"What did you say, Saint?"

"You heard, woman. I love you, and Alessandro. I don't give a damn about expansion. It's us I want. Grief and anger got the better of me, and this is my fault. I take ownership, and I would never, ever forgive myself if something happened to you."

"I'm not going anywhere, Saint. I love you, too," Mira repeated back meekly, hauling my heart through the wringer. On top of the information she had confessed to me, her words of love quenched an internal fire. After all the trials and tribulations of our fighting to be together, the tragic circumstances of it all, we were banded together now, fighting for our famiglias' legacies.

"Does that mean you're coming home to me?"

"Yes." Simple answer, but the three letters carried such weight. "What you saw matches up with what Falcone told me. The streets are talking, and your brother is too arrogant to keep his scummy mouth clamped. It seems he made a deal with the Callahan brothers."

A section of Mira's raspberry-stained mouth tugged into a sardonic smirk. "That's no surprise. He's always been a loudmouth."

Chapter 26

Mira

A bell notification sounded off in my purse, but all my brain could show me was Alessandro's face in my mind's eye. One of my men was safe, but my father was in the hospital...shot. I didn't want to think about burying him. We'd only just rekindled our connection, and if I was being honest with myself, the heart-to-heart we'd had was the most honest talk we'd ever had in life.

Frankie Saliano was larger than life. He was the city of Chicago, and that was saying something for a city with close to three million people living in it.

After digging in my purse, I called Clara. "Hey, hey. Are you okay there?"

"Completely safe and fine. Alessandro is watching Aladdin. Do you want me to put him on the line?"

"Yes, yes," I jabbered. "Put him on." The phone slipped forward, but I caught it with Saint reaching out his hand to help. Waiting for my little boy's voice to grace my ears, I gulped hard, silently praying for my father. Putting the phone on speaker, I made sure Saint could hear too.

"Hi, Mommy. Are you coming home soon? I'm bored. I want

to play with grandpa again!" he called out with a giggle. "He's funny. I like him, and he's got hair growing out of his ears." Tears streamed down my face as I chuckled at his lack of filter and childlike innocence. Saint briefly shut his eyes in relief and torture as our son mentioned my father's name. I had never heard "funny" and "Frankie Saliano" mentioned in the same sentence together. "Cutthroat" and "barbaric" were more his lane, but when I recycled an old memory of him playing hide and seek with us and his animated faces, I saw how he could be.

My father loved kids and was good with them. He gave back to the hospitals, cutting checks to the community hospitals, but in the same breath, he stole the livelihood of mom-and-pop businesses by making them pay street and security taxes and feeding them drugs. A complicated hero wasn't the right word for him.

"Yes, sweetheart. I'll be home soon. Daddy's coming, too." I stemmed the flow of tears, knowing they wouldn't help anything, swiping them from my face.

"Hey, Alessandro. That's a good movie you're watching," Saint sang into the phone, keeping as much normalcy in his voice as he could.

"I like the genie. He's funny, too. Bye!" He cut off the phone accidentally, not giving it back to Clara. As far as my son knew, it was a normal, windy Chicago day, and that's how I wanted him to remember it.

Saint's eyes were boring into me and checking if I would fall to pieces, but I wanted to rewind a play-by-play from the restaurant.

"Saint. Who are the Callahan brothers? Do we need to be worried about them?"

Saint licked his lips as we sliced through the thick traffic and took the back streets. "We do need to be worried about everyone right now. Nobody can be trusted."

Knots locked themselves together as he told me a truth I didn't wanna hear. The bell sound kept going. "What if it's Marco? I can't talk to him. I want to rip his throat out with my bare hands. Was he the one who shot my father?" Pure silence covered the space between us, and in the gap, the answer was clear. "Marco shot him, didn't he?"

"It was your brother." His jaw clenched hard. "I'm sorry. I saw him point the gun and aim it. The Callahan brothers shot in his direction, too, but Marco's gun hit him. If the cops are on their game, they can trace it back to him."

"The cops," I sneered. "Whose side are they on? The Saliano's or Riccini's? This can go either way."

My phone kept interrupting my speculations, but as far as cops were concerned, I didn't trust any of them. "I'm aware, but the cops on the scene were from our camp."

"I can't believe Marco shot at Dad. How could he do that?"

"Easy. He wants the throne and the peace treaty to be over. Do you think he knows about you not being Frankie's? Or about Alessandro?"

"Fuck! That would explain why he's fucked me over so many times. But he's my father's son, though from his actions...he's a man that's just like my mother, Angelica." I bit down my bottom lip, willing the phone to stop ringing. I wanted nothing to do with the Salianos.

"Hey, Mira. Look at me." I shifted my head to Saint, disappointment and fear cloaking me. "We—you, me, and Alessandro are family. I'm going to make this right. I'm the motherfucking Don, and Marco isn't equipped or finessed enough to handle the seat of a Don like your father."

"Maybe..." I rested my face on my elbow, watching the traffic roll by. My phone kept buzzing. "Who the hell is calling me?"

"Check it. Whoever it is, keep it cool, Mira. Be strong for me, baby. Don't let them know nothing." Saint sliced a finger over his neck viciously.

Opening my bag, contents spilled out, but I ignored them. I looked at the caller ID: unknown number. I answered it anyway. "Hello?"

"Mira, it's Antonio. Are you okay? You safe?"

"I'm fine," I cut back. "I'm with Saint. He's here." I put the phone on speaker. I had no secrets from him, and if we were going to win this fight, we would have to take every step together.

"Phew. Stay undercover. Callahan and the gangs are at it. Your father got shot. Did you know that? Did you see the shooter?"

"No, I didn't. I saw nothing. Do you know the hospital Dad's at?" Being part of a mob famiglia had taught me how to compartmentalize my feelings early. I shut them down in the vault, taking up my ice queen persona—the same one I'd summoned back in Paris to seduce Saint before I started having feelings for him.

"He's at the Chicago Memorial. I'm getting the room sorted. We gotta move quick in case people wanna come in and finish the job."

"How can you cover him in the public health system? I'm coming there as soon as..." I zipped my mouth shut. The Saliano camp knew nothing about Alessandro, and it would be hard to keep him under wraps. But with volatility on the streets, I had to keep my son safe.

Saint trusted me, not blinking an eye at my near-miss. From the stormy look in his eye, he wasn't about to let anything happen to his child, regardless of who knew. "We can't. That's where I step in. I got our forces on the ground, but the Callahans are high on the list, and they're low-level thugs. The main sticking point being they're in cahoots with the Prentice family...arms dealers, and it's not pretty."

Saint jumped in. "Cover him the best you can, and I'll get Lupo involved. I smoothed it over with the Prentices. We've been talking, and as far as I'm aware, there's no beef on our side. Shouldn't be with the Callahans, either, but it's a double cross. You got a gutter rat over there."

"Saint," Antonio replied, surprised he was offering insight, but everything had changed after the meeting with my father. "You know about the Callahans already? Funny how you think the rats are coming from the Saliano side," he hit back with sarcasm.

"Maybe so, but can you blame me? I've had the pleasure of connecting with the Callahans of late." He didn't specify his reasoning as a stab of resentment bubbled. I told Saint not to pursue a war, but for me to play judge would have been hypocritical. I'd been the one to set off an entire chain of events leading to years of street war between two rival famiglias.

It was as if Saint read my mind, clutching up my balled-up fingers. There were so many things unspoken between us. I curled my fingers around his, grateful for the quiet gesture of reassurance.

You got past Lupo without him detecting you. Maybe someone else could, too. Get off the fucking phone, Antonio, so I can talk to Clara.

Many irrational thoughts attached their tentacles to the worst-case scenarios rocking my brain. No point calling her now. We had arrived at my apartment.

The garage door opened to the parking lot. Saint withdrew his gun, checking the space as it was full of dark shadows, a prime location for enemies to lurk.

"Right. We'll do our best. I don't think bringing you and yours down here is the best plan. Stay back," Antonio warned as I shook my head.

"Can't do, Antonio. My wife is a Saliano. She wants to see her father. He set this up. The peace treaty is still in place. I'm coming through to support my wife, and I'm coming with my crew. Don't forget the peace treaty."

"Tuh, for how long?" Antonio snorted with an ugly chuckle. Insensitive bastard, but what to expect from a consigliere? He probably couldn't care less about wanting my father out of the way. Now he'll report to Marco. Maybe Donato knows, too. Can't trust any of my family. The one I did trust is dead. What kind of life is this for my son?

A long silence hung in the balance from Saint. "I'm going through a tunnel. Talk later, Antonio." He hung up the phone on my behalf. "You don't need that joker in your ear. I take aversion to his tone. But at least it seems that none of them know about Alessandro. A small blessing right now."

"I agree," I trembled. We looked at one another for a moment in the cover of the car, our forged connection unshakeable. Saint's eyes penetrated through the empty parking lot. Not a person in sight. His warm hand wrapped around the base of my neck, kneading at the tiny knots that had formed. Closing my eyes, I leaned back slightly, enjoying the touch of his deft fingers.

Saint still smelled of cashmere and musk mingled with sweat and grime—a tough combination to beat. His lips sought mine tenderly, providing solace and love in a place where only charcoal roses bloomed.

"I love you. I love our son. Let's get upstairs, then. Good with that?"

We were working like a family unit. Finally, the walls had been broken down, and we were presenting a unified front.

Chapter 27

Saint

Marco's head was about to be on a platter. Teaming up with the Callahan brothers, that fucking weasel.

I got Mira inside, drawing my gun, not giving a fuck who saw me armed in her apartment building. When we arrived at her door, three of my foot soldiers were surrounding it.

"Good job."

"Aye, boss. All clear. It's quiet up here. No word of anything."

"Perfect. You can sign off this post, but I need you to follow us, okay? Make sure you're fully loaded."

"Sure. Sure. We're ready," one of them answered.

I looked him square in the eye. "I hope you're ready to die. There's a possibility that you don't get a second shot at this. Got it?"

"We know the drill. Ain't none of us getting shot today. We're down. Falcone know?"

"No, but he's about to."

Mira was already inside, dropping to her knees to hug

Alessandro. He hugged his mom back, but a confused look crossed his face. He didn't know what all the fuss was about.

Kids really are resilient...

I stepped in after her, Clara visibly shaken by my presence. I soothed her nerves.

"It's okay, Clara. I'm not an ogre or anything. You're safe and welcome to visit Mira anytime." A sense of urgency and duty put me back on track.

"Uh, thanks, sorry, I've just never been in this situation before," she gushed with wide eyes.

"Never have I. Trust me." I slid my gun back into my holster, picking up my phone to call Falcone to make sure the hospital was secured. "Great minds," I smirked.

"Yeah, something like that. Listen, Frankie's in a bad way and that's coming from the inside. I got as much information as I could. You better get down here."

"On the way, make sure the building is secured. Give me another three on the ground."

"Ten steps ahead. We got four down here."

"Good," I replied.

"Be ready, Saint. If Frankie keels over, it's done, and every day will be a walking nightmare until we get rid of Marco. He's not the sit-down-at-the-table guy."

"I know. Alright, gotta go." I dropped the call and looked at Mira. "Hey, we gotta go. We need to go to Chicago Memorial first before we head to mine. Frankie's not in a good way. Let's go, little man." I held my hand to Alessandro, who looked at us as if we were aliens. My first test as a father, and with chaos all around us. He slowly put his small hand into mine, and instantly, I knew what my purpose was.

"Clara, thank you again."

"Sure, no problem. This is..."

"It's a lot to take in. Take a deep breath."

"Bran, I changed my mind. Follow Clara, make sure she gets home safe, then come to Chicago Memorial."

"Is that necessary?" Clara asked as we hit the elevator to the ground floor.

"Yes, it is," both me and Mira stated firmly.

"Alrighty then." Clara separated from us as we headed to the car and fitted Alessandro in a car seat. Mira rushed to the front seat.

"Let's go, Saint. Please tell me he's going to be okay. I can't believe this. I still can't believe it. We have to hurry! I know he's not my real father, but he's the only father I've ever known."

"*Est-ce que ça va* (Are you okay?)?" Alessandro asked.

"Mommy's okay. Thanks for asking."

"Not telling him?" I quipped.

"No, no way. I can't do that to him, or myself." Mira turned the radio on, likely to distract herself and our son.

"I want you to stay in the car when we get to the hospital. It's going to be volatile, and I'm pretty sure your brother is going to be there."

"I want to see my father, but Saint, find out everything you can. I have to know he's okay. I don't have a good feeling about this. I'm sure I can find a way to come in. I can't swear in front of Alessandro, but I have a bunch of expletives in store for Marco."

"I want you to stay in the car when we get there. We can't risk

Alessandro being seen."

"How will I see my father? I can't sit in the parking lot and do nothing," she fired back, but the conviction in my eyes set the tone.

"Mira. I said no. Stay in the car. I should take you straight to my house, but I know you. It's better we know now than you tormenting yourself. But remember, there are too many variables that I don't want to get into right now, and I'm sure you can work a few of them out." I cocked my chin upward, staring into the mirror. Alessandro had floated through this whole thing and was swinging his legs, humming to himself with a Transformer in his hand.

Mira pouted, but her being alive and upset with me was better than dead and six feet under. By the time we arrived at the hospital, thirty minutes had passed, and every minute counted. I did my best to conceal my gun, leaning forward to kiss Mira's soft pillow-like lips. Maybe it was for the last time, but I wouldn't tell her that.

"I love you. So much, you don't even know." I reached a hand back to hold onto Alessandro's leg, wanting to feel his flesh before I stepped out of the car. He giggled, wriggling free of my hands. "Daddy!"

My chest swelled with pride as he called my name so easily. That's the thing about children; they loved freely and unconditionally. I'd given up loving this way a long time ago until Mira, and now my Alessandro. But today, inside, my heart was nothing but pure hate for the man who'd triggered a world of pain for us.

The guys who guarded Clara at Mira's apartment parked right behind me, putting my mind at ease that my famiglia would be safe while I entered the hospital.

"I love you, too. Be safe, Saint. We need you." Mira's brow bunched up, her eyes troubled and full of pain. I already knew the answer about her father. In a way, it was a false charade, but one that had to play out this way. I had to be sure.

"This won't take long. I'll make sure he's okay, and I'll be back." I rubbed Mira's knee, strands of her honey-colored hair falling forward, her warm eyes staring back at me, hopeful.

As I stole that one last glance at Mira, I remembered why I loved her and how strong she was.

There was no other for me. She was my ride-or-die until the very end.

I stepped out of the car. "Look after them. I don't want a single hair on their head touched. You hear me?"

"Loud and clear."

"Good. Don't let my wife slip by you again like she did at the apartment. All eyes on the car. Otherwise, you both won't have legs to walk by the time I'm finished with you. *Capice?*"

"No problem, Saint. We got the assignment."

"Fucking aye." Letting spit fly to the left, I kept my eyes on moving to the hospital with one thing in mind. I called Falcone on my phone.

"Where are you?"

"Inside. Not good, buddy. I don't think you should come in here," Falcone relayed grimly.

Too late. I was already striding through the double emergency doors. I looked in all directions, only seeing injured patrons, but none of my team until I looked further up the corridor, where I saw two men all in black. Salianos. I recognized Antonio's face.

My phone was still locked in my hand. "Falcone," I hissed.

"Right behind you. Chill." A dark aura slid up beside me. "Boss."

"Is he alive?"

"Nope."

"Fuck!" I put my hand out to slam on the sterile white wall in front of the nurse's station but refrained. I turned my attention to the stunned women behind their station.

"Yes, can I help you?"

"Ah, I'm looking for Frankie Saliano's room. I'm his son-in-law. Can I see him?"

The woman looked at the computer, but it was cold when her gaze returned to mine.

"No. I'm afraid we can't let you into his room unless you are immediate family."

"Can you give me the verdict on his health? Did he pull through?" I asked, determined to hear the answer from the horse's mouth. Footsteps from around the hospital corner had me stand up straight with Falcone and the boys dropping their hands to their guns.

"I can't give out that information, sorry." The nurse shook her head, and I got to walking, not wanting a showdown in the middle of the hospital. Marco, with his inverted thick eyebrows and stocky crab walk, stalked behind me.

His crew closed the gap right before the parking lot exit. "Nice of you to pay a visit. It's pretty fucking foul considering you're the one responsible for my father's death."

Guns clocked into position and passersby avoided us, giving ten men facing off a wide berth. I drew mine. "You piece of dogshit. Who do you think you're talking to? You were the one who shot your father so you could claim his spot. I got eyes on the streets of Chicago. Is that the narrative you're trying to spin?"

Marco's face exploded into a crimson-splotched mess as he drew his gun, pointing it up high, a snarl curling on his pencil-thin lips. Four men of his own had him surrounded. A couple of his foot soldiers were discreet in pointing the barrels of their guns at us, hiding them under their jackets, only the muzzles poking out.

Mira, I'm willing if I have to die for you today, but I'm not going down to this fucker.

Donato, apparently, had taken a leave of absence, but Lupo spoke next.

"What are you going to do right now? Shoot Saint in broad daylight? You haven't thought this through enough."

"Shut up!" Marco yelled, globs of spit flying.

My eyes were full of fire, ready to end his life.

He waved his gun around floppily. "The peace treaty is over, and my father is dead. I'm the Don now. We ain't reforming another, either."

Dirty gray clouds lined the skyline, the Chicago wind howling through, setting the backdrop for violence. A standoff as I stood unyielding, Marco's podgy fingers on the trigger, my heart forcing blood around my body rapidly. There was no room for error, lest Chicago Memorial was about to be a killing field with more emergency causalities than the hospital cared for.

After a few long seconds, Marco dropped his gun, chuckling darkly.

"I'm going to give you a hall pass on this one, but only for today. Wouldn't be any fun for me to kill you yet." He wiped the excess sweat from his brow. "Besides, our famiglias have enjoyed many a fight together. I think it's good for business. I wanna show goodwill today. Mira's lost her father, and that's gotta hurt." A slick smile emerged on Marco's face. I noted he'd called Frankie her father, so he didn't know of Mira's true lineage.

You fucking pig. You've got no family loyalty. That's not how the mob works. He's your fucking father by blood.

"No, you need to be out of commission, Marco," I retorted.

He took a step forward.

"Oh yeah? We'll see, we'll see." Marco grinned. "No peace treaty means we do it like the days of old. You might be a little rusty. I hope you're ready, bitch."

Chapter 28

Mira

I didn't trust Marco. I pressed my face to the glass, looking out at my husband. Rolling the window down, I strained my ears to listen in. Saint's gun was lowered, but his finger stayed on the trigger. A bunch of people were staring in our direction, but with the heavy hitters next to my car, they wouldn't come closer. It surprised me that the cops weren't close by, but given both famiglias' network with them, maybe they wanted mob business to stay mob business.

Saint watched as Marco and his crew walked away, his jaw ticking. He turned towards the car, walking fast, his eyes moving wildly as he checked our surroundings.

Anybody who lived in Chicago long enough knew about the street warfare and not to risk getting caught in the crossfire.

"Falcone, we're gonna need new recruits. I need everyone at the meeting spot tomorrow morning. We got a war on our hands," he said when he was closer.

War on our hands? That could only mean one thing.

I clutched my throat, my windpipe threatening to close over.

Please. Don't let it be true.

Saint's back was turned, but he was close to the car.

"Tomorrow?" Falcone squeaked, the high winds of Chicago almost taking me off my feet.

"Yes. Tomorrow. Tonight, I spend it with my famiglia. Mira has information on Marco. She grew up with him, and I sense anything she knows will be valuable to help take him down. I have to talk to her first. We're a team. He's not completely stupid," Saint added, tapping his hand on the car.

That could only mean one thing...no, no, it can't be.

I started feeling woozy, but still hopeful I was in another world—one where my father was alive. Saint kept talking, and I should have rolled up the window, but I had to know.

"He had enough sneakiness to team up with those who had a niggle with me. He capitalized," Saint remarked.

"Hmm. Makes sense about your wife. She's gotta have intel," Falcone added smoothly. "In terms of Marco, he's a fucking idiot. Those Callahans on deck for her father's shooting are the kids. Not the old blood Callahans," Falcone reasoned.

What? Callahan. Marco. What a shitty day. I rubbed my chest, feeling itchy and finding it hard to breathe.

"You heard right. Callahan offspring," Falcone continued. "Alastair wouldn't move like that. He's got street thug in him, but he's calmed down these days. He wants to do proper business. Otherwise, you wouldn't have made the call to work with him."

"Exactly. He has street capital I want," Saint concluded, his shoes scuffing the ground as I listened to every sound coming from their mouths.

"Right, right. I called him, and he said the shooting had

nothing to do with him, but he's had trouble with his sons rebelling," Falcone responded.

"You believe him?" Saint inquired. Personally, I didn't. He had to know what his sons were up to.

Why couldn't my father have listened to me about Marco? Why?

"Can't be sure, so not full trust, but there's merit. The only way to find out is to test him," Falcone said smartly.

"Let me get my family home. Keep in communication," Saint concluded.

"You're already thinking like your father. Let's take this one step further," Lupo chimed in.

"You got that right. See you guys later. I gotta deliver the news, and we need to get the details of the funeral."

My heart sank. No running from the truth. The man I'd loved and wanted to respect me all these years was dead.

"You can't go, and neither can Mira," Lupo pushed vehemently.

"I know. Find out where he'll be buried, so Mira has a place to pay her respects," Saint quipped. I couldn't hold my tongue any longer, but the denial lingered.

"Pay my respects. What do you mean pay my respects, Saint? Please!"

"Guys, gotta go," Saint told them quickly. The crew mumbled goodbye, parting ways as I sank back into my seat.

"Saint. What did you mean just now? Pay my respects?" I asked once he settled in beside me. He scooped up my slender fingers, the same ones I loved running through his hair. Stroking the side of my face, he dived in, telling me the truth.

"Mira." He cast his eyes down. "Frankie's dead."

I expected to flip out, but I shifted, twisting in my seat to see if Alessandro was okay. His head of exuberant glossy curls hung around his head in a lion's mane. He would need to be a lion to tackle the legacy he was due to inherit, but for now, the little man slept.

I switched back to the front, Saint giving me time to ingest the painful information.

"I don't trust any of the Salianos. Antonio, Donato, Marco, the soldiers—none of them. They're dead to me, Saint, but Marco is playing with the wrong one. I know his drawbacks, and his weaknesses. He won't be able to run the streets like you, Saint. You're the true king."

Fire raged through my system, and all I wanted was Marco's tombstone marked.

"Mira, don't worry about me. Did you hear what I just told you about your father?"

"Saint, I heard you. I was listening outside the window. I've lost so many, I have no more tears left to cry." The chilling emptiness in my speech surprised even me.

The agony written on Saint's face was telling. "I hate this. You having to experience the weight of being part of a mob family. Since Alessandro's belongings are at your apartment, let's double back for now. We'll go to mine when you're ready. I'm not leaving you. We're not having any more nights apart." He picked up my limp fingers, kissing them before cranking the engine, bound for home. We arrived nearly half an hour later.

Because of the madness, Saint never got to see how I set up a nest for myself. Alessandro's toys were on the living room floor, facing a large flat-screen TV. Fruit was left out on the white and gray marble top. A modern space with enough room for us both. A vase of flowers on the table. A nice linen scent ran through the space, and I wanted the apartment to feel cozy.

I had learned how to make a house a home. Small photos in frames sat on the built-in wooden wall shelves. Me, Alessandro, and Clara. Saint picked up the photo of my father and mother holding my hand in an old black-and-white picture.

"Is this Frankie and Angelica?" he asked once I emerged from putting Alessandro down.

"Yes. I was young then. I don't know why I kept it." I shrugged, but at least I had a happy memory of better times for us all. I'd folded the photo, and Saint turned it over, putting two and two together that Marco was out of the picture.

"I'm glad you did." Saint gently put the picture down, draping an arm around my chest from behind and kissing my shoulder. "Mira, I'm here for you. If you need to cry, cry. We both lost." I picked up the photo, thumbing over a younger but menacing face of a man who had terrorized Chicago streets for so long.

A weird snort came out. "What a day. I told my father so many times not to listen to my brother," I replied bitterly. "Marco set this up for so long. I can see it now. From Paris to today. He's been plotting this whole time."

Saint massaged my shoulders, clusters of knots becoming apparent as he kneaded, and my resistance dropped. "Is Alessandro down?" he asked in a rough whisper as I moaned at the beauty of his strong fingers.

"Yes, he's fast asleep. That boy would sleep through a fire. That might be a problem later."

Protectively, he rubbed the top of my collarbone, swaying with me, kissing my ear. Saint was my sanctuary.

"Good, I want him to sleep. Let's shower together. I wanna ease your mind for a while." He kept working on dissolving the knots, letting out a hard sigh. "There you go. We can worry about mafia shit tomorrow. I love you."

I raised my arm to rub his. "I love you, too, Saint. A shower would be good."

I led the way as I salivated, thinking of Saint soaping down my body. Confidently, I stepped into the apartment bathroom, closing the door behind me and locking it so Alessandro couldn't get in. My son would be safe here. Three of Saint's men were standing right outside our door, plus a few more in the lobby.

Pulling his shirt overhead, I observed the bruising on Saint's chest, running a hand over my fighter. I kissed there lightly, Saint wincing. "It's fine," he said, unbuckling his jeans, his hard arousal bursting free.

"Does it hurt?"

"No, I can't feel it. Nothing new. It will heal." His raspy, sexy voice took me places far away.

If the house were burning down around us, the primitive fire inside Saint would still burn harder. I wriggled out of my ribbed sweater, standing in my panties with my come-hither mouth, cinnamon eyes, and hair, a tumbled mane of gold.

I licked my tongue out over my top lip, admiring Saint's muscular frame of compact power. I turned on the water and the radio near the basin. He stood watching me with his cool blue eyes as I observed the scratches and cuts on his body.

I unclasped my bra, my bountiful breasts hanging free. Despite my slight frame, my breasts were big enough for a whole handful. Saint dropped his underwear, matching me, his cock glistening with pre-cum. An amused glint rose as I silently entered the warmth of the water.

Saint jumped in behind me, handing me my coconut and

vanilla-scented body wash. Spurts of hot water hit his face as I let the warm water wash death and grime away.

"Put it on this." I handed him a loofah as he scrubbed it over my body, his blood running down the drain. My breasts were swollen, my nipples hard with arousal. I turned to slide them down his chest.

Water ran over my sensual lips, Saint claiming them, water mingling, our tongues dancing. Saint's touch took away the pain, if only for a little while.

I soaped him down with the loofah, body wash lathering over his tired, tense limbs, all the way down to his feet. My hand stroked between his sturdy legs as I closed over his stiff cock with my mouth.

Saint put his hands on the shower tile to steady himself, a hard gasp escaping his lips. "Dammit, Mira," he growled, my lips working magic, the water dissolving the street-butchering he'd engaged in. I wanted more. Had to have more of him.

My jaw loosened, slinking his cock deeper into the hot, slippery cavern of my mouth. I worked him until he removed his cock from my mouth, easing me up.

I slicked back my hair from the water. Saint took his time, repeated the intimate motions of lathering me clean, cupping my breasts as a reward. He flicked his tongue back and forth, fire shooting in my veins. Saint was bringing me alive again.

Saint's tongue swirled in circle motions down my body to my pussy, first guiding his fingers inward, massaging and probing. I was grinding against his fingers, wanting more.

Angles were tight, so round two was reserved for the bedroom. "Wrap your legs around me, baby." I gargled through the water, the extra element making it more exciting. I wrapped myself around him. He held me tight, digging his fingers into my thighs, using the wall as leverage.

Thrusting, Saint penetrated my hot pussy, my mouth opening with pleasure. I rocked in rhythm against the wall, pushing my hips forward, supporting the motion. We were one, Saint and I. Destined to live this life and heal each other's wounded hearts.

Between the sheets of cascading water and the busy Chicago streets, Saint brought rolling waves of orgasm to me in the shower, my legs shaking once he let me free. I looked down at his hard-on, thick and ready for more. "We haven't finished..."

In the days that followed, Saint and I moved together. I was his shadow, and that's how I wanted it until he ran the streets completely. An ambitious plan, but one I knew we could master together.

We lay in bed talking one night, Saint speaking his mind.

"The Salianos aren't the same anymore. Marco, as the Don, is not good for Chicago as a whole. Your father was a man of class—yes, brutality, but class. He put the streets of Chicago on the map. Marco is a clumsy fool."

"Exactly why we're going to dominate and take my brother out completely. There is no more Saliano." I put my index finger on his fleshy lip, rolling it down, replacing it with a raw kiss.

I was different now. A true mafia wife.

Chapter 29

Saint

"Do you still have the book?"

I stared at Mira blankly. We were sitting at the kitchen table drinking coffee, a morning ritual I loved. She would sit right in front of the window where her face was illuminated, her legs crossed, sipping her hot brew. Every morning, my blood pumped with the same everlasting fire it had since Paris. Mira and I were soulmates, but now, the sorrow had left her eyes and been replaced with intensity.

"The book? What book?" I had a meeting with Falcone and Lupo, but unlike in the early days, they were coming to the house for the meeting. I had nothing to hide from Mira, and she was as much a part of the game plan as my Riccini street family.

"Your book that holds your trade secrets. The one I saw in Paris."

I laughed with my nose pitched over my coffee cup. I was past the hurt now and could see the funny side of it. I never thought the moment would come, but it had.

"Ohhh, that book." I got up, walked to the sink, before kissing her temple. "Let me go get the destroyer. It doesn't hold weight anymore since Marco has all the suppliers on deck."

"Marco is a dummy. He probably lost the photos. When are Falcone and Lupo getting here?" she said curtly.

"Any minute. All business this morning, aren't you?" I wrapped my arms around her from the back, soaking in her delicious vanilla scent I'd missed so much.

"Yes. Hey, I'm a Riccini wife. I have to be."

"Damn straight, and you're doing a fine job, too. Have I told you how sexy you look sitting under the light?" I breathed, wanting a quickie but knowing it couldn't happen. Her light giggle brought me so much joy. We were up early, but Alessandro was an early riser, too, so I sensed he would be up shortly.

"Yes, you have. Stop Saint! We're not giving Falcone and Lupo a show."

"No? Why not?" I dipped down, slipping my hand up her pencil skirt. She quickly shoved it away, continuing to laugh. God, how I loved her.

"Saint Riccini!" The doorbell rang as the intercom video came on.

"Aye, knucklehead, let us up," Lupo said affectionately. I pointed him to the door.

"See, answer that! Go get the door," Mira said.

"Ha-ha, we'll pick this up later." I winked at her before heading over to the intercom, letting Falcone and Lupo in. Alessandro entered, wiping sleep out of his eyes, staring at the men. "Who are they, Mommy?"

"Your uncles. Get used to seeing them around," Mira said. I smirked as she sat Alessandro up to eat.

"Come in when you can." I blew a kiss at her, and minutes later, she came in.

"Alright, Mira. We know you're busy with Alessandro. Any insights for us?"

"Yes, I have plenty." I watched my woman in action, and it lit a fire in my loins so hot, I had to readjust myself. "Chip away at Marco. He's more of a brawn type of person, not brains. Be strategic and wear down his operation. Marco has territory in the Chicago hub. I remember that area from when I was a kid, and Dad telling me it was his most lucrative area. Find their warehouses, and hit them fast, simultaneously. It will make Marco scramble. He talks tough, but when you hit him between the eyes, he will buckle."

"She's right. I told you—we need more recruits on ground," I said to Falcone.

He nodded. "Already done. I need to initiate them first. This will be an excellent exercise. Add some vandalism to the buildings, and the mayor's not gonna be so happy about that. Throw in some looting, and we got ourselves a winner."

"Exactly," I replied, sitting upright, the wheels turning.

"Brilliant plan, Mira. Hit the Back of the Yards and Englewood. Get your best crews to talk heavy on the ground and spread the word," I added.

"Blow up their hotspots. Call them in. Use your drug runners to make calls, so the Salianos are always under surveillance. It's going to irritate the cops." Mira dug in deeper. She was a natural. Her father should have let her in earlier, but now that I'd spoken to Frankie, I understood why he hadn't. I was a lucky man. She could have taken the Salianos to new heights.

"Nice. I like it. How's he likely to retaliate?" I asked.

"Like a bitch." She crossed her arms. "He'll gang up. Same thing he used to do to me when I outsmarted him. He's sneaky. Is he still affiliated with the Callahan boys? Have you confirmed if the Don knew?" she inquired.

Lupo leaned over his knee. "Our guess is he didn't. There's been no word about seeing them together. They are both injured, anyway, thanks to Saint."

"Should have shot straight through their heads," I scoffed, anger still roiling at my misstep.

Lupo continued, "Both aren't hanging out in their usual spots. We cut a small deal with them to see how they'd handle coke in their area. They didn't waver. Money returned on time, and legitimate."

"They're drug traffickers, but they're good at what they do and move bricks at a quicker rate than anybody in Chicago. That's why I wanted them involved in the cartel in the first place," I mentioned.

"Hmm. Might work. Your cartel idea might be the best way to take Marco down. Four famiglias working together with deeper contracts and networks. It can only work because Frankie's no longer with us." She clasped her fingers around her cross, welling up, but not letting a tear hit the ground.

I sent her a look of adoration. "I messed up. I feel responsible, and in my haste, I think I needed the right players in the game. Alonzo Lombardi would be a better pick. He has the Las Vegas circuit on lock, and we've started implanting our people on the inside."

"I have no doubt between the three of us we've got enough firepower to contain Marco and take the bottom out of his drug operation," Lupo stated.

"Don't count him out too quickly. He's got an underhanded side, and he'll wait to strike, like he did with my father. You have to end him all the way," Mira told Lupo with an empty stare.

"Understood."

Alessandro banged on the door. "Mommy! Mommy, what are you doing in there? I want to come in."

"Duty calls. Let me know if you need anything else. If you give me your black book, Saint, I'll call the dealers and work on them. Maybe we can offer cash incentives for them to get intel for us?"

I stared at her with admiration. "Can do."

Day One...

"Yeah. Englewood? What happened?" Falcone was on the phone at past midnight. I jolted up from my slumber, annoyed as I was snuggled in with Mira, where I wanted to be.

"Arson. The boys called it in. The cops are here. Chinatown, another call in. Two dead. McKinley Park, boom! Fucking outta here. Cops everywhere. Your wife is a genius. Tell her from me."

"I will, but Falcone..."

"Yeah, boss?"

"Call me in the morning. I'm trying to fucking sleep."

"Got it, got it. I get excited when I get to play street god. Night, night."

I clicked off the call, groaning into Mira's back.

"Who was it?" she asked drowsily.

"Falcone. Your plan's working. By the way, he said to tell you, you're a genius."

"Ha!" Her belly shook from laughter. "When my brother gives up and is six feet under, then I'll feel better." She rolled to the side, dragging my fingers around her stomach.

"You want him dead, Mira?" Mira pretended to be asleep as I kissed her shoulder.

"I don't know how I feel, Saint. Go to sleep." She tapped me. "Alessandro will come in here otherwise if he hears you talking. He'll think it's playtime."

"My God. Our son, where did he get all this energy from? He sleeps for a couple of hours and then gets up!"

"He's yours."

Day Five...

"He hit back, and we lost a couple, but the cops are riding him hard. His place got raided last night." Mira and I were in our usual morning spots, me admiring her as she sat in the sunlight with her coffee.

A deviant smirk crossed her face. "See. He's not organized. Shame the Callahans had to lose their son, but they tried to double-cross us. That's what they deserve."

"Fuck, you're a sexy woman when you talk dirty like that," I growled hard, wanting to fuck her on the table. She put her coffee cup down.

"Come and get it, Saint. I got time if you got time. You look handsome in that sky-blue shirt. It matches your eyes."

Blood pumped hard through my veins, my cock rising to the occasion, but Alessandro bounding in with his high-top sneakers, demanding his mother's attention, stopped all that. Fatherhood was a different ball game.

My phone rang, flatlining my hard-on.

"We need you at Oak Park. We got trouble. Marco's trying to

run his own version of our game," Falcone mentioned.

"Any stock lost?"

"No, but the cops are down here, and you're probably gonna get a call. Thought I'd give you the heads up."

"Good. I'm on the way." I switched into game mode, kissing my son's face.

"You and Mommy have a good day. Daddy's gotta go to work." I left a wet smooch on the side of his face. I was craving more father/son time. I hugged him a little longer, knowing that my life was on the line every time I stepped outside the door.

I kissed Mira hard. "Hold it down for me, baby."

"Of course. Love you."

"Love you, too. And oh, can we do dinner tonight? I have something for you. I can cook."

Mira leaned her warm face against the shirt sleeve of my arm, and then looked up at me with shock on her face. "You wanna cook? I would love that, and it sounds weird, but I miss you."

I stroked her hair, twirling it at the ends. "It doesn't sound weird, and yes, I want to cook for you both." I kissed the soft pillows of her lips, wanting to stay but needing to go. "See you tonight. I'll try to make it home before eight," I replied huskily.

"We'd both love that." I watched Mira relax, glad I could do that to her.

I managed to keep good on my promise and let the day go when I arrived back. Seeing Mira giggling with Alessandro in the living room instantly put the beast inside me back in the box. She grounded me in a way that was hard to articulate.

Loosening my tie, a smile drifted over my face. If only Riza were here. She would have loved Mira like I did. I patted the velvet ring box in my pocket. I'd had enough time to swing by the jeweler and pick up the five-carat pink diamond cluster. Mira deserved the best money could buy, and I wanted to do things the right way. Now we were a real family.

"Honey, I'm home," I called out, Alessandro running towards me. I hoisted him in the air. "Hey, how's my little man?"

"Good, Dad. I made a Lego house!" I flashed Mira a sweet look as she joined him, kissing my cheek.

"Really? I wanna hear all about it. Let me wash up and get ready to cook. You can tell me all about it." Mira looked a little lost with her hands in her jean pockets.

"I, umm, put everything out for the pasta. Sure you don't need me to help?"

"Baby, I can cook. I want to. You don't have to do it every time, but if you pour me a Scotch and tell me about your day while I'm cooking, that works."

I squeezed her hand, my nerves a little frazzled.

"Okay."

Twenty minutes later, I stepped out of the bathroom with the radio playing in the background, a breeze floating through the kitchen window. Alessandro followed me like a shadow as I put a stool next to the stove so I could talk to him.

"Tell me about your Lego house. You're going to have plenty more houses to take care of when you're older, so that's a good start."

"Am I?" Alessandro climbed on the stool with his too-bright eyes as I ruffled his hair. God, it felt good being with them. My father had been right about focusing on my family.

Mira greeted me on the other side with a Scotch on the rocks.

"Here we go, handsome."

I pulled one of the knives out of its wooden chopping block, slicing effortlessly through the chives. I leaned over to Mira, kissing her, loving her soft scent. "Thank you, sweetheart. Have a nice day?"

"I did. I finished up what I needed to do." She winked. "It's even better now you're home."

I grinned, turning the hot water on. "Don't try to seduce me while I'm cooking. I gotta concentrate if I'm gonna bring this garlic and white wine pasta to life. Riza and I used to cook together. Let's see if I can remember." Now the good memories of Riza were starting to surface. It didn't ache so much in my chest to talk about her.

"I didn't know you liked to cook?"

"There's a lot we have to learn about one another. I'm excited about the next chapter for us." The sparkle was back in Mira's eyes, and it felt like the perfect moment. I watched closely as she poured herself a wine, leaning on the other side of the bench. Spur of the moment, but oh so right.

"There is, but I'm enjoying the ride."

"Me too. Mira..." I hesitated, sprinkling sea salt in the bubbling hot water.

"Yes?"

"Reach in my pocket."

"What's in your pocket, Dad?" Alessandro asked.

"You'll see in a minute."

Quizzically, Mira regarded me. "Okay, what are you up to?"

A wide smile broke on my face as she lifted the velvet box out of my right pocket. The whites of Mira's eyes shone through, her mouth parting as she clicked the box open. My pulse quickened, hoping she liked it.

"Saint. What tha-this...you?"

I nodded as Alessandro gasped, pointing to the ring, jumping down from his spot on the stool. Seeing the water boiling on the stove and knowing it would need a few more minutes before it boiled over, I dropped to one knee in front of the love of my life.

"For you, my love. My one and only. I'm glad you came to Paris and rocked my world. We belong together and I wanna do this thing called life with you right. It's five carats, and I hope it fits. Let's renew our vows and be married because we want to, not because of a peace treaty."

I stopped momentarily. Mira's jaw slackened as I pulled the exquisite ring out of its slot, gliding it on her shaky finger. Her eyes darted between the ring and me.

"Yes. To all of it." She gasped as if she was having trouble breathing. "I-Saint." Mira threw her arms around me as the hot water spat. Instinctively, I put a hand out to block Alessandro from the tiny spurt of hot water hitting him. I quickly kissed Mira, laughing and turning to switch the stove off.

"Daddy, daddy! The water, the water!"

"I got you. Stand behind me. Maybe I need Riza here after all." I chuckled, feeling complete. There were never to be any dull moments in my life. I had it all.

Day Fifteen...

"Saint, holy shit. So fucking good." I let Mira up for breath, our bodies mixed with sex sweat. Panting, I laid on my back, feeling like everything was coming together.

"I'm insatiable when it comes to you, Mira. We make a deadly team."

"We do, but we've got a ways to go. Keep your eye on the prize, baby."

I semi-growled, tickling her. "I have my eye on it already. I've won already."

Mira cupped my face. "No, we've both won. We've got each other."

Chapter 30

Mira

"Have you spoken to Kracken and Hilton? Aren't they working with the Zig Zag crew? They were in your book?" Things were progressing for Saint and me. We were taking Marco down step by step, hour by hour. I texted Clara about vow arrangements in between. Such was the juxtaposition of my life, and I loved it.

ME: *Can we get the venue we talked about?*

CLARA: *Yes! It's free on the date you want. I'm so excited! Btw, freesias or lilies?*

ME: *Hmm. Both. Lilies mean fertility and purity. I don't know about the pure part, but fertility. Well...*

CLARA: *Omg. You and Saint are having another baby?*

ME: *Maybe in the future. I can see it.*

CLARA: *I love you two together. Both florals it is! Talk soon, bride.*

Excited, I returned my attention to Saint.

"They were suppliers in Englewood, but Marco stole them years ago. We're in talks with them, and they're coming on board with us. Interesting information. Both told me Marco is falling apart, screaming. He can't handle the pressure." Saint's smirk cemented it for me. We were taking hold of Chicago streets.

Alessandro stood tucked under my arm, staring up at me. I was his source of entertainment now, considering school hadn't started. Besides, we had to clear the streets first and put things right.

"*Bonjour, maman!*"

"*Bonjour,* Alessandro. What shall we eat this morning?" I was settling into a routine with him, and even though I'd never been so tired, I finally felt like I had an actual family.

Alessandro stood back, spreading his arms wide. "Pancakes! I want pancakes! Can you put the smiley face on it, like you did last time?"

"Yes, I can do that. Come on, do you want to make them together?" It amazed me how much more Alessandro was adopting his father's mannerisms. Another mini-me Saint. A chuckle rose from my mouth as I observed him setting up his tiny plastic stool so he could stand next to me at the kitchen bench top.

Saint's body heat cruised on me, a light kiss gracing my shoulder. "Keep going, and I'm going to put another baby in you."

"Huh?" I chuckled, Saint's warm hands around my waist. He

brought a peace to me I'd never experienced. It was surreal that we were in this place, with all the chaos breaking out on the street.

Saint nuzzled his head into the crevice between my shoulder and head. I breathed in his musky cologne, loving the way I fitted in between his arms.

Alessandro and I had our pancakes perfected, so he was a pro at it. His little hands were busy gathering ingredients from the pantry, and I hoped for a disaster-free floor. The last time we made them, flour ended up on the floor, not in the bowl.

I kept a watchful eye. "You're so good with him. You look happy. Would you want another one?"

"When things calm down, we can talk about it, but right now...we have to focus on taking Marco out of commission." As soon as his name ejected from my lips, my phone buzzed.

Saint kissed my shoulder again as I scrambled to pick up the phone. I didn't want him hearing Alessandro in the background, and on some levels, I wondered if he already knew.

"Good morning, sister. Are you having fun over there?" His sarcasm cut through the phone. Saint mouthed to ask who it was. I covered the phone before answering Saint.

"Marco."

"You good to handle it?" he whispered in a low voice.

"Yes." Saint didn't question me anymore. He still protected me, but he'd seen what I was capable of, so he let me do what I needed to do.

"What do you want? Are you ready to lie down and die now?" I snuck away from the counter, making sure I was out of Alessandro's earshot, but his ears were like sponges picking up information. Saint filled the gap, distracting him.

"I was going to ask you the same thing."

Shaking from anger, I fired back at him. "You killed my father. You're a dog and not fit to be a Saliano. Stand down. You can't think you're a Don. Donato and Antonio must be pulling their fucking hair out over there."

He was silent with no comeback, and I wanted nothing to do with him. Ever.

"You've always been resourceful, Mira, but I've got a few plans for the Riccinis that you don't see coming. Watch your back."

"I look forward to seeing what they are. Do you admit to killing your own blood father?"

"I don't know what you're talking about. I loved Frankie boy. You felt like you couldn't attend the funeral. I'm sorry. I would have loved to see you there." A hard lump worked its way down my throat as I held in the hate.

"He's not my father. I'm a De Luca, but I loved him like one. Maybe that's why I never liked you. You're no fucking brother of mine."

"What? What are you talking about?"

I smirked ruefully. "Oh, you didn't realize? Angelica killed my family and stole me from the hospital, but I'll tell you something...I was more of a loyal loving family member to my father than his own son. You're a piece of shit!"

"Fucking bitch. I knew you didn't look like a single one of us. Fuck you and Saint Riccini," he let out, and I hoped he choked on the news. Boy, it felt glorious to dig up the bones of our family's past.

"Marco, I've got your number. I see you. You won't be Don for long."

"Back your dogs off, Mira. I'm warning yo..."

I hung up, not wanting to hear his spew any longer. I dropped the phone in my back pocket, switching back to family mode. I walked back into the kitchen, Saint's eyes following me.

"And?"

"Empty threats, but be careful out there. He's crumbling." All the ingredients were laid out on the counter and Alessandro's sleeves were rolled up. "Impressive, Saint."

"If I had time, I would make the pancakes with you, but I gotta go. Back by lunch. Are you good to make the calls?"

"Yes. I got you."

Saint gave me a saucy look, tapping me on the ass, and landing a juicy kiss before he left.

"You definitely do."

My thoughts turned back to Frankie as I watched Alessandro pour flour into a measuring jug. I hated seeing a film from Frankie's funeral. I hadn't gotten to say my goodbyes, but he ended up being buried right next to my mother. Lupo had delivered the news to me.

"Sorry, Mira. It's tragic what's happened, but in this business, you come in thinking you're gonna die. All you can do is hope you've contributed enough to take care of your family."

"Lupo, thank you for finding out."

My father taught me many lessons, but they weren't gift-wrapped with a pretty bow. He gave them to me the way he knew how. The Saliano way.

A wry smirk found its way to my face as I skipped through the timeline of my life. Paris, getting the information to my father, Ella and his knowledge of her and what she'd done to keep my boy safe.

"You've always been watching out for me, haven't you, Papa?" I muttered while encouraging Alessandro. My silver cross dangled forward as I checked the consistency of the mix.

"Whoa! Look at that, Mom! So cool. I like cooking. It's fun."

"You say that now..."

"No, I like it. I hope I can do it at school." Alessandro's comment about being out in the open triggered me to hunt down as many dealers as I could and coerce them to our side.

"I hope so, too. Maybe you'll be a chef." I wanted Alessandro to have the option for what he wanted to do in the future, and for me and Saint to run the streets until it was time.

Monitoring Alessandro, I let him crack the eggs open into the flour. We were having a lot of fun together. He wiped his nose, and a pinch of flour smeared over his nose.

"Look at you with the flour. You're a funny boy!" He giggled joyously as he poured the mixture into the hot frying pan with my careful supervision.

"Now we wait, and you can flip them over with the spatula."

"Okay!"

The pancakes turned out beautifully, and it was only once Alessandro was planted in front of the TV screen that I got back to mob business.

Turns out I hadn't taken photos of all the pages back in Paris. Made sense—I'd been in a rush. There were three more pages of dealers, and I spent the rest of the afternoon buying them off while Saint handled the grittier affairs.

"We've got a nice fat signing bonus for you. We treat our dealers well. Yes...you can keep that territory over at Little

Village, but your revenue was down by two thousand from the normal amount of weight you move. Uh, how are the kids?" Me adding my nurturing touch changed things. It got Salianos' dealers to turn on him. I was ten for ten by the time I struck my pen through the list.

Lupo rang at five in the afternoon, my ear ringing from so many phone calls.

"Hey! You should have worked in sales because I have a swag of dealers at the meeting spot."

Grinning, I nodded. "I hope all the street soldiers are there in case. We have to test their loyalty when they jump ship."

I could hear industrial machinery in the background, knowing they were probably in a warehouse on the outskirts of Chicago. "We'll break them in. Trust me, but I never thought I'd see the day when we'd get the Little Village dealers walking in here. We've been trying to take those guys out for years!"

I tapped my worn-out pen against my teeth. "Some things, Lupo, just need a woman's touch, but you're a consigliere. You have your own magic to conduct."

"Indeed, I do. I agree with you, so would my wife."

"Speaking of your wife, bring her over for the ceremony. I'll be sending invites later on this week, but consider this an official invite. Bring the kids, too."

"Ah, the wife will be happy. We will be there. Thanks for sending the dealers through. See you for family dinner on Sunday."

"Done and look forward to it." I put the phone down, happy the Riccinis had their tradition. Even though I'd never met Riza, I knew she would be proud of her twin and the legacy we were building.

Saint's early appearance shocked me. I stared up at the round clock on our mantelpiece. I looked at him with a puzzled frown as he was holding his hands behind his back.

"Wow. You're here. It's only 8:30. I expected you later."

"Daddy, Daddy!" Alessandro ran to Saint. He was tall enough now to get his arms around most of Saint's waist.

Saint placed a loving hand on his back. "Hey, little man. How were the pancakes? Did you save me any?"

Alessandro tilted his head back. "Ah hah, you weren't here. It's all in my tummy. None for you." Saint tickled him.

"You ate it all. I got more food here. Tiramisu for later. A Riccini favorite."

A merry-go-round game went on for a minute or two, but once Alessandro got his share of dessert, the mayhem calmed.

"How's my lady?"

"She's doing great. I thought it would take longer, but dealers are folding like a house of cards. Okay out there?"

Saint's stubbled jaw was extra sexy to me, and his icy blue eyes twinkled. "Better. Only lost two today, but it's better. The Boston nightclub venture is working out. We have that stream of income now and new dealers on the side. It got a little heated down there for the meet, but it's shaping up."

Alessandro ended up in my lap as he bounced on my knee, his curls shining in the light.

My boys.

Chapter 31

Saint

Four weeks later...

This time, it was different. We were reciting our vows to one another because we wanted to. The first wedding had been a courthouse affair, reciting after the judge. No feelings. No love. No meaning. But now, things were different. The bond I had with Mira was unbreakable. The Riccinis weren't overly religious, and although Mira kept her cross close to her chest, she'd wanted an outdoor ceremony.

We'd hired out a discreet estate right outside of Chicago. Mira had requested a large indoor gazebo to be erected, so the Chicago wind didn't interfere with proceedings.

She would have whatever she wanted. Standing in the aisle with the celebrant in my navy-blue suit with a charcoal tie, I smiled a little. I'd kept my hair long like Mira wanted. I didn't mind the concession because it felt like heaven when she ran her fingers through my hair at the end of the day.

She'd wanted to keep some traditions. *"No, you have to let me go to the apartment without you. You can't see me until the day. Think you can survive?"*

"*No, I don't think I can. Why don't you stay here?*"

"*You'll cope. It's good to see if you can take care of your son without me. You do a good job.*"

I'd done pretty well. Alessandro and I had fun. I'd cooked with him, but he'd pined for his mother like I did.

Inside the gazebo, the guest chairs were white. Less than twenty of them. Few knew about our son, and I wanted to keep it that way. Only close Riccinis and Mira's childhood friends. Ella made the trip, and Alessandro was overjoyed to see her.

Before the ceremony, I'd thanked her after Mira revealed she'd cared for my son for the first five years of his precious life. "*Thank you, Ella. You did a wonderful job with him. How are things in Paris? Ready to come back? If you are, you have a job. Frankie spoke highly of you.*"

The shock on Ella's face brought a chuckle. "*I thought...I thought you would hate me because I took care of him.*"

I shook my head at her. "*No. The opposite. In the end, it was the right decision to keep my son safe until he's strong and old enough to understand the legacy he's about to carry.*"

"*I'm honored. I've been working at a café. Nothing special. I would love to come back to America permanently,*" she gushed.

"*Say no more. I will make sure you have a nice apartment, and you're comfortable. I wouldn't trust anyone else with my kin. Alessandro and more to come. Welcome to the Riccini famiglia.*" I kissed her cheek.

"*Thank you, Saint. I accept,*" she replied graciously.

"*Good, good. Now, I have to get ready to say my vows to my beautiful wife.*"

I stood in position, admiring the white freesias, jasmine, and roses my wife had picked out. Mira had exquisite, sophisticated tastes, and her planning the event excited her. My heart pounded harder than it ever had in life, even when I'd had a gun held at my temple at age fourteen. Mira and Alessandro meant everything to me.

Lupo, who stood beside me as the best man, whispered in my ear, "Marriage is a wonderful thing. You've picked the right one to stand beside you. Proud of you both." Tears pricked my eyes, and I knew it was due to be an emotional day for me. The two other people I wished to be here the most were Riza and Nick, but I hoped they were watching from up high.

"Thanks, Lupo," I choked out. "Man, I'm nervous. This normal?" I arched my eyebrow, my palms sweaty.

"Yes. Completely normal. You got it. Enjoy the moment."

The celebrant, who was the same one to marry my mother and father, smiled at me, his glasses hanging at the edge of his nose. "Here we are again. I love weddings." I let out a nervous whoosh as the music started. It was customary for the bride to be a little late, and Mira was making me wait, but as soon as the music played and she walked down the aisle, her cream sleeveless dress fitted to her like a glove, she knocked the wind right out of me. I stroked a hand down over my chest, awestruck by her beauty, toughness, and daintiness all rolled into this phenomenal woman.

The wedding music played in the background, but all I saw was Mira shining with Alessandro beside her in his vest, his hair slicked to the side and his curls kicked up in a curve. My emotions spilled over as tears slid down my face. My famiglia had been restored, not the same as before, but different—and better in some ways. I flicked a look towards my mother, a wide smile on her face, tears rolling down her cheeks. This day couldn't get any better.

Falcone whispered under his breath. "I can't take this shit. I don't cry, but this is fucking beautiful." His outburst broke the waterworks as all in attendance chuckled. Trust Falcone, my main hitter, to come out with the goods at the right time.

Mira's makeup was minimal, but she didn't need it. Her cheeks were shiny with a light bronze glow, her lips stained rose-pink.

Alessandro was quiet, taking everything in as he walked the aisle hand in hand with my beloved. Mira's hair was upswept, a pearl clasp holding the updo together, her champagne locks glowing under the skylight. The music stopped, and I took her hands.

"Hi, Saint," she said demurely.

"Baby, you look amazing. I love you so much."

"I love you." Mira's warm eyes almost undid me. The love we shared ran through us in this two-handed circle we'd created. "You look very handsome. Don't cry. You're going to make me cry." Mira's glossy lips quivered, and I put a thumb on the imprint of her chin to soothe her.

"We got it. Together, we have each other. Come on. It's just you and me right now. We've done this before—only this time it's a million times better."

Alessandro leaned on Mira's leg. "Hey, what about me?" I bobbed down to pick my son up, even though he was a little heavy.

"What about you? You're part of us, too." I pinched his nose, smiling at the celebrant, unaware that the ladies were sniffling with tears.

I overheard one of them say. "I want somebody to look at me like that. Wow."

A wide grin opened on my face. Yes. Our love was one of a kind. The sky light illuminated our faces, and everything was fucking perfect. "You can start now," I told the celebrant, my son in my arms.

"We gather here today for the vow renewal of Saint Riccini and Mira Riccini. Both of you have been through insurmountable tests in order to be with us here today. This is what marriage is: a test of courage, vulnerability, compromise, and most of all, enduring love."

Mira's face streaked with makeup, but no matter if she cried or was happy, she was even more beautiful to me.

After the ceremony, we partied, danced, and drank like Italians do.

No hiccups, no phones, no bullshit. I expected there to be when I turned my phone on, but all I got were messages of deliveries passing through without interruption.

The next morning, worse for wear but on a high, I shook off my mildly irritating hangover, dragging myself to the kitchen. Light filled the space up through the parted venetians at 5 am. I was up early before Mira and Alessandro, giving me time to reflect. We'd been running and gunning so long that I hadn't had the time to catch my breath and wanted to take Mira on a honeymoon. I made myself a coffee, smiling.

"I think I did good, Pop. What you say?" I said. We would still be awake if Nick and Riza had been at the ceremony. We would play dominoes or a board game until the sun streamed through the window. Both of them were party animals. Gratitude struck as Riza's face cut in before I could get too sad.

That, along with a phone call. I scraped it up, answering with one hand, drinking my coffee.

"Saint. Robinson here."

"Morning."

"Morning. Will you be at Café Roma this afternoon?"

"I will at three."

"Good." Code for a cop. I'd struck out on luck. Another ally in my back pocket, and no slouch, either. The new head of the narcotics division, who I was about to make a rich man with "kickbacks." Yeah, life was good.

Mira shuffled in, yawning. "Can you make me a cup, too? I'm so tired."

"Sure. Why are you up? Did I wake you?"

"Yes, you left a dent in the side of the bed." She smiled dozily.

"Hmm, coffee coming right up."

"I can't believe Marco's operations are done. It's happened so fast. I thought it would take years."

"Hard and fast, that's what you told me," I replied, laughing at myself as I quickly handed her the warm cup. She poked me in the side as I fingered a tendril of flaxseed-colored locks. Mira's presence in my life had changed everything. I was more mellow and more compassionate, and that's not the man I used to be. I stared at her for a minute longer, pinching myself.

"I've got a meeting this afternoon with the head of narcotics. This is it—the nail in the coffin. If you want to talk about shutting your brother down, he's the guy to do it."

Mira cuddled her cup but sank into my arms. I put my cup down, hugging her back.

"I think your brother is the best thing that's ever happened to us. You know that?"

Mira pushed back to look at my face for the punchline, but I was serious. "You're kidding...you have to be."

"No. The Salianos have their ways. Your father, he showed you his love the only way a made man knows how, and your brother pushed you into my arms. I gotta thank him for it. He's a low-key genius. I should have toasted to Marco yesterday for bringing us together."

Mira jutted out her lip. "You have a nice perspective, but he's not in my good books."

"I think it's done. I got this crazy idea that the Riccinis and Salianos will be able to merge territories after all this time. Crazy, I know, but maybe it will happen."

Mira covered her palm over my temple. "Saint Riccini, you're coming down with something."

"Nope, but I do want to take you on a honeymoon."

Mira dropped her coffee to the side, draping her arms around my neck. I dropped my hands down, skimming her arm and resting my hands on her ass with a tweak. Her mouth opened as I sunk into her world, her lips parting, the perfume of Mira's feminine scent firing up every neuron in me. She whimpered as I cupped her ass in my hands. We had to find new inventive ways to get around Alessandro dropping in to sleep between us some nights.

"Hmm, can we start the honeymoon now? It will have to be soon though." She winked as we came up for breath.

"I wish. Trust me, I plan to make it as soon as possible. Pick anywhere you wanna go, and I'll take you. How soon?"

Mira grinned. "Soon, as in before I pop because Alessandro's going to have playmates."

My heart knocked on my chest. "What? You're...are you?" I rubbed her belly in shock.

Mira nodded happily. "That's why I wasn't drinking. I'm thinking our little love babies were conceived after we got back from going to see Frankie...nearly two months now. I found out I was pregnant last week."

I raked a hand through my hair, alarmed, but fucking over the moon about the news. Still, I asked her the question. "I saw you with a glass..."

"No, you saw me with sparkling apple juice. Clara swapped my drink out so you wouldn't know."

I scooped Mira up, lifting her feet off the floor. "I fucking love you so much. Did you say playmates, by the way?"

"Yes, we're having twins."

"I may be 39, but my boys are still fertile."

"I love you, Saint Riccini. I can't wait to expand this family with you."

One Riccini lineage might have wilted, but another replaced it, stronger than ever. Two famiglias were merging to reign on the streets of Chi-town.

Cross to Bear: Mafia Billionaire Daddy Series (Book 1)

Epilogue

Mira

Two years and seven months later

"Don't worry. I already started the barbecue for the hot dogs. Alessandro, can you help your mother bring out the small chairs for the twins? I think we've got everything then."

Nearly three years later, with one girl twin and one boy twin delivered successfully, I was preparing for their second birthday. They say terrible twos, but so far, Enzo and Aria were amusing themselves and giggling in the backyard, Ella watching over them.

We'd moved not long after I revealed my pregnancy to Saint. He wanted room for his children to play and move around. There was even talk of a cat and a dog.

Alessandro's hair had morphed into a lion's mane of unruly curls, thus needing to be cut every four weeks. Saint was doing a great job setting up the table for the event. Both sides of the famiglia were arriving with gifts and well wishes for the twins.

I'd cut my hair to a manageable, sleek bob. It became too

bothersome with the twins and Alessandro. "Okay, Dad, be right back."

He was a real man of the house, and it brought a contented sigh to my lips seeing how well Saint handled fatherhood. The doorbell rang to our gated estate, and I checked the visitors through the intercom and camera. Rosa De Luca, and Prima De Luca, my aunt, and cousin from my birth family, had arrived. I knew their faces off by heart. I'd stared at their pictures for so long.

Falcone had surprised me with their details once we won over the Chicago territory. Apparently, I'd gained his respect at a high level. *"Listen, I feel bad about what your mother had me do back in the day, and I want to help. I think I found one of your cousins and your mother's sister on the De Luca side. I got their numbers right here if you wanna give them a call."*

"You-you found them?"

"Yeah, yeah. On account of feeling bad about what I'd done. You've repaid this family ten times over. You're a Riccini through and through. Your father...he gave us a run for our money back in the day. I respect the guy. We're all linked, so I did my best. The rest is with you. I understand if it's too painful for you, but here they are."

He'd left me in the office, torn between the painful tragedies of the past and the present, glossy Kodak photographs lodged in my hand. My aunt Rosa was on the plumper side, but she had my eyes—the same almond shape—and the same nose. She looked like me. My cousin Prima was slender, yet taller than me with golden hair, again the same regal nose, and tiny cute lips. I'd bawled my eyes out, only for Saint to burst in and ask if I was okay.

"My family. The De Lucas. Falcone found a couple of them."

"Oh, honey. Do you want to see them? I can arrange to have them flown here so you can meet them." Saint had been, as his name

suggested, a saint throughout all my pregnancy mood swings and running our street empire. He never complained and seemed to be loving his role as father and Don.

I'd agreed, but it had taken me nearly a year and a half to reach out to them, and now I was about to meet them in the flesh. My stomach bubbled with worry if they would hate or reject me. After all, my "mother" had ordered the hit on their whole famiglia. Saint wasn't taking chances. He had them patted down at the gate, but they cleared the security check.

I let them in as I checked on the twins' cake in the refrigerator. I licked a little of the icing off my finger. It was too good not to. "Hey, there you are. Your family is here. You're busted. Is it good?"

I dipped a little more on my finger for Saint to lick off. His full mouth sucked the icing off my finger, his eyes darkening as he probed into mine. "Damn, that's fucking good." My mouth parted, mesmerized.

"I want to be the icing."

"You can be later..." he kissed my neck as the De Lucas showed up at the door. I tucked my bob behind my ears and wiped down my white capris. Both had large boxes in hand, and I took them.

"Hi! Thank you so much for coming. We have the guest house set up for you. I'm waiting for everyone to arrive before I take you there. Please come in and meet my husband, Saint."

"Hi, ladies. Nice to meet you. I hope you enjoy your stay here. If you need anything, shout out." Saint smiled at me affectionately, understanding it was a deeply personal time for me. "I'll be barbecuing and pretending to keep our kids in order." The De Lucas laughed, and that was the first icebreaker.

"Thank you, Mira," Rosa said nervously, her eyes twitching, and my cousin Prima had her hands clasped in front of her shyly.

She was stunning and reminded me of an Italian model with her evocative beauty. Her eyes were cinnamon, with the same gold flecks in the light as mine.

I took their gifts inside, where all the other guests were slowly gathering, welcoming them into our new decadent home.

"Drink?" I offered. "I sure could use one," I said shakily, unsure how to start the conversation with my long-lost family members.

"Yes, gin and tonic for me. For you, Prima?"

"Thanks, I like the hard stuff. Scotch and coke."

I chuckled. "You and the husband both." I made both their drinks, poured myself a white wine, and guided them into our luscious garden, away from all the ruckus of guest arrivals. The aroma of barbecue and caramelized onion filled the air. I loved our sprawling grounds with its garden. I enjoyed being in it.

As we walked a little, I started the best way I knew how.

"Please don't hate me. I'm so sorry about everything. I wish I'd been able to find you before. I'm so sorry." My voice trembled on the edge of cracking, but Rosa grabbed my hands, rubbing over them.

"Please. Please. Stop. We know. You had nothing to do with this. Yes, you were planted into the Saliano famiglia, but we De Lucas come from mafia roots. The bakery we ran for thirty years was a cover. We wanted nothing to do with the corruption of it all." Rosa's bombshell threw me for a loop.

"I might need several drinks," I muttered, staring out at all Saint and I had built. The vision Saint had of both famiglias merging came true after the first year. We were not only in Chicago but affiliated with Boston. Talks of a cartel were next up on the table.

"Yes. It's a shame, but we escaped to New York, hoping to hide out in the big city, but, ah, here we cannot run from the mafia," Prima advised as we sipped and walked.

"I have so many questions, and I'm sure Saint does, too. I can't believe we...I mean, you were part of a mob family, too." With her affectionate eyes, my aunt put a gentle hand on my shoulder.

"You're our famiglia, too. You are part of us, Mira. We are your blood. We accept you and yours. I brought the photo album to show you. We can look later, but today we celebrate the twins!" My aunt had a twinkle in her drooped-over eyes, and kindness rang out through her voice as she raised her glass, clinking with mine.

"I can't believe this. You're here. I'm too overwhelmed." Taking a sip, I shook my head. "I've wanted the truth for so long." I hugged them both, excited to get to know them and the rest of the famiglia.

"We are, too, Mira. We're overjoyed you're safe and happy."

I was more than safe and happy. I wanted for nothing, and I had already set up trust funds for the twins and Alessandro. It was as if the universe was giving Saint a do-over with twins of his own.

The day was a tremendous success, and the twins loved all the attention and gifts. Everyone was full and happy, seated in the lounge and chatting. Alessandro, the twins, Saint, and I were bunched up on the couch as Rosa flipped through the old sepia and black and white photos of my mother and father.

"Wow. They look so smart. My mother..." I clapped a hand over my mouth in awe of the photos. Saint rubbed my hand with his thumb.

"You look like her. You've got great genes," he said softly as Falcone interrupted us.

"Ah, ladies and gents, sorry to interrupt, but Marco is here to pay his respects."

Saint's jaw flickered, his fists balling up, but Falcone gave him a signal that it was okay. "I got it. Let me speak to him," I said firmly. I wanted to see the look on his face.

When I opened the door, Marco's expression was sheepish, his shoulders folded in, his eyes pitiful. A small wrapped package with a bow on top was in his hands.

"Hey, Marco." I cracked the door but didn't want him in my house. We were on speaking terms, but not to a place where he could break bread with us. "How are you keeping?"

"Good, Mira." He licked his lips, shoving the present at me. "Here's a gift for the twins." I took the gift, holding it to my chest.

"Thank you." He rocked back and forth on his heels, shoving his hands in his pockets. I waited, not saying a single word.

Silence. I knew Marco was a proud man and I didn't expect an apology from him.

Seeing him now, I felt nothing. No sadness. No pain. Not even numbness. Maybe pity would have been the closest emotion, but that was it. "Good luck on your side."

He lingered for a moment, his lips thinning remorsefully. "Okay. See you 'round, Mira." I closed the door gently. Falcone stepped up to the door to ensure he headed out the gates and didn't double back.

Marco had been demoted to foot soldier and was barely spoken of, other than to say he was Frankie Saliano's wayward son. Antonio and Donato were foot soldiers too, trying to prove their worth daily.

I smiled, adding his present to the others. Both Lupo and Saint looked at me expectantly.

"Well?"

"I sorted it out. He paid his respects, and now I'm back with my real famiglia. Come on, let's look at more photos." Saint grinned, kissing me softly.

"You are a queen fit for this king. Nicely done."

A peace treaty and an unbreakable bond. So I was a mafia woman born and bred. Right where I belonged all along.

~ THE END ~

Book 2 of this series is now available!

OTHER SERIES' BY THE AUTHOR

Billionaire Daddy Series

Swoon to the irresistible charms of these powerful, rich, and protective lovers. A riveting collection of 5 standalone, fade-to-black, two hour reads.

Mountain Man Daddy Series

Starting afresh in a sleepy mountain town sounds like the perfect plan, but the women in this series didn't expect sparks to fly in their quest to rediscover who they are after a rough patch in life. Their mountain men swooped in with their quiet confidence and powerful presence, proving that they had made the right decision. A heart throbbing collection of 4 standalone, steamy, three hour reads.

Hadsan Cove Series

What do you get when you mix a second chance at love, a cozy beach town, and already established relationships? A heartwarming collection of 4 standalone, steamy, three hour reads. Best part...you'll get to experience each and every couple's milestones as the main characters become secondary characters in the next book.

Printed in Great Britain
by Amazon